A SHAKESPEARE IN THE VINEYARD MYSTERY

TWISTED VINES

CAROLE PRICE

FIVE STAR

A part of Gale, Cengage Learning

GALE
CENGAGE Learning·

Detroit • New York • San Francisco • New Haven, Conn • Waterville, Maine • London

GALE
CENGAGE Learning

LIBRARY OF CONGRESS CATALOGING-IN-PUBLICATION DATA

Price, Carole (Carole Joyce) , 1935–
    Twisted vines : a Shakespeare in the vineyard mystery / Carole Price. — 1st ed.
        p. cm.
    ISBN 978-1-4328-2602-4 — ISBN 1-4328-2602-6 1. Life change events—Fiction. 2. Theaters—California, Northern—Fiction. 3. Shakespearean actors and actresses—Fiction. 4. Vineyards—California—Napa Valley—Fiction. 5. Murder—Investigation—Fiction. I. Title.
PS3616.R525T85 2012
813'.6—dc23   2012013196

First Edition. First Printing: August 2012
Published in conjunction with Tekno Books and Ed Gorman
Find us on Facebook–https://www.facebook.com/FiveStarCengage
Visit our Web site–http://www.gale.cengage.com/fivestar/
Contact Five Star™ Publishing at FiveStar@cengage.com

Printed in Mexico
1 2 3 4 5 6 7 16 15 14 13 12

TWISTED VINES

For my husband Cliff and daughters Carla and Krista.

ACKNOWLEDGMENTS

First of all, I must thank my family: my husband, Cliff, for his unwavering support and his critical eye for consistency throughout the book; my daughters Carla (also my Web designer) and Krista for not laughing (too much) about the mysterious objects that decorate my den; and Shilo, my little mixed terrier companion who came into my life unexpectedly.

I am indebted to Sgt. John Hurd of the Livermore Police Department for patiently answering countless questions and giving me the opportunity to become a volunteer. Livermore's Citizens Police Academy provided opportunities for me to understand how a police department functions. I'm also indebted to Sgt. Garwood Jorgenson (retired) for his advice on weapons, and to other officers who allowed me to ride along on their graveyard shifts. Thank you, Jackie Robertson (retired), for helping me to understand what a crime analyst does. Any errors in police procedures are entirely mine.

What would I have done without Gary Drummond, Livermore's Historian? I am fortunate to have met and worked with Gary when I moved from Ohio to Livermore, California. When I decided to set my book in a real city, I knew I had to get my facts straight or alert readers would surely discover my mistakes. Gary provided me with photos and information from the last hundred years, when Joaquin Murietta stopped at Murietta's Well for a drink on a hot summer day.

I'm indebted to Stefan and Betty Folkendt who owned Folk-

Acknowledgments

endt Crest vineyard in Livermore before moving to Hawaii. Stefan generously provided me with information on growing grapes and what is required for each season until harvest.

Special thanks to Judy Melinek, San Francisco Forensic Pathologist, Dan Apperson (retired), Alameda Coroner's Bureau/Oakland, and Dr. D. P. Lyle for setting me straight on medical procedures.

This book would not have been possible if it were not for the meticulous reviews and professional expertise of my Friday critique group: Penny Warner, Ann Parker, Colleen Casey, Janet Finsilver, and Staci McLaughlin. Other writers who critiqued my work over the years and offered their support are Camille Minichino, Mike Cooper, Margaret Dumas, Claire Johnson, Rena Leith, and Gordon Yano.

Finally, my sincere appreciation to Five Star Publishing for making this book a reality. Special thanks goes to my editors, Alice Duncan and Tracey Matthews, for making this book a better read.

CHAPTER 1

Crime analyst Cait Pepper finally finished clearing her desk Monday morning at the Columbus police station when the phone rang. She reached over a stack of case files and flipped on the speaker.

"Pepper," she answered as she tucked a strand of her curly hair behind her right ear.

"Is this Caitlyn Tilson Pepper?" a soft male voice asked.

The use of her full name surprised her. "It is. How can I help you?"

"Ms. Pepper, my name is Stanton Lane. I'm Tasha Bening's attorney. I'm sorry to inform you that your aunt has passed on. As Mrs. Bening's sole heir, it's imperative that you come to California immediately."

Cait retrieved her most current case file. "I don't have an aunt, Mr. Lane. You have the wrong person." She was about to hang up when the man continued.

"But you *are* Caitlyn Tilson Pepper, born at Mount Carmel Hospital in Columbus, Ohio, thirty-five years ago?"

"Yes, but apparently not the one you're looking for." She flipped open the file she was about to hand over to one of their detectives.

"I understand Mrs. Bening's sudden death has come as a shock, considering she'd been in excellent health—"

"I told you, Mr. Lane, I don't have an aunt—"

He ignored her interruption and continued. "However,

9

because of the substantial inheritance involved, decisions have to be made as quickly as possible. The Shakespeare festival she was deeply committed to is already scheduled and the actors are under contract."

Shakespeare festival? Actors?

"Mr. Lane, you're assuming I know what you're talking about. I assure you I don't. Now if you'll excuse me, I have work to do."

He cleared his throat. "I'm not only Mrs. Bening's attorney, but a personal friend as well. Unfortunately, she told me only what she thought I needed to know to prepare her trust, not details about her relationship with you." He paused. "There is a stipulation in the trust that you may find difficult to honor."

Cait struggled to curb her growing annoyance. She didn't need this just before her vacation.

"Ms. Pepper—"

"Mr. Lane," she interrupted. "Apparently, you haven't done your homework. It's *Mrs.* Pepper. And I'm a crime analyst for the Columbus Police Department. You can stop trying to con me into believing I've inherited some bogus property in California."

"I apologize," he said. "I only meant to save us both time and—"

"As I said, I do not have an aunt. Good luck in finding the bona fide heir."

Her finger was poised over the disconnect button when she heard him plead, "Wait, Mrs. Pepper. Please. I'll fax a copy of the trust to you right now. I've taken the liberty of booking a flight for you. Your ticket is waiting at the American Airlines counter at the Columbus Airport for tomorrow's flight to San Francisco. It leaves at twelve fifty-eight P.M. and arrives at SFO at five forty-five. I'll meet you. So you'll recognize me, I'll be wearing a—"

"Let me guess. A single red rose tucked in your lapel? Spare me the drama. I'm not going to California tomorrow, next week, or next month."

Cait pressed the speaker button and broke the connection. "Unbelievable," she mumbled.

"What if it's legit?"

Cait looked up and saw Detective Sergeant Shep Church grinning and leaning against the doorframe. Tall, trim, and almost every female's dream date.

"And what if this elusive Aunt Tasha did leave you a bucket of money?" he continued. "You could retire and I could inherit your office."

She shook her head. "In case you didn't know, today is April Fool's Day. That call was obviously a joke."

The fax machine whined and papers began to spit out. Cait glanced over. "You've got to be kidding." She stepped behind her desk and watched as the Lane & Lane Attorneys at Law letterhead spilled from the machine.

Shep walked over and sat on the edge of her desk. "As I said, what if it's legit?"

"It's someone's idea of a joke, Shep. I'm not amused."

He rose and bent over the emerging document. "I don't know, Cait. Looks like the real thing. And the timing couldn't be better. You've sold your house, cleared your calendar, and probably have nothing but a haircut and a manicure scheduled for the week."

She rolled her eyes.

He grinned and wiggled his eyebrows. "Free ticket to sunny California? With nothing to do but step off the plane, soak up some golden rays, and collect your inheritance?"

"The timing's too damn convenient, don't you think? I inherit a fortune just as I'm trying to put my life back together? Not likely." She ignored the pages from the fax machine, handed him the file folder, and walked to the door. "What I do need is a cup of strong black coffee."

He waved the fax over the shredder. "Sure you don't want to read this? Looks like this so-called Tasha Tilson Bening person meant business when she named you her heir."

Cait froze. "What did you say?" Before Shep could answer, she yanked the shiny paper from his hand and sat back down at her desk. "Tilson?" she mumbled as she scanned the fax. A chill ran down her spine.

CHAPTER 2

As the plane touched down in San Francisco Tuesday evening, Cait again questioned her decision to fly cross-country on a potential ruse. Yet the remote chance she was the rightful heir of this mysterious aunt—whose family name she happened to share—piqued her interest.

She called the attorney back and agreed to use the ticket held for her at the airport but insisted on making her own car and hotel reservations, even though at his expense.

After spending the night at the Sheraton Four Points Hotel, Cait was back in her rented Saturn by nine o'clock and on the 101S freeway headed toward the San Mateo Bridge.

She arrived in Livermore an hour before her scheduled appointment at eleven with Mr. Lane and found Peet's Coffee a few blocks from his office. She reread the trust Lane had faxed her as she sat at a window table with a cup of black coffee. The same uneasy sensation she'd had when she first read the trust rolled around in the pit of her stomach. Tilson wasn't a common name. If her dad, Randolph Tilson, and this Tasha Bening were siblings, why had her parents kept it a secret?

Cait lost track of time and was surprised to see it was almost eleven o'clock. She finished her coffee, spilling a couple of drops on her blouse as she tucked the trust papers back in her handbag. She left the coffee shop and drove the few short blocks to a small house similar to others with business signs in the windows.

She went in and walked up to the receptionist. "My name is Cait Pepper. I have an appointment with Mr. Lane."

The blonde young woman stood; her dimples flashed as she smiled. "He's waiting for you, Mrs. Pepper. You can go straight back."

Cait studied Stanton Lane as he walked from behind a beautifully polished oak desk to shake her hand. He stood a stout five-nine, and was expensively dressed from his gray pinstripe suit, pink shirt, and gray silk tie to the fancy gold cuff links peeking out from his sleeves. He sported a silver buzz haircut that suggested a military heritage. His cheeks had a slight droop like tired saddlebags. She guessed him to be in his early sixties.

As they shook hands, something akin to startled recognition appeared momentarily in his blue eyes as he stared at Cait. He took a step back and scrutinized her with unnerving intensity, his eyes raking her from her head to her shoes. Cait felt like a bug under a microscope.

"Do I pass inspection, Mr. Lane?"

"I don't mean to embarrass you, Mrs. Pepper," he said. "I knew Tasha for ten years, and your resemblance to her is uncanny."

Noticing his flushed cheeks, she said, "You didn't embarrass me."

He walked back around his desk. "How was your flight?"

"Long, but the Sheraton near the airport was lovely. I hope I didn't abuse your offer." Cait felt a twinge of guilt for her indulgent hotel selection.

He smiled and motioned to the burgundy leather chairs facing his desk. "Not at all. You're here, and that's what's important. As I said on the phone, time is of the essence. I trust you read the fax I sent."

She sat down. "Several times."

"Tasha's trust is short and straightforward," he said as he sat

14

down behind his desk. "You're her only heir. There were no children. Hilton Bening, Tasha's husband, passed away almost a year ago."

Cait moved to the edge of her seat. "Mr. Lane, I came a long way on short notice, interrupting my vacation time. Could you show me proof that I am this woman's niece? I can't quite wrap my brain around this mystery aunt of mine."

"You truly knew nothing about her?" Lane asked.

"No. My parents died in a plane crash five years ago," Cait replied. "There's no one left to ask."

Lane interlaced his fingers and stared at them for a moment as if gathering his thoughts. "Your father, Randolph Tilson, and Tasha Tilson Bening shared the same birthday. They were twins."

"Really? Well then, that solves that. My father was an only child."

"I'm afraid that's not true." He opened a folder on his desk. "Tasha was an extremely private person, but she seemed to know a lot about you, your career as a police officer and later as a crime analyst."

Cait's hands began to sweat. "How did she know about me? And if she really was my aunt, why suddenly care about a niece she'd had no use for until now?"

"I'm sorry, Mrs. Pepper—"

"Cait. Please call me Cait. I was divorcing my husband when he suddenly passed away, and I never got around to changing my name back to Tilson."

Lane sat back in his chair. "I'm sorry, Cait, but I don't really know why she never contacted you. Maybe your father kept in touch with her. When Tasha died, I lost a very dear friend. She was as bright and lively the day before she died as she was when I met her." He placed his hands on his desk. "Your inheritance is very real, I assure you. After going through her house, maybe you'll find something that will put your mind at ease about accepting your inheritance." He cleared his throat. "As I mentioned on the phone, there is one condition."

Here it comes. "And that is?"

He paused, then said, "The estate cannot be sold. If you choose not to move to California to manage it, the estate will go to a specified foundation for the arts."

Cait sat still, too overwhelmed to speak.

Lane checked his watch. "You'll have an opportunity this afternoon to see the estate. Unfortunately, I'm due in court, but afterward I'll take you there."

Cait cleared her throat. "Just how big is her estate?"

His gaze dropped to the file folder before him. "Quite sizeable. There's the big house, vineyard, and two Shakespeare theaters. All told, about twenty acres. Naturally, there's the financial means to manage it. But why don't we wait until we tour the property? You'll have a better understanding of what's involved." He glanced again at his watch. "I expect to be out of court by two."

She rose. "Where is the house? I'm sure I can find it on my own."

"Very good, then." Lane pulled a map of Livermore out of a drawer and traced the route with a red pen. "Do you have a cell phone?"

"Of course, and a good sense of direction."

He jotted a phone number on the sheet. "It's not far, maybe fifteen minutes. Call my clerk if there's a problem." He handed the map to Cait and then reached into his jacket pocket and produced a key. "This will unlock the front door." He stood and they shook hands. "I'll see you there after two unless I'm lucky and get out sooner," he said, smoothing the front of his jacket.

She thanked him and turned to leave.

"Cait?"

She looked back.

Lane's eyes lightly misted. "Thank you for coming. Tasha would have been very pleased."

Cait nodded, hoping she wouldn't live to regret this trip.

CHAPTER 3

As Cait turned into the entrance of the estate, she noticed foot-high polished gold letters mounted on a stone wall—Bening Vineyard & Shakespeare Festival. She accelerated up the steep driveway and passed rows of grapevines forming straight rows on both sides like young cadets standing at attention. She trembled with anxiety and slowed after nearly grazing a grapevine at the edge of the driveway.

She pulled up in front of a three-story yellow house with a long porch. Stained-glass windows sparkled where the sun glanced off them. She stepped out of the car and stood a moment appraising the house before climbing the stone steps to a massive oak front door. As she reached for a brass knocker that resembled a Harlequin mask, a deep male voice from behind startled her.

"Can I help you?"

Cait whirled and dropped the key.

A tall muscular man stood before her. As she stepped back, she made a quick assessment of him—attractive in an earthy way, black hair cropped close like a skullcap, broad shoulders, and ice blue eyes. She also noticed a hole in the knee of his jeans, a tan leather vest over a blue work shirt, and thick forearms where his sleeves were rolled up.

His eyes rolled over her. "Should I call the cops or wait until you plead your case?"

"I wasn't told anyone would be here."

"Their mistake. I'm the stage manager for the festival."

She noticed a bulge beneath his vest. "Since when do stage managers pack a gun?"

His eyes narrowed.

I really should stop taunting people, especially when they're armed.

"You're good," he said. "But I still want to know what you're doing here. You a lawyer?"

"Not even close." She allowed herself a self-satisfied smile. "It seems I've inherited this place. Technically, that makes me your boss."

He raised his eyebrows but didn't respond.

Cait studied the man as closely as he did her and thought him to be in his late thirties and more rugged-looking than classically handsome. Under his scrutiny, she became aware of her unruly hair and the coffee stains on her new silk blouse. His half smile did nothing to dispel her discomfort, and she cursed herself for allowing him his moment of chauvinistic pleasure.

He held his hand out, blocking her way. "ID?"

She debated—driver's license or law enforcement identification—then reached in her handbag for her Ohio driver's license and handed it to him.

He scowled and stared up at her. "*You're* Cait Pepper?"

"Isn't that what it says?" She reached over and tapped her license with a peach fingernail.

"You're Tasha's niece?"

Geesh. Everyone knew but me. "So it seems."

He returned her ID. "I wasn't told you were coming."

"Don't feel bad. I didn't know I had an aunt until Monday when Tasha's attorney called. Do you know Stanton Lane?"

"Yeah, I know him." He stared at her for a long time before reaching into his jeans pocket and pulling out a key. "Name's Royal Tanner." He unlocked the door and held it open for her.

She picked up her key from where it had fallen on the porch, dropped it in her handbag and stepped inside. Sunlight spilled through stained-glass windows and highlighted a faded Persian rug surrounded by buffed hardwood floors that hinted at the house's Victorian heritage. She surveyed the interior of what appeared to be a great room, empty except for a polished mahogany grand piano set in the curve of the staircase. The walls were lined with gilded frames of Shakespearean characters. She tipped her head back and looked up at a massive crystal chandelier.

Tanner closed the door behind him. "The house is haunted. It's been remodeled, but it's still an old house." He watched Cait with a cocked eyebrow. "Old houses sometimes have ghostly residents that refuse to leave. But don't worry. I'm told they're friendly."

She ignored the comment and circled the room, well aware of him watching her. "Where's the rest of the furniture?"

"They seldom entertained in this room, but when they did they brought in tables and chairs from storage. What furniture the Benings couldn't use upstairs in their living quarters, they either donated or used in their theaters." He ushered her across the room toward a hallway that led to smaller rooms. "These rooms were to serve as her gift shop until she could have one built."

Cait stuck her head in one of the doors. Unopened boxes and crates were stacked in the middle of the room. "What's in those?"

"Merchandise Tasha ordered—puppets, tapestries, drama masks. Everything Shakespearean, I'm told." His gaze swept over her. "You're up to this, aren't you?"

She turned to him. "Mr. Tanner, I don't have the luxury of time, and—"

"But you do like Shakespeare?"

She sighed with impatience. "I was an English-lit major in

college. After graduation, I chose a different path."

He grinned. "There's always *Shakespeare for Dummies.* You like wine?"

"White and dry."

"That's good since you're surrounded by vineyards." He turned. "Kitchen's back this way. Has all that jazzy stuff you women think you need but never use."

She shot him a dark look. She wasn't fond of cooking, but loved the large kitchen—black speckled granite counters, stainless steel appliances, and particularly the stained-glass window over the sink with its rendition of a vineyard.

He pointed to an open doorway at the back of the kitchen. "That's an office Tasha's secretary uses. Ready to go upstairs?"

With a last look at the kitchen, she nodded. "Sure."

On the second floor, he showed her a sitting room, small bedroom, bath, and kitchenette.

Cait thought about her late husband's taste for chrome, glass, and black leather. This house suited her better with its muted greens, pumpkin, creams, and choice antique pieces. A wall of shelves filled with art books and leather-bound classics caught her attention, but before she had a chance to examine them, Tanner steered her toward a door tucked away in a small alcove.

He held the door open. "This way up to the master bedroom."

"What, no elevator, Mr. Tanner?" she said, then regretted her snap comment.

"Watch your manners," he said. "And, by the way, it's RT." He urged her up the stairs.

A king-size sleigh bed almost filled the back wall. Its downy coverlet of ivory with a mix of green and royal blue provided a cheerful contrast to the cooler blue walls. Sunlight flickered through bay windows at the front of the room and spread across two white wicker chairs and a chaise lounge covered in shades of tan. To the right of the bay was a niche just large enough for

Tasha's desk, chair, computer and printer.

"You plan to move in?" RT asked.

"I already have a home, thanks very much."

"You're not thinking of selling this place, are you?"

"Are you always this direct?"

He crossed his arms. "I'd like to know your intentions."

"I've barely had time to catch my breath, but I couldn't sell if I wanted to. If I don't move to California, the estate will be turned over to a foundation. Which reminds me, I need a hotel reservation. Any suggestions?"

"If you're not going to stay here, try over by the local airport. You might find the Hilton to suit your taste."

"Thanks. I'll check it out." Suddenly overwhelmed with the burden of her inheritance, she sank down on the edge of the bed and ran her hand over the coverlet. "How did Tasha die?"

He hesitated. "Didn't Lane tell you?"

"Mr. Lane seems to have a limited vocabulary, but he indicated heart failure."

He stared down at Cait. "According to the autopsy report, the cause of her death is undetermined."

"Really? Where did she die?"

"In this bed."

Cait frowned and stood up, not because she was skittish, but because the site of a sudden death was considered a crime scene until judged otherwise. However, it had been a couple of weeks now since Tasha died.

Cait was surprised to find Stanton Lane waiting for them inside the front door when they returned downstairs.

Lane smiled. "I see you've met."

"We've just finished a brief tour," she said. "I didn't expect you so soon."

"I got lucky. Case was dismissed," he said.

A door banged from the back of the house.

"Probably Marcus," RT said.

A rangy man in his late twenties strolled into the room. He froze when he saw them.

"Marcus Singer," RT said, "meet Cait Pepper, Tasha's niece. Marcus was Tasha's secretary."

Marcus stood erect and silent as if ready for military inspection, his beady eyes riveted on Cait.

Her first impression of the man was that he was physically bankrupt, but when they shook hands he almost cracked her knuckles. He wore his arrogance in the form of a white starched shirt opened halfway to his belt buckle. She thought his spiky strawberry-blond hair looked stiff enough to pick a lock. "Hello, Marcus. Have I inherited you too?"

Marcus blinked and then shrugged.

Lane coughed. "Well, then, shall we go outside? I'm sure you'd like to see the theaters."

Marcus Singer backed away and disappeared around a corner. Cait wondered where the Benings had found him—on Craigslist?

Cait and RT followed Lane out the back door.

"That's Tasha's meditation garden." Lane pointed out across the path. "She began each day here with a cup of chamomile tea."

Cait walked over to look at a small copper sign imprinted with "MEDITATION." A bird dropping dotted the first "I." A white marble dolphin rested nearby on a pedestal surrounded by a patch of fragrant lime thyme. It reminded her of a verse she'd seen—*Thyme in a garden is time well spent.* She felt a twinge of empathy for the aunt she'd never known.

"You okay?" RT asked.

She shook off an odd feeling of reverence as she left the garden. "I'm fine. So where are the theaters?"

"Not far," RT said.

They followed a brick path through a row of cypress trees then into an open area of wildflowers before coming to a trellis flanked by terra-cotta oil jugs.

Lane opened the ornate gate beneath the trellis. "The theater complex is through here."

RT hesitated and pointed to a raised platform to the right of the brick courtyard. "Tasha wanted a Green Show similar to the one where she worked at the Oregon Shakespeare Festival, so Marcus built this for her." He turned his back to Lane and leaned close to Cait. He whispered, "Don't be too quick to let your inheritance go. This place was important to Tasha."

Startled by the concern in his voice, she said, "I won't. What's a Green Show?"

His voice back to normal, he said, "It's a short routine of music and dance; a perspective on the play the audience will see. Marcus can explain better than I and tell you which of the plays will showcase a Green Show."

Lane had walked ahead and waited for them to catch up. "We'll start with the Blackfriars Theater." He crossed the courtyard and proceeded up a path that ended at a plain small white building. He pulled a set of keys from his pocket and unlocked the door.

Cait stumbled as she stepped inside the theater.

RT grabbed her arm to steady her.

"Watch those cords," Lane cautioned.

The dark theater made Cait think of the old fantastical Duke of Dark Corners from *Measure for Measure*. When Lane hit the lights, the theater still appeared dark. The walls and stage were painted black. Wooden shutters, screens and trellises were positioned to block sunlight. Tiered benches surrounded the stage. "Wow," Cait said. "This *is* small."

"It only seats a hundred and forty," Lane said. "Some plays

are best suited for small, intimate settings like this. It's mostly used for experimental and, shall I say, risky productions?"

Cait stepped up onto the stage and looked out over the seating. "I love it. I wish I could stay here long enough to see a play."

"I hope you will," Lane said. "Remember when I said time was of the essence? *Tongue of a Bird* is scheduled to open the season on this stage since it's an indoor theater." He glanced at RT. "Mr. Tanner can explain better than I about the plays since he is stage manager."

Cait sensed tension in Lane's voice every time he mentioned RT. She wondered if it was resentment or jealousy.

"Let's move on," RT said, his voice gruff.

They left the Blackfriars Theater and crossed the courtyard to the Elizabethan and around to the back where two men were measuring large sheets of plywood and another was installing wiring.

"This theater isn't finished?" she asked.

RT slid his hands in the pockets of his jeans and frowned. "It was until a couple of months ago, just before Tasha died."

"What happened?" she asked.

"Fire," he said.

Cait stared up at the theater. "What caused it?"

"Arson."

Her head snapped around. "My God. Do the police know who started it?"

"No," Lane said. "I warned Tasha about building up here. The house has been here a long time, but she had to have her Shakespeare festival 'to keep the arts alive,' she insisted."

Surprised by the sudden sharp tone of Lane's voice, Cait stared at him and noticed an odd expression cross his face. Was it regret? Fear? Or indigestion?

Lane turned away.

"Well, good for Tasha," Cait said. "If more people got involved in the arts, maybe there'd be less crime in this world." She glanced at RT and thought she saw his eyes sparkle with suppressed laughter.

Lane glanced back. "You're new here, Cait. You don't understand. People in this valley don't want their hills disturbed. If you want to build something, keep it low so as not to obstruct the view. And not on top of a hill." He flushed as if he'd said too much.

Cait's dealings with lawyers were usually limited to tax issues—those of her parents' and her deceased husband's estate. She had yet to find out what Stanton Lane was capable of, but apparently he had strong opinions about the environment.

"I have an early court date tomorrow," Lane said abruptly. "Do you plan to stay at the house?"

"No," she said, "I wouldn't feel right about it. I understand there are hotels near the airport."

"There are. If you're ready to leave, I'll show you how to get there."

She glanced at the theater. "Can't we go inside the theater?"

"I'll take you through tomorrow," RT said. "Maybe the contractors will be finished by then."

Disappointed, Cait nodded and started to follow Lane back toward the house and their cars. When she looked over her shoulder, she saw RT watching. "I'll catch up," she told Lane and walked back to RT.

"Forget something?" RT asked.

"I wanted to thank you for the house tour," she said, "and to ask what you meant about not giving up my inheritance. I had the feeling you wanted to tell me something other than about the Green Show."

He hesitated. "Be careful. That's all."

Cait studied his body language—rigid and tough—and

wondered what underlying meaning his warning had that could affect her inheritance and her visit. She nodded and backed away. "See you tomorrow."

"I doubt Mr. Tanner knows squat about Shakespeare," Lane said when she caught up with him. "Tasha said he was a family friend, but something doesn't quite ring true with him."

"Mr. Lane, I work in law enforcement, and one of the basic rules of survival is to observe and analyze people."

Only later did Cait think back on her words to Lane as she immersed herself in the world of Shakespearean actors and found most were not what they appeared to be.

CHAPTER 4

Cait's inheritance seemed less a gift and more like an albatross tightly wound around her neck. The strained conduct between RT and Stanton Lane coupled with Marcus Singer's odd behavior had her head swimming. And the fire at the Elizabethan Theater compounded her apprehension. What could anyone hope to gain from burning it down? She drew in a deep breath and clutched the wheel as she drove, tempted to grab the next plane back to Ohio while at the same time knowing her curiosity had been aroused.

She took the airport exit as Lane had indicated, and shortly pulled into the Sheraton. When she got to her room, she opened her laptop and checked her e-mail. She deleted all but one from her friend Samantha in Columbus wishing her luck with the inheritance and asking her to sample some wines for her. After sending a reply off, she stretched out on the bed to think about RT's warning but was soon sound asleep.

The phone rang, startling Cait. She fought her way out of a nightmare of floating drama masks and gnarly grapevines entangled around her ankles and looked at the red numbers on the bedside clock—4:00 A.M. She grabbed the phone. "Hello?"

"It's RT. There's been another fire at the Elizabethan Theater. I suggest you get over here now. The police will want to talk to you."

She bolted up to the edge of the bed. "I'll come right away." Since she was still wearing the same blouse and slacks from earlier in the day, she grabbed her handbag and keys and left the hotel. It hadn't occurred to her until she was on the road to wonder how RT had known which hotel she was staying in.

Police vehicles were parked on the road at the foot of the driveway. Red and blue lights flashed against the black night. A police officer stopped Cait from going up. She rolled her window down and read his badge—THOM. He held a radio in one hand and a flashlight in the other.

"You can't go up there, ma'am."

Cait dug in her purse for her ID and held it up for him to see. "I'm Cait Pepper. I just inherited this place." As strange as that sounded to her, she automatically accepted the responsibility.

He took her ID and flashed his light on it, then returned it to her and motioned for her to continue on. "Drive carefully."

She accelerated up the drive. At the top, she parked off to the side to leave room for emergency vehicles, jumped out and ran toward the theater.

The flames had been extinguished, but smoke billowed out from the charred remains at the rear of the theater. A photographer walking the perimeter snapped pictures as a fire truck arrived from another direction with sirens wailing. Firemen dragging heavy hoses forced Cait back. She saw RT and a fireman heading her way. "What happened?"

"Nothing definite yet, but a good possibility it was arson," the fireman said.

Another firefighter—a female with a dog—approached. The dog lunged impatiently on the end of his leash. "Tork and I are going in now," she said.

The fireman nodded. "Be careful."

Cait studied the dog. "That's an accelerant detection dog, isn't it?"

"Sure is." She gave the dog a friendly pat and hurried off.

Cait knew weirdoes set fires for the thrill of watching the blaze, while others sometimes hung around and offered to help. She looked at RT. "Notice anyone hanging around that shouldn't be up here?"

He wiped his hands on a dirty towel hanging from his pocket. "No. Not when I made my rounds at eleven and not now."

"By the look of things," the fireman said, "the fire didn't burn long. Damned lucky the winds are down and summer hasn't set in yet. Wouldn't take long for a fire to sweep across these hills when they're dry."

"Excuse me," Cait said, and hurried after the female firefighter and dog amid the smoke-choking air as bits of charred paper floated and swirled around the theater. She covered her nose and mouth with her hands as she skirted around hoses and pools of water, but the firefighter disappeared through the charred doorway before Cait could catch up with her.

"Found the point of origin," someone hollered. "Not sure if it was deliberately set, but if I had to bet on it, I'd say it was."

Cait stopped one of the firefighters as he exited the smoldering structure. "Excuse me. Arsonists usually leave a fingerprint. Some kind of pattern. How long before you'll know for sure that it's arson?"

He stared at her. "Who are you?"

"Cait Pepper. I just inherited this place." She wrapped her arms around herself against the cold night air and grimaced at the rankness of the smoke. She wondered about those who chose to work fire scenes on a daily basis. Of course, there were plenty who'd say the same about her choice of profession as a cop and later a crime analyst.

The firefighter removed his hat and wiped his forehead with his sleeve. "I'm sorry, ma'am. At least the fire was confined to the rear of the theater. We'll let you know as soon as we're sure what started it." He replaced his hat and hurried off.

RT walked up to her. "Come on, Cait. There's nothing we can do here. Let's go up to the house so you can get warm." As he turned, she saw his gun nestled at the small of his back.

"I saw a fire truck come from a different direction," she said, as they jumped puddles of water. "You didn't tell me there was another way up here."

He stopped and turned toward her. "You haven't been around long enough to find out. For all I know, you'll be back on the next plane to Ohio."

Her hands clenched into fists at her sides. "Hey, I didn't ask for this—"

"Neither did I," he snapped. Then, "Look, I'm sorry, Cait. The fire . . . sometimes I wonder why I'm still here."

Frustration flared between them like lightning.

"Same for me. I'd intended my vacation to be spent on getting my life back together." Cait turned and walked ahead of RT before she said something she would later regret. When she reached the house, she entered through the back and then stood in the middle of the kitchen not knowing what to do next. She would not allow anger or exhaustion to overcome good judgment, even though she felt as if she'd been tossed into a frenzied ring of fire. She pulled a stool out, sat down, and rested her forehead on her arms.

When she heard the back door open, she looked up and saw RT heading to the coffeepot and watched as he filled it with water and opened a bag of Peet's coffee. The desire for a cup of coffee made her dizzy.

"Look, I'm sorry I yelled at you," he said, "but you've got some attitude. Must get you in a lot of trouble." He turned and smiled. "Truce?"

She nodded.

A knock came at the back door.

RT opened it to the fire marshal.

31

"Bad news," the man said. "Definitely arson."

RT nodded. "I figured as much, since this is the second attempt. I'm making coffee if you guys want some."

"Thanks, appreciate it, but we're okay."

Cait joined them at the door. "How was it set?"

"The wigs were torched. They're a total loss." He backed out of the doorway. "We'll be here for a while." He turned and left.

The percolator slowed and then stopped. RT filled two mugs and handed one to Cait. They sat at the counter, drinking coffee. RT hung his head and closed his eyes.

Cait watched him over the rim of her cup. "What's wrong? I hope you're not blaming yourself for the fire."

He looked up, his eyes weary. "It's not that."

"I don't understand."

"I came here to protect Tasha. Now she's dead, and I'm no closer to knowing who killed her or why anyone would want to destroy her theater."

Cait froze. "What did you say?"

"Sorry," he said. "I shouldn't have said that."

"But you did, and now I need an explanation."

He took a long drag of coffee. "Look, if I said you have nothing to fear from me, would you believe it?"

She wondered where he was heading with this, but her instinct was to trust him. "Maybe."

He stared hard at Cait, then nodded. "I don't believe Tasha died from a heart attack. I think she was murdered. I just can't prove it."

CHAPTER 5

Cait's inheritance just took a turn for the worse, like a scene from one of Shakespeare's plays. She set her mug down, splashing coffee on the counter. "Do you have evidence suggesting murder?"

RT rose. "Stay here. There's something I want to show you." He left, and the back door slammed behind him.

Murdered? He's got to be kidding. As she reached for a paper napkin to wipe up the spill, her instincts told her he wasn't.

When the back door burst open, she assumed RT was back. A cold draft swept across the kitchen along with a woman as tiny as a wren. She flounced into the kitchen like a turbulent weather front, her hand fanning her nose.

"Sweet Jesus." She coughed, blinked a few times, and then froze when she saw Cait sitting at the counter. "Who are you?"

"I could ask the same of you," Cait said.

"Rachel Cross, a neighbor who called nine-one-one."

Cait sized the woman up—size zero, mid-fifties, striking. Clad in narrow-fitting white jeans, tight red sweater, bleached blonde hair piled on top of her head and held in place with rhinestone clips.

Cait forced a smile. "I'm Cait Pepper. Tasha's niece."

Rachel's eyes popped, her jaw dropped. She stared hard at Cait. "Impossible. Tasha and I are close friends, and never once has she mentioned having a niece." She glanced around the kitchen. "Where is she?"

Stunned, Cait rose, pulled a stool out, and prayed for RT's quick return. "Why don't you sit down? There's fresh coffee." *She's a close friend and doesn't know Tasha's dead?*

Rachel climbed onto the stool, her feet dangling. "I have a strange feeling I'm going to need that coffee."

"Cream? Sugar?"

"Black. None of that fancy latté stuff."

"How close a neighbor are you?" Cait asked as she filled a coffee mug.

"Close. Just across the road." Rachel narrowed her eyes on Cait. "Are you staying at the house?"

"No, I'm at a local hotel." She set the coffee in front of Rachel. "Have you any idea who would want to burn the theater?"

"Of course not." Rachel blew on her coffee. "Those firefighters wouldn't let me near the theater, but I managed to get under that yellow tape before some big lug picked me up and set me back down on the other side." She brushed at her cashmere sweater. "Will you look at this? Soot!"

Cait tried not to laugh.

RT walked in the door and stopped when he saw Rachel. "Rachel? I thought you were still frolicking about Europe."

"Be nice, RT. That exhausting tour finally ended, thank God. My last commitment for a while, and just in time to help Tasha with her festival." She rubbed her nose. "What is going on around here, RT? Why is someone determined to torch the Elizabethan?"

Cait looked from one to the other. "I guess you know each other."

"We sure do," Rachel smiled. "RT is Tasha's favorite person." She frowned. "Well, second to Hilton, of course."

Cait saw RT's jaw tighten and wondered if he'd caught on that Rachel was unaware Tasha was dead.

RT set a folder on the counter. "Rachel is a Shakespearean

actress, Cait."

"So where *is* Tasha?" Rachel fluffed her coiffure.

Cait hated this part of being a police officer. Giving family and friends bad news depressed her for days. She looked at RT.

"Well?" Rachel asked.

RT slipped his arm across Rachel's shoulder. "Tasha's dead. I thought you knew. Ben was supposed to call and tell you."

Rachel's face drained of color. "Dead?"

Cait and RT exchanged looks.

"Are you okay, Rachel?" he asked.

"Of course I'm not okay! What happened? When did she die?"

"Two weeks ago. March twenty-first. An apparent heart attack," he said.

She pressed her fist to her lips and stared at him. "Rubbish. She had regular checkups. Ask Marcus. He'll tell you. He always drove her to her doctor's appointment."

Cait watched Rachel with interest. As a cop and crime analyst, she was familiar with this kind of denial, but wondered why Rachel hadn't shed tears if she was the close friend she claimed to be. Then she chastised herself. Everyone handled bad news differently.

Rachel picked up her coffee mug. "Tasha would be turning in her grave if she knew there'd been another fire. Her heart and soul went into her Shakespeare festival." Her eyes snapped on Cait. "*I'll* see to it that the festival thrives."

Was that a warning? Cait analyzed Rachel's odd behavior: No tears or anger at her husband for not telling her Tasha had died. "Rachel, do you think Tasha's death is related to the fires?"

"What are you suggesting?" Rachel grabbed RT's arm. "She's a stranger, RT. Are you sure she's Tasha's niece? Maybe she had something to do with the fire."

"Calm down," RT said. "Talk to Stanton Lane. He called

and asked her to come."

"Stan would have told me about her."

"You were out of the country, Rachel," he said.

"I didn't know I had an aunt, Rachel," Cait said. "Not until Mr. Lane called. And I didn't set the fire. Why would I?"

"Why don't I take you home, Rachel?" RT said.

She slid off the stool. "Fine." At the door, Rachel stopped and looked back at Cait. "I don't understand why Tasha didn't tell me about you or why you didn't know about her. She had a wonderful spirit, like a harmonious flock of birds. Energy flared off her like a live electric wire. We didn't always agree, but actors are sensitive people and highly opinionated." She grasped RT's arm and flung her head back. "Tasha expected the Bard to translate into big business for Livermore. I intend to see that happens."

After RT and Rachel left, Cait rinsed the mugs and left them in the sink.

Her eyes lit on the folder RT had dropped on the counter. She picked it up, opened it, and saw Tasha's autopsy report.

Cait knew there had to be good reason for an autopsy. Most jurisdictions operated under similar guidelines. Violent deaths—homicides and suicides—and those considered suspicious, sudden, or unexpected required an autopsy.

She sat at the counter to read it. An examination of the body showed no evidence of heart disease, but Tasha's potassium-chloride level was exceptionally high. Potassium occurred naturally in the body and was necessary for life. Cait had a deficiency as a teenager. As a result, she had to eat a banana every day.

Her eyes slid down the page until she came across succinyl-choline, a familiar word from an unsolved case she had assisted on. She learned that all bodies have elevated potassium at the time an autopsy is done, which is why pathologists don't usually test for it. Cait frowned. Succinylcholine paralyzes the body's muscles. The victim's awake and alert, but can't speak or bat an eye. Death is quick, only three or four minutes. *This must be what concerns RT.*

She continued to search for any mention of injection sites on Tasha's arms or thighs, but found none. The autopsy only suggested the possibility of injection as a way to increase the level of potassium. Cait thought that only someone who understood how the drug worked could use it as a tool for murder. She also thought that succinylcholine could be stolen from a hospital or even bought on the Internet. She made a mental note to see Tasha's doctor.

What she next read disturbed her.

Breast and uterine tissues, striations over the breasts and abdomen.

Her throat tightened as she reread it. Had Tasha given birth? If so, what happened to the baby?

After the toxicology tests for blood, the cause of death was "undetermined death for a sixty-three-year-old woman."

The pathologist findings were electronically signed, as well as the death certificate.

CHAPTER 6

A white envelope slid from the folder and fell to the floor. Cait slipped off the stool and leaned down to pick it up. It was addressed to Mr. and Mrs. R. R. Tanner, San Diego, California. She peeked inside the envelope and saw it was empty.

"The letter was destroyed," RT said from the doorway.

Startled, Cait jumped.

RT picked the envelope up and tossed it in the trash. Then he poured coffee into a mug and sat down at the counter. "The letter was from Tasha." He tested his coffee. "She sent it after the first fire at the Elizabethan." He set his cup down and stared hard at Cait. "Before we talk about what's in that folder, I want to know your intentions and if you're really interested in Tasha's theaters. If not, I'll call her friends at the Oregon Shakespeare Festival and ask if anyone is available to come here to help Rachel with the festival."

His blue eyes bore into Cait's, radiating fierce and uncompromising determination; his jaw held a stubborn set. Normally, Cait could size people up in quick-time; at this moment she felt totally helpless. Two days in California wasn't long enough to know whom she could trust or to understand the full extent of her inheritance. Every hour held yet another surprise. How could she give RT what he obviously was asking for—a commitment to Tasha's festival—until she understood what it would mean for her own future?

To stall for time, she went to the end of the counter and

38

absently picked up a pipe she'd noticed earlier, its bowl resting on a small china plate.

"That was Hilton's," RT said, his voice soft. "Tasha kept it there because it made her feel he'd be back."

Cait brought the pipe to her nose and sniffed. "English. Same as my dad smoked." She put it down. "RT, all I can promise for now is to stay until things settle down a bit."

He nodded. "What about your job?"

"I'm on vacation. I read the autopsy report, and I want to know how Tasha died as much as you do and why someone set fire to the theater. Until three days ago I'd never heard of Tasha Bening or Livermore, California. I have a lot to catch up on."

He smiled. "Okay. I can live with that. I guess I should apologize for rushing you, but my time here is limited too." He ran his hand over his hair. "We seem to have the same goals. Maybe together we can figure this out before we return to our jobs. Agreed?"

"Works for me." She picked up her coffee and finished it. "Is your family here with you?"

He frowned. "What?"

"The envelope. Mr. and Mrs. Tanner. That's you, isn't it?"

A corner of his lips curled. "It was addressed to my folks."

"Oh. So . . . you're not married?"

He leaned close enough for her to catch a whiff of woodsy cologne. "That's none of your business." He rinsed his coffee mug at the sink and pulled the plug on the percolator. He turned and asked, "Where's your husband, Mrs. Pepper?"

Cait froze. She never knew how to answer that question. Widowed? Divorced? "I'm widowed."

His face softened. "I'm sorry. That's not my business either."

"It's okay," she said, and changed the subject. "Don't take this the wrong way, but I have to ask. Why do I feel you're out of your element as stage manager? You know, like the righteous

Detective Kojak versus the bumbling Inspector Clousseau?"

He reared back with laughter; his eyes sparkled. "Oh, man. Do you watch those old reruns too?"

She grinned. "I love them." To hear him laugh like that eased the tension between them, but he didn't answer her question. She'd been up since four and was exhausted. A glance at the wall clock indicted eight forty-five.

"You're okay, Cait Pepper. I think I like you."

She felt her cheeks pinken. "We've agreed to share information about the Bening estate and everyone connected to it. Right?"

RT straddled a stool. His smile slid away, the intensity in his eyes deep enough to touch the soles of her shoes. "Right."

"Then tell me about Hilton Bening. Mr. Lane said he died nine months ago."

"Seven. He died last September. He was the love of Tasha's life. They were devoted to each other," he said.

"That's not very long ago. How did he die?"

"Riding accident. He fell from his horse at his ranch."

"I'm sorry. I'd like to see the ranch sometime."

"I'll take you."

"Thanks. I'd appreciate it." She glanced around the kitchen. "I feel I'm invading someone's privacy by being here. I got the impression Rachel intended for me to feel like a trespasser."

"You never know with Rachel, but she'll come around." He leaned against the counter. "When Hilton died, my mom came up and spent a couple of days with Tasha. Mom met her when they appeared together in a play." He rubbed his hand over his jaw. "Tasha had a crystal-clear vision of what she wanted to do here: workshops and summer seminars for high-school seniors to learn set design, props, costumes, all that behind-the-scenes stuff. Everything her parents refused to allow her to do. They thought acting was a frivolous vocation. She left home right after high school and never looked back."

"She sounds like a strong woman."

He smiled. "Yes, as I said, she knew what she wanted. A tea is planned in a few weeks, something you'll want to talk to Rachel about."

She frowned. "I'll be gone by then."

"Still, I think you should talk to her about it. This *is* your inheritance. Last year, to help promote her Shakespeare festival, Tasha held a tea in the front room and invited all the local officials. Some faculty and students from Las Positas College were also included."

"There's no furniture in the front room. Is someone going to play the piano while the guests stand around sipping tea?"

He chuckled. "A little respect here, please. It's a Steinway that makes even me sound good. Marcus set up tables and chairs from storage. The same will be done this year." He glanced at his watch. "I have a call to make. Are you staying or going back to the hotel?"

"I'll stay here for a while. I want to look around."

"Catch you later, then," he said and left.

She was starved. She found a fresh container of milk in the refrigerator, an unopened box of Cheerios in the cupboard, and settled down at the counter to eat. She noticed the folder with Tasha's autopsy report was missing. They'd never gotten around to discussing its contents.

After she ate and rinsed her dishes, Cait peered into the three rooms RT said were intended to be a gift shop. Boxes needed to be opened and the merchandise displayed on the shelves, but she was too tired to do it now and returned to the kitchen. She went into the office where Marcus worked, but he wasn't there. A door led to the outside.

The air had cleared of smoke; the sun was brilliant. She was surprised to see RT in Tasha's meditation garden, his cell phone to his ear. He was sitting on a patch of grass, his head back against a white marble pedestal, a smile on his face.

He looks happy, she thought.

RT saw her, said a few words into the phone, and then snapped it shut and stood.

"Sorry. I didn't mean to interrupt," she said.

"No problem."

Cait hesitated and then sat down on the marble bench. Everywhere she looked, lupine and wild mustard were straining toward the sun, and she understood why Tasha began each day in this garden. "This is nice."

"Yeah, it is," he said.

She glanced up at RT. Even among their peers, cops don't share information about their cases unless they were working on the same one. Respecting need-to-know logic was ingrained into her and often overlapped her personal life. But with her time here so short, there was only one way to learn and that was to ask. "Will you be going back to San Diego after you leave here?"

He stared off into the distance. "For a while. But I travel a lot."

"Really? You make a living at that?" *Geez, Cait.*

He looked down at her. "As you've probably guessed, stage manager was a cover."

She smiled. "Yeah, I thought so."

"I'm a Navy SEAL. I go wherever I'm sent."

That RT was involved in covert activities didn't surprise Cait. He was sharp, serious, and had a take-charge attitude. But a SEAL? She'd have to think on that.

"Lost your tongue?" His bitten-back smile bordered on arrogance.

"I'm trying to visualize a match between the elite Naval Special Operations unit and Royal Tanner. Now I understand why Tasha wanted you here."

"Yeah. I hope I'm here long enough to get the bastard who murdered her and Hilton."

She stared at him. "Whoa. Wait a minute. You think both were murdered?"

RT shook his head as if to dismiss what he'd just said.

"I thought we were sharing information. Tell me about Hilton."

"I told you. He fell off his horse. Let it go at that."

Frustrated, she said, "Is that what a SEAL would do? Let it go? Why did you become a SEAL?"

He placed his hands at the small of his back and stretched. "To be where expectations and demands to perform were high." He grinned. "And I liked their toys."

She sighed. She could relate to that. "Were you working out of the country when Tasha sent that letter?"

He sat next to her on the bench. Seconds ticked by before he answered. "Our missions are unreported and unknown to the general public. What we do is classified. But it so happens that when Tasha's letter came, I was teaching a class in Coronado, a small island town in San Diego Bay where SEALs are trained."

"I wouldn't guess you to be a teacher."

He raised an eyebrow. "Hey, I'm a good teacher."

She smiled. "Okay, but I doubt that's why you became a SEAL. To be confined in a classroom."

He scowled. "True, but I didn't have a choice at the time. There was an incident where I hurt my back."

"What happened?"

The faraway look in his eyes chilled her, as if he were revisiting the incident. A look that told her the subject was closed. "You ask a lot of questions."

"I know."

"Look," he said, "I'm sorry."

She nodded. "Then tell me about Marcus Singer," she said to change the subject.

He pursed his lips. "When I met him, I thought he was beyond saving. His attitude toward me was bad until he saw I wasn't looking to send him back to prison. When guys get out, trust is not something they hold dear and close."

Surprised, she said, "What was he in prison for?"

"Theft. He's smart, computer literate, and he chauffeured Tasha around town because she hated to drive." When he smiled, creases fanned around the corners of his denim-blue eyes. "Now, that wouldn't be you, would it? You're too independent."

"Not in this lifetime." She jumped when a white puff of fur with china-blue eyes walked across her foot. "Hey. Where'd you come from?" She held her hand out, but the cat ignored her.

"I found her sitting outside my trailer one morning," RT said. "I call her Velcro for obvious reasons. Tasha fed her, so I guess she thinks she belongs here." He leaned over and slid his hand down the cat's back. "I lifted Marcus's prints and had them run through the system. That's how I learned he had a record."

"Tasha didn't tell you?"

"Nope. I asked her about it, but all she would say was she believed in giving a person a second chance. She did admit, however, that Hilton hadn't been as trusting about hiring him. Marcus spent a couple of years at Folsom Prison—that's near Sacramento."

Cait thought back to yesterday—was it only yesterday?—when she'd met Marcus, and how he'd ignored her. Keeping track of parolees and probationers was what she now did for a living.

Before she could tell RT about her job, he asked, "Did Stanton Lane say if Tasha left Marcus anything in her will?"

She shook her head. "No, but I suppose it's possible they had a verbal agreement. If so, I'll honor it."

He stood. "I have work to do. I suggest you go back to the hotel and get some rest."

After RT left, Cait pulled her cell phone from her belt and called Shep Church, her mentor and friend at the Columbus Police Department.

"Hey, how's it going?" Shep answered.

"Well, let's see. There have been two deaths, both possible murders. Fire by arson at one of the theaters. An ex-con who was Tasha's secretary. An actress who thinks I'm an imposter. And a Navy SEAL."

"A SEAL? Where does he fit into the picture?"

"Family friend called in by Tasha to find out who wanted to harm her and her husband. I've only been here since yesterday, but it feels like a lifetime."

"What was your aunt thinking to draw you into this mess?"

"I don't know. Maybe she resented me for some reason."

"Cait, I'm sorry. Can you turn this inheritance down?"

She stretched her neck and rotated her tight shoulders. "I can't, but I wish I had my Glock."

"Want me to see about sending it to you?"

"Not yet. Maybe things will get better," she said.

"You like this SEAL? Is he single?"

"I know how your mind works, so don't go there. I need another man to mess with my life like a bird needs an airplane. Good-bye, Shep."

He laughed. "But who's going to guard you while you sleep?"

"The tooth fairy."

CHAPTER 7

Talking with Shep brought the best part of her job to mind—the camaraderie of teamwork, the support system to back her up. When she closed a case, she had friends to share the victory with; when it all went up in smoke, she had the squad to commiserate with. They were family. In Livermore, she was on her own, except for RT. She truly hoped she could trust him.

Cait rose and took a last look at the sparkling green hills, and went back inside the house and up to the third-floor bedroom. Two large cherry wardrobes stood side by side across from the foot of the bed. She opened the double doors to the one on the left and caught a whiff of lavender. Padded hangers held evening dresses, business suits, and casual weekend wear. A glimpse of herself in the long mirror on the inside of one of the doors showed dark circles under her eyes. She closed the doors.

The second wardrobe held empty hangers, a pair of worn and dusty brown cowboy boots on the flooring, and a strong presence of tobacco. She closed those doors and turned to look around the room.

Stacks of books lay on the floor next to the bed. Two more were on the bedside table—a book of Shakespeare quotes and one opened and placed face down. Cait picked it up and read the title—*Howdunit. How Crimes Are Committed and Solved.* She eased down on the side of the bed and leafed through it. No turned corners or sentences highlighted to indicate any particular interest Tasha might have had, but Cait took the presence of the book as an indication that Tasha experienced real fear when she contacted RT.

She closed the book and replaced it on the table and went over to the office niche. She sat down at the desk and opened the bottom file drawer. She riffled through the hanging folders and decided it was a job for another time and closed the drawer. The belly drawer appeared to be stuck. She worked her hand around inside until it released with a burst, spilling pens and pencils and paper clips into her lap.

She reached in and pulled out a date book with the Bard's face stenciled on the brown leather cover. A ribbon bookmarked a page and fell open to March. Tasha died in March, two weeks before Stanton Lane called Cait on April first. Some joke, she thought as she turned the pages.

Tasha had jotted reminders about the festival on most of the pages, but when Cait came to September and saw the twenty-second circled in red, she got a chill. Written in red and underscored was a simple notation: *C36.*

You've got to be kidding. She kept track of my birthday?

Cait couldn't wrap her mind around this mysterious aunt who knew all about her, left her this large estate, yet had never sent her a birthday card.

She shook her head and turned another page. December 22 was covered with a big red heart. Maybe Hilton's birthday, she thought. January had only initials that meant nothing to Cait. February 9 had a phone number with area code she recognized as Ashland, Oregon, where her college roommate lived before moving to Santa Cruz, California, with her husband.

March 7 had a local phone number and the name Novak. Tasha died March 21. RT was convinced Tasha was murdered. Cait wanted to know who Novak was and used the desk phone to call.

"Novak Investigations," a sugary female voice answered.

Cait sat up straighter. *Investigations?*

"Hello?"

"Hi. I came across this number and the name Novak in my aunt's date book and was curious who it was."

"That would be Karl Novak. We only have one investigator and his part-time deputy."

"I see. Then maybe you could tell me if Tasha Bening was a client." She expected an ambiguous answer.

"May I ask who's calling?"

Surprised, Cait said, "Cait Pepper. Mrs. Bening's niece."

"Please hold. I'll see if Mr. Novak's available."

Moments later a deep male voice came on the line. "You're calling about Tasha Bening?"

"That's right. She was my aunt. She had your name and number, but I didn't realize you were a private investigator. Would you mind telling me why she contacted you?"

"Because I'm a PI. She never hired me."

Cait didn't like the defensive tone of his voice. "Mr. Novak, Tasha must have said why she called."

"When people call here, they usually have a problem."

Cait felt a stab of frustration. *Arrogant jerk.* "Tell you what. I'll stop by tomorrow. Where are you located?"

He cleared his throat. "Look, I'll save you a trip. Mrs. Bening thought someone murdered her husband and thought someone wanted to kill her too. I suggested she come in to talk, but she said she'd have to think about it. Didn't surprise me. Some people are too embarrassed to admit they have a problem and then change their mind when I question them about it. She hung up, but an hour or so later she called back and wanted to know where she could buy a gun."

Cait thought about the book on the bedside table. "What did you tell her?"

"I told her where she could buy one, but that it would take

time for a permit. I told her I could help her, but she hung up again. That was the last I heard from her."

"Did you follow up to see if she was okay?"

"Why would I? I told you, she never hired me. I got clients that need my help. I forgot about her until I heard she'd died."

Cait asked a couple more questions but knew she'd get nothing further from Novak and thanked him for his time and hung up.

Tasha's fear and interest in buying a gun explained the *Howdunit* book. Cait thought about the coroner's autopsy report but knew it wasn't conclusive enough to stand up in a court of law. The case had gone cold before Cait had even been summoned to California. Tasha had already been cremated. But Cait had worked with less, and the phone call to Novak proved RT's instincts were right.

She pushed the date book aside, stood, stretched, and again rotated her shoulders to loosen the kinks. She missed the rush of pushing her body to the limit during workouts. Police officers were required to stay in shape, but her job as a crime analyst kept her behind a desk more than she liked.

She went to the window at the rear of the bedroom. From her vantage point she saw a road the fire truck must have taken up to the Elizabethan Theater. *The arsonist could have used that same route. If I stay at the house while I'm here, I can keep an eye on the estate and the people who come and go.*

Cait returned to the Sheraton and checked out. Back at the house, she changed into shorts and a long-sleeved T-shirt and then headed out the back for a run. She set off across the yard, through the squeaky trellis gate, and into the theater courtyard. She slowed as she crossed the bricks when she heard voices coming from the direction of the Elizabethan Theater.

The smell of burned wood, plastic and paint had blown out

with the wind, but the fire marshal was still there talking to a man she hadn't seen before. When they saw her, they motioned for her to join them.

"Ms. Pepper," the fire marshal said.

"It's Cait, please. I thought you'd left."

He shook his head. "Still poking around. We were just discussing that if someone wanted to destroy the entire theater—and I'm not saying that wasn't the intent—they could have done a more thorough job of it."

"Maybe there wasn't time," she said, "or whoever it was was frightened off."

"In the middle of the night?"

She felt her cheeks flush. "Good point." She glanced at the other man.

"This is Detective Rook with the Livermore Police Department," the fire marshal said.

Cait shook the detective's offered hand. "Nice to meet you." He appeared average—his height, light-brown hair, tan suit—until she looked into his brown eyes flecked with gold. His smile reminded her of Shep.

"I understand you just inherited the Bening estate," Rook said. "I'm sure a fire wasn't exactly the welcome you anticipated."

"It's one of several challenges I've encountered since coming here, Detective."

He pulled a card from his inside jacket pocket and handed it to her. "Call if I can be of assistance."

She glanced at the card before slipping it in her pocket. "Thanks. I've decided to stay at the house while I'm here. Easier to keep an eye on things. You'll know where to find me if you need to."

"I'll be leaving shortly," the fireman said.

She nodded and then backed off to continue her run. She

traversed the steeper part of the hill down to the road, jumping over rocks and roots. She wouldn't have noticed the horseback rider on top of the hill if the horse hadn't snorted. She shielded her eyes from the sun with her hand and then waved when she recognized Marcus Singer. Instead of acknowledging her, he turned the horse, slapped the reins, and disappeared from view.

She dismissed him from her mind to concentrate on her run until she saw a man hiking up the hill. As they came closer to each other, she noticed a couple of serious-looking cameras around his neck and a collapsed tripod in his hand.

He stopped and grinned. "You must be Cait."

She shielded her eyes from the sun. "Why is that?"

He laughed. "RT described you. I'm Ilia Kubiak." He shook his blond hair out of his eyes.

"Then you have the advantage," she said. "Are you planning to photograph the Bening estate?"

"Sure am. I'm a freelance photographer promoting tourism in the Livermore Valley. Tasha liked my work and gave me an open invitation to take photos of her Shakespeare festival, the house, and the grounds." He unsnapped a pocket on his shorts, removed a card, and handed it to her. "I'm on the board of Valley Artists."

She took his card, glanced at it and slipped it in her pocket with Detective Rook's. "Then I guess I'll be seeing a lot of you while I'm here."

"I promise to stay out of your way. Heard you met Livermore's other famous Shakespearean actress," he said.

"You must mean Rachel Cross. We met. I also met Marcus Singer. Do you know him?" She nodded towards the top of the hill. "I think it was him I saw on horseback a little bit ago."

"Sure, I know him. Careful with that one. He's got the personality of a pit bull."

Cait laughed. "I'll buy a leash." She jogged in place. "I should get going."

"RT and I are ordering pizza tonight. Come join us. Your kitchen, seven o'clock."

"I've never been one to turn down pizza."

Cait stood in the large tiled shower after her run, eyes closed, and reflected on her inheritance and wondered if her arrival in Livermore had anything to do with the fire at the Elizabethan Theater. Then she remembered there had been another fire at the same theater not long before Tasha died. She opened her eyes and turned the water off. As she toweled herself dry, she thought about what Lane mentioned about building on top of the hills and considered the possibility of an environmentalist setting both fires.

After she dressed and blow-dried her hair, Cait settled on the chaise lounge in the bay window and opened her laptop to check her e-mail. Nothing urgent demanded her attention, so she sent a quick message to Shep and her friend Samantha to let them know she'd moved into the house. If they didn't hear from her, they'd at least know where to start looking. She glanced at the time on her laptop: 6:45. She opened a blank Word document and started to record everything that had happened since her arrival in Livermore. Her fingers flew across the keys until she glanced at her watch and saw she was late for pizza. She saved the document, closed her laptop, and went downstairs.

The kitchen was dark and still. Had she misunderstood the time? She turned the light on, peeked in the dark office, and then pulled a stool out from the counter and sat down to wait for the guys to show.

A loud crack and fractured glass broke the silence.

Cait jumped off the stool and instinctively dove to the floor and scrambled under the counter between the stools, scraping her arm on a piece of splintered glass that had shot across the room.

Defenseless without her gun or cell phone, she grabbed hold of a stool leg, the closest thing she had for a weapon. Her pounding heart was amplified in the silence that followed the blast.

A door banged open.

Footsteps crossed the tile floor.

"Cait! Are you in here?"

She recognized RT's voice and peeked out from beneath the counter. He was standing in the middle of the kitchen, a gun clutched in his hand. Ilia stood close behind him.

"Cait!"

"I'm here." She crawled out and pulled herself up on shaky legs.

He rushed over and grabbed her arm. "Are you all right?"

She brushed at her arms and clothes, grateful she hadn't sprung a bullet leak. "I will be. It's not the first time I've been shot at."

"Your arm's cut," Ilia said.

"What? When were you shot at?" RT said.

She grabbed a paper towel by the sink, wet it, and dabbed at the cut. "Not here. Long time ago. You didn't see anyone out there?"

RT unclipped his cell phone from his waist and punched in a number. "No. I'm calling Detective Rook, and then I'll search the grounds." He looked at Ilia. "Stay here."

The doorbell chimed.

CHAPTER 8

"Isn't there some kind of security system in this house?" Ilia asked as he bit into a slice of pizza.

"I wouldn't know," Cait said.

RT returned from searching the grounds looking like a thundercloud. He grabbed a slice of pizza. "No one's out there now." As he ate, he stooped to examine the end of the counter riddled with birdshot. "Rook's in San Francisco. He'll come by in the morning."

"Dispatch could have sent someone else," she said.

"I can handle it. I'll take you back to your hotel when you're finished eating."

"I checked out. I'm staying here."

He reached for another slice of pizza. "No, you're not. He might try again. The Benings never bothered to alarm the house. They thought it was safe way up here on this hill."

"I can take care of myself." She reached for a slice of pizza.

RT raised his eyebrow. "Then I'll sleep here, too. On the sofa upstairs in the sitting room."

"I don't think so. Thanks for the pizza." She grabbed her can of Coke and walked out.

Friday morning Cait awoke to heavy silence. No traffic. No sound of children's voices as they headed off to school. No barking dogs. The quiet unnerved her. After living in a neighborhood full of kids in Columbus, the numbing silence would take getting used to. She eased over to the edge of the bed and glanced at the clock: eight o'clock. She would have been at her desk or in a meeting at the police station by now.

She jumped into the shower and let the hot water cascade over her until her skin turned red and her frustrations ran down the drain. Last night's shooting upset her, but this morning she was determined to find the culprit.

She dressed and then sat in the bay window and opened her laptop. She wanted a record of everything that happened last night, beginning with the time of the shot. She typed for an hour. When she had nothing else to add, she closed her laptop and went downstairs. Someone had swept the floor of glass and boarded up the window in the door.

RT came in the back door carrying a plate covered in foil. He stopped when he saw Cait. "I brought breakfast. You didn't eat your share of pizza last night. Detective Rook will be here shortly." He set the plate on the counter and removed the foil, opened a drawer, took out a fork and handed it to her. "You look better than the last time I saw you."

"Amazing what a little sleep and a hot shower can do." Cait inhaled the aroma of scrambled eggs, bacon, and buttered toast. Her stomach rolled with the force of a hurricane. She picked up the fork and started to eat. "This is so good. Can I have this every morning for as long as I'm here?"

"Don't you wish." He poured two mugs of coffee and set one down in front of her, then leaned against the counter and watched her as he drank his own coffee. "Sleep well in Tasha's bed?"

"Apparently so." She devoured everything on the plate. "Too bad I didn't inherit you instead of Marcus."

"It's too bad I didn't get much sleep because I worried about you all night."

She paused with her fork in the air. "Believe me, I *can* look after myself." She licked bacon grease from her finger. "If you were that worried, you should have let Dispatch send an officer."

He glared at her over the rim of his coffee mug. "If I thought I needed backup, I'd have asked for it."

"You and Detective Rook must be best buddies if you were willing to wait until this morning for him." She sipped her coffee. "I should have stayed up and helped you search the grounds."

"You should have stayed at the hotel." He picked up her empty plate and carried it to the sink. "I've been trying to figure out why you're a target. It's not like your inheritance is tied up in some court battle with lots of family members scrambling for their share."

"I thought about that too," she said.

The doorbell chimed.

"That'll be Rook." He left the kitchen to answer the door.

Cait rinsed and dried RT's plate and set it aside. She heard voices and turned to see RT and Detective Rook walk in. "I never expected to see you again so soon, Detective."

Rook smiled. "Sorry I couldn't be here last night, Ms. Pepper."

"Why is everyone so formal? Call me Cait."

He nodded and looked her over. "Were you hurt?"

"Just a small cut from broken glass." She noticed how his hair brushed his open collar, his spit-polished shoes, and the firm press in his tan slacks. Just like Shep, she thought.

RT poured a cup of coffee and handed it to Rook.

"Thanks," Rook said. "Tell me about last night," he said as he examined the indentations on the end of the counter.

"Not much to tell. It happened fast," she said. "Someone was either a poor shot or intentionally missed to scare me out of town."

There was a glint in Rook's eyes when he asked, "Have you annoyed anyone since coming here?"

RT laughed.

She glared at him. "Everyone, it seems. Particularly Marcus."

He frowned. "How's that?"

She shrugged. "He won't talk to me. He lurks and watches. Really weird."

"Weird doesn't necessarily mean dangerous," Rook said.

She shrugged. "I know, but have you met him?"

Rook took his time answering as he drank his coffee. "I have."

"Then you understand." She'd dealt with enough weird ones to know how combative they could be on the outside yet gentle inside. It took time to understand them, but she doubted that would happen with Marcus before she returned to Ohio.

"I could have an officer posted here for a couple days," Rook said, "but I doubt that would deter someone from trying again. At least RT is here."

Cait glanced at RT, who cocked his eyebrow at her. "He has a job to go back to. So do I, for that matter. I'll be more watchful from now on, so don't bother sending someone."

Rook looked at RT. "Have you shared your suspicions with her about Tasha's death?"

RT nodded. "She had a right to know."

"I read the coroner's report," Cait said. "Tasha could have been injected with drugs, maybe given an IV to hurry up the process. Thing is, I saw no mention that they looked for needle marks on her arms or thighs."

Rook set his coffee mug down on the counter. "You're talking about her high level of potassium. The coroner ruled her death as—"

"Undetermined for a woman her age. I know. But don't you find it interesting that her bedside reading material was about how crimes are committed and solved?"

Rook and RT had puzzled looks on their faces.

She savored the moment. "Just saying. And then there's her call to the PI."

"Who?" Rook and RT said in unison.

"Karl Novak. I have his phone number if you'd like it. You should call him. Tasha didn't hire him, but she was interested in buying a gun."

"What? She never mentioned anything about a gun to me," RT said. "She must have contacted him before she got hold of me."

"Sweet Jesus," Rook said. "How did you learn all that?"

She smiled. "I found his name and number in her date book. Anyone for more coffee?"

"You've been busy," Rook said.

She turned back from the coffeepot. "My time here is short. I really can protect myself."

"That's what they all say before it's too late," Rook said. "We're professionals. It's what we do, Cait."

"Is that so?" She reached for her handbag she'd brought downstairs with her and took out her police credentials. She held them up.

She detected a hint of amusement in Rook's eyes, but her satisfaction dimmed to twinges of guilt when she looked at RT. He'd trusted her with his identity as a SEAL. As bad as she felt about deceiving him, she wouldn't have done things differently. Not until she'd separated in her mind the good guys from the bad guys.

She drew a deep breath. "I was a police officer for seven years, a crime analyst the last four. Among other things, I track convicted offenders—sex, narcotic, and arson—who are required by law to register and are on probation or parole. I spend enough time at the shooting range to stay in the top three of my department. You don't have to remind me I'm out of my jurisdiction, Detective, but please, don't waste my talents. I want to help." She shot a quick glance at RT.

Rook shook his head in disbelief and grinned. "Okay, just don't try to be a hero."

"Not my style. But this is my inheritance, and I have a right to protect it." She noticed RT heading to the back door. "Where are you going?"

"I have a call to make," he mumbled. The door banged behind him.

"I think I just stole his thunder." She was more concerned she'd lost his trust and what it would take to redeem it.

"Let's get to work here," Rook said.

She opened a drawer and removed a saucer with seven small-diameter pellets. "I gathered these off the floor last night."

"Where were you when he started shooting?" He tipped the dish of pellets into his hand.

"Right here on this stool. There was a loud crack, glass shattered, and I dove to the floor and under the counter."

He ran his fingers over the side of the counter where the pellets had hit and then walked to the door. He turned and looked back. "He shot right through the window?"

"Yeah."

Rook pushed the pellets around in his hand with his finger. "They're small, mostly used for small game. Not much stopping power unless at close range, twenty to thirty feet or so. Which means—"

"I know what birdshot is."

"—that I agree with you," he continued. "He didn't intend to kill you. He wanted to frighten you." He stared at the pellets. "I used ones like these when they first came out and never had a clean kill." He pulled a knife from his pocket.

Cait recognized the Leatherman. She had one. A birthday gift from her husband. She loved that it housed multiple tools, yet collapsed to the size of a pocketknife. She found a box of sandwich bags in a drawer, pulled one out and held it open for Rook as he stooped to dig pellets out of the wood.

When he finished, he rose and took the bag from her. "Thanks." He checked his watch. "I've got a meeting at headquarters in twenty minutes. Have RT give me a call."

She nodded. As she walked Rook to the front door, she asked him something that had been bothering her. "Who found Tasha?"

"Marcus Singer."

Cait wrapped RT's breakfast plate in a kitchen towel and left the house to find him. She went around to the front of the house and followed a dirt and gravel path that ran between pink and white oleander. As she approached a large open area, she saw a vintage twenty-four-foot silver Airstream trailer hitched to a black Hummer. As she raised her hand to knock, the door flung open. She jumped back, startled.

"What do you want, Cait?" RT asked.

A rush of heat flushed her cheeks. She held up the towel. "I brought your plate."

He leaned against the doorjamb, arms crossed over his chest, feet crossed at his ankles.

"Detective Rook left. He wants you to call him."

"You should have told me, Cait. I felt like a damn fool."

She nodded, feeling like a child. "I know. I'm sorry. I intended to . . . it just never seemed to be the right time. And I needed to be sure about you." She turned and started to walk away.

"Hey," he called.

She looked back.

"Can I have my plate?"

CHAPTER 9

Cait returned to the house. She heard a soft humming coming from the back office and assumed Marcus was there. The room was empty, but the computer was on. She sat down at the desk, tapped the space bar, and watched as folders filled the screen. When she clicked on one titled *Festival Schedule*, a list of all the plays planned for this season opened up. Marcus had organized everything about the festival, even the actors' quirks and demands. She turned the printer on and ran off a copy of the schedule.

Blackfriars Theater: (2nd yr.) Rehearsals week of 4/26

Fri.-Sat., May 3–4 & 10–11 / *Tongue of a Bird* (internal journey for the search of an abducted girl)

Fri.-Sat., June 5–6 & 12–13 / *Macbeth* (a tragedy—where the crown is the central image to the play, the reason Macbeth commits the first murder)

Fri.-Sat., July 4–5 (only) / *The Royal Family* (a comedy—this season's brandied truffle)

Elizabethan Theater: (1st yr.) Rehearsals - May

Fri.-Sat., June—1st weekend / *Hamlet, Prince of Denmark* (a tragedy of revenge—the ultimate ghost story)

Fri.-Sat., July—1st weekend / *King Henry III* (history)

Fri.-Sat., Aug.—1st weekend / *The Tempest* (a comedy of wonder and magic)

Fri.-Sat., Sept.—1st weekend / *Midsummer Night's Dream* (a comedy—magical; fairies who lived in an enchanted wood)

When Stanton Lane called Cait to tell her about her inheritance, he had stressed that time was of the essence and that she needed to be in Livermore to help with the festival. After looking over the schedule, she understood the urgency, but wondered why Marcus or Rachel hadn't given her a copy and discussed it with her.

Cait turned the printer off, left the office and went down the hall to the gift shop where boxes waited to be opened and the gifts priced and displayed on the shelves. She crouched in front of one of the boxes and peeled the tape back, tearing a fingernail in the process. She cautiously removed green Styrofoam popcorn and found Harlequin masks, pens with purple plumes, and bubble-wrapped busts of the Bard. She set each item on the floor and started on another box. Books, cards, puzzles, and notepads filled this one. She held up a black Bard coffee mug as a flash of light went off behind her. Startled, she fell back on her heels and dropped the mug.

"Oh, Gosh, I'm sorry, Cait. I didn't mean to frighten you." Ilia held his hand out to help her up.

She picked up the mug and checked it for cracks. "No harm done."

"Tasha spent weeks deciding what to order, what would sell, and how much to sell them for." He smiled. "She was like a kid waiting for Christmas. Unfortunately, most of these boxes arrived the day after she died."

She nodded. "Life isn't always fair, is it?"

He shifted his feet and shook his head. "Have you seen RT?"

"Check his trailer. He was there a little while ago."

"I did. By the way. The back door was unlocked."

"That's probably my fault. I'll be more careful." She stooped to gather up a few of the items and set them on the shelves. "Detective Rook came by earlier, but I'm sure he'll be back. He'll want to talk with you about what you saw last night."

"I'll be around for a while." He tinkered with his camera. "You going to be all right, Cait? Maybe you should take RT's advice and go back to the hotel until the police find who took those shots at you."

She turned to face him. "Ilia, if someone wanted to kill me, he could have. I'm going to tell you something that I'd rather not get around just yet."

He slid his hands in his jeans pockets. "Okay."

"I work in law enforcement. I was a cop before becoming a crime analyst." She smiled. "So maybe you don't need to worry so much about me."

His face went blank for several seconds; he looked at her and said, "Oh, man. Does RT know?"

"Yeah, he knows."

"So . . . do you know about RT, that he's—" His neck flushed.

She grinned. "A SEAL. Yes. Now that that's out of the way, do you have time to help me unpack some of these boxes?"

He whistled softly. "Yeah. Sure."

"That would be great." She turned and picked up the schedule for the festival she'd printed and showed it to him. "Have you seen this?"

He looked at it. "Sure. Tasha showed it to me. She asked me to take pictures of the Elizabethan opening this year like I did last year for the Blackfriars."

"Was there a good turnout?"

"Oh, yeah. Tasha was excited. She thought the valley deserved a theater for more modern, controversial, and experimental plays. That's why she built the Blackfriars. She was curious to see how those types of plays would be accepted in this valley. The Elizabethan was built for the more traditional Shakespearean plays." He picked up a Harlequin mask and held it up to his face. "What do you think?"

She laughed. "I think you look silly. Do other vineyards put on Shakespeare plays?"

"A couple, but Tasha's theaters are built specifically for those types of plays."

"Well, art is powerful food for the soul," Cait said.

Ilia grinned. "You sound just like Tasha. My parents saw *Macbeth* on the small stage at the Oregon Shakespeare Festival a few years ago. It was considered experimental then. Tasha loved the intimacy of the smaller theater and wanted to try *Macbeth* at the Blackfriars this year." He set the mask aside. "It's sad she won't know how well it goes over." He returned the schedule to her.

Cait thought of her own parents, their love of the theater, and the blazing plane crash that took their lives five years ago. She glanced at the schedule again and then set it on the glass counter. "There's a good balance of plays: comedies, histories, and a tragedy. I'm sorry I won't be here to see them."

Ilia took his camera from around his neck and set it on a shelf. "You're not staying?"

She sighed. "I don't know. I have a job to go back to. Now, if you could open some of these boxes, I'll check the items off on the invoices."

"Sounds like a plan. Marcus can make more shelves if you run out of space."

"Ha. Getting him to do something for me would be a miracle." Cait placed her hands at the small of her back, stretched, and stared up at the stained-glass window behind the counter. She walked over for a closer look.

"Marcus doesn't like many people, but he'll come around." He stood beside her. "Tasha wanted this house for its stained-glass windows as much as the land," Ilia said.

"They're beautiful," Cait said. "I used to dream of owning a glass studio until I did the math and realized I couldn't turn out lamps and windows fast enough to pay the mortgage. Did you know Christianity was the prime influence in the development of this type of art?" She turned and saw RT leaning against the doorjamb watching her.

"Let's take a ride," RT said.

She didn't want him behind a wheel if he was still angry with her. "I'm busy."

"Ilia can take over. Let's go."

It annoyed her how easily he could manipulate her and was about to refuse until he mentioned food.

"I'll feed you if you promise not to snarl at me."

Ilia chuckled.

"In your dreams," she said, and winked at Ilia.

Cait had hated her husband's Hummer and sold it soon after he died, to a lieutenant in her police department who had an ego to match the vehicle. Roger's love for his Hummer had been only a fraction less than for his classic '32 Ruxton. Between his cars and his part-time job as police chaplain, there'd been little time to mend their soured marriage. Except when he tried to get her pregnant. Each time she failed to conceive, he blamed her.

"I haven't decided how long I should stand here holding the door open for you, but time's running out," RT said.

She shook off the ugly memory that still haunted her and climbed into RT's Hummer. Cait glanced at RT as he drove, his blue eyes glued to the road ahead of them, his strong hands gripped on the wheel. She noticed flecks of silver sprinkled at the tips of his side hair.

"You're staring at me," he said.

She blushed and looked away.

"Relax," he said. "We're going to be in each other's company for a while. Don't you want to know where we're going?"

"Lunch, I thought." She stared out the window at the

vineyards they passed and thought what a difference they were from her real life of city streets and exhaust fumes. "Do you know much about Tasha's family?"

He glanced over at her. "Mostly what my mom told me. Kids don't pay much attention to their parents' friends, but I liked Tasha and Hilton. It's rare to see older couples openly display their love for each other, hold hands, smooch, but they did and weren't embarrassed by it. They had the kind of marriage most people would envy."

Cait had yet to hear a negative word from anyone about Tasha. No one is that perfect, she thought. Not even her own parents, whom she loved dearly. Every family had secrets; obviously hers did or she wouldn't be in California, heir to a property from an aunt she'd never known or heard about. "Do we have a destination or are we just driving aimlessly?"

"I never do anything aimlessly if I can help it. And, yes, we have a destination, but I thought you might like to see some of the local wineries. If you decide not to stay, at least you'll have something to think back on."

As if I could forget this trip, she thought.

"Here's a little history for you about this Tri-Valley region. Its rugged landscape and dry Mediterranean climate are perfect for growing grapes." He glanced at her and noticed her frown. "Okay, so maybe you're not interested."

"I am. It's just that I'd forgotten about the vineyard. When Stanton Lane called, he didn't mention the vineyard, but stressed it was urgent I come here because of the Shakespeare festival. He said it would soon open and decisions had to be made about the future of the estate." She shifted in her seat. "It's like an albatross around my neck, a burden that could strangle me."

"A lot's been thrown at you. Forget about the vineyard for now. I've got it covered. The vines will start to flower in May.

After that, the shoots will need to be thinned. We'll talk about this before I leave, but I'll look into arranging help for you. Okay?"

"Thanks. How soon will that be?"

He laughed. "I'll let you know when I know, but probably by the end of the month."

"Between the theaters, vineyard, and ranch the Benings must have been busy."

RT slowed and pulled off to the side and parked beside Wenté Winery. He turned to face Cait. "The theaters are seasonal work. Hilton's ranch is in good hands. We'll go there after lunch. That's why I wanted you to come out with me. Hilton and Tasha planted twelve acres, half in Cabernet and half in Chardonnay. Two years ago, they completed their first harvest and sold their grapes to local wineries." He glanced out the windshield as a gang of motorcyclists whizzed past them. "There are incredible resources around here for anyone wanting to start a small vineyard; you could join the local winemakers association to learn the art of cultivating grapes. There's also Las Positas College across the freeway; it has an enology/viticulture program, and the student interns work in the vineyards." He nodded at the winery beside them. "Would you like to go in and sample some local wines?"

Her head throbbed as she tried to absorb all that RT had said. "I don't think so. You talk as though I'm here to stay. I do police work. I do lunch. I *do not* do winemaking."

He laughed. "Then let's *do* lunch. Garré Winery is just down the road. Then we'll go to the ranch." He waited for a dozen yellow-jerseyed bikers to pass before pulling out onto the road.

CHAPTER 10

Lunch at the quiet Mediterranean-style café at Garré Winery helped soothe Cait's frayed nerves. Over crab salad and a glass of Chardonnay, she listened to RT describe the accident that killed Hilton Bening. It brought back sad memories of her best friend in high school who died when his horse missed a hurdle during a competition.

"Hilton cherished his horse," RT concluded.

She understood the bond between an animal and its owner. She'd grown up with dogs and assumed there'd always be one in her life. Unfortunately, her husband thought pets brought diseases and dirt into a house and forbade her to have one. "What happened to his horse?"

He swirled the wine in his glass. "He's still at the ranch. Some people would have put the horse down after the accident, but not Tasha. As far as I know, she never went back to the ranch to see Faro."

"It would have been hard for her. Mr. Lane said Hilton left the ranch to his manager."

"He did. Bo Tuck's also a veterinarian; he and his family love that place." He pushed his chair back. "Ready to go?"

"Absolutely," she said. "Thanks for lunch."

When they pulled out of the parking lot, he stopped at the edge of the road. "Do you golf?"

"No, but I'd like to try it sometime," she said.

He pointed to a hilly road that ran through vineyards ahead

of them. "There's a public golf course out there—Poppy Ridge. Stunning views of the vineyards and a first-class restaurant. You should drive out there while you're here."

She squinted into the sun. "Maybe I will."

They drove in silence until RT turned onto Mines Road, drove a little way, and then pulled off to the side. "Murrieta's Well winery is back in there. Legend has it Joaquin Murrieta and his band of desperadoes watered their horses there." He turned in his seat to face her. "If you decide to move here, besides great wine, there are tons of art events and even a rodeo. Give it a chance, Cait." Before she could think of an answer, he pulled out, but soon braked hard to miss a pair of peacocks at the edge of the road.

Cait sat silent the rest of the way and stared out the window at the horses and the few scattered houses. About three miles out, RT turned left and drove through a tall arch with "BEN-ING RANCH" and a horse emblazoned in cast iron across the top. He wound along a dirt-and-gravel lane lined with pristine white fencing on their left and eucalyptus trees on their right.

"Bo's the veterinarian for lots of folks around here," RT said. "He's a hard worker, a demanding manager, and respected by his employees and the community. You'll like him."

"Does he know we're coming?"

"Nope." He pulled up to the front of a freshly painted red barn and parked next to a dusty white trailer with a horse's head decal on the side. As soon as he shut the motor off, a tall man appeared in the doorway.

The man approached with his hand outstretched. "RT. About time you came to see us. Joy's been buggin' me to pieces." They gripped hands and then he tipped his hat to Cait. "Ma'am."

He reminded Cait of a Cincinnati Bengals halfback she admired: six-three, broad shoulders, narrow hips, and tight jeans. The sleeves of his blue denim shirt were rolled up, displaying powerful forearms. She fought the urge to remove his black Stetson to see if his eyes were as blue as the halfback's.

"Bo Tuck, meet Cait Pepper, Tasha's niece and heir to the Bening vineyard and Shakespeare festival."

Bo's hand swallowed Cait's as they shook. "I've been expecting you."

Cait smiled. "Really?"

"It was a matter of time. These hills are known to spill secrets."

"I'll have to remember that," she said.

"Cait wanted to see the ranch," RT said. "I thought now was as good a time as any if it's okay with you. She never had the opportunity to know the Benings so maybe this will help some."

Bo looked at Cait with questioning eyes. "Sure thing. I was just feeding the horses, so let's talk as we walk."

"I'd like that," she said as she followed him into the barn. Harnesses and tack hung from nails along one wall in the barn. Bo fed biscuits to the horses as they went. The few horses in the barn were stabled in individual stalls with fresh mats of straw and were tied onto sliding ropes that allowed them room to lie down.

"I have one trainer, a few stable hands, and several laborers. Hilton wanted to expand the operation to include a larger breeding program, including his own stallion."

Cait thought about Tasha's own plans for her Shakespeare theaters. Unfortunately, neither Bening lived to see their plans come to fruition. "Will you carry out his wishes?"

"I'll do what I can since he so generously left us this place to live in." He looked at her from under the brim of his hat. "But it takes money to make money."

She wondered how much money it took to run the Bening estate. Something she would have to ask Lane about. He'd said there were no money worries, that the estate was in good shape, but she wanted to see the numbers and decided to make an appointment to see him. The house definitely needed an alarm system, she thought. And the theaters, if they didn't already have one.

Bo asked, "Know anything about horses, Cait?"

She laughed. "I'm a city gal, Bo. Barely know one end of a horse from another."

"That's an easy fix if you're interested. I have several horses that'll go easy on you."

"That I'll have to think about." She looked at RT. "Do you ride?"

"Some. Haven't had much opportunity lately," RT said.

"There you go, then. Here's your opportunity," Bo said. "Let's head on out back. I'll show you some of our other horses." He led them to a paddock enclosed with the same white fencing they'd followed in. Bo propped his foot on the bottom rung and whistled. An extraordinarily graceful horse seemed to float over the ground like a shadow as he trotted to the rail. "This here's Blackjack. He's an Arabian stallion, the purest and oldest of all breeds, and the most beautiful in my estimation." He offered his hand to the horse. "What's up, son?"

The horse snorted, allowing Bo to stroke his neck. From his glossy bay coat to his long black tail, Cait thought the horse presented a picture of royalty. She glimpsed in Bo's hand a sugar cube, which disappeared quickly when he offered it to the horse.

Cait had never ridden or been around horses, and admitted their size scared her a little, but when a colt trotted over to greet them, she held her hand out for him to sniff. As she stroked its chestnut neck, she said, "Bo, I understand Hilton's horse is still here. Can I see him?"

Bo shot a look at RT, then dipped his head. "He's over here." He led them to a small pasture with one horse. "That's Faro, but don't expect him to greet you."

Touched by his seclusion, she said, "He's so handsome."

"Yes, he is. There's none better," Bo said. The chestnut quarter horse kept his distance, his eyes on the three intruders, his ears laid back in intense irritation. "I'm grateful Tasha wanted to keep him even though she never came back to visit him. The accident wasn't Faro's fault."

Cait noticed Bo dig the toe of his boot into the ground with force, as if to stress each word. His head was down and the brim of his hat shaded his face so she couldn't see his expression, but if the tone of his voice were any indication, it would reflect great sadness. "What happened, Bo?"

Bo looked up at Cait, scrunched his eyes and leaned back against the fence. "It's old news now. I best get back to feeding the horses."

Respectful of his reluctance to talk about the accident that killed Hilton, the pain lurking behind Bo's eyes struck Cait. *This is a man still mourning the loss of his friend.*

"You're welcome to come anytime, Cait," Bo said on their way back to RT's Hummer. "RT, Joy wants to know when you intend to come and ride." He pushed his hat back and smiled at Cait. "Joy's my daughter. She thinks RT's cool."

"Really?" Cait looked at RT and raised her eyebrow.

"At least someone does," RT said. "Tell Joy I promise to come see her."

Cait watched Bo through the window as RT backed the Hummer around and wondered if there was another reason he still found it so difficult to talk about Hilton's accident.

They were quiet on the drive back to the house, but when RT stopped at the foot of the driveway he pointed across the road. "Over there is where Rachel lives in a house that's been in her family for generations."

Cait couldn't see any houses for the trees and shrubs.

"There's just Rachel, her husband, Ben Bauer, and the sheep he raises," RT continued.

"Bauer? She kept her own name?"

"Yeah, probably for stage purposes. She let Tasha know when this property came on the market. Tasha and Hilton looked at it and grabbed it up quick because it's close to Hilton's ranch, it's private, and has the land to fit into Tasha's plans for a Shakespeare festival." He accelerated up the driveway.

RT let Cait out before he turned to go to his place. "Thanks for taking me to the ranch," she said. "I like Bo, but for someone who inherited a nice spread, he doesn't seem very happy."

"Look who's talking. I haven't seen you jumping through hoops over your inheritance."

"I guess that makes me an ungrateful brat," she snapped. She slammed the door shut and walked away. Upstairs in the bedroom, she sat in the bay window and thought about Hilton and Bo Tuck. She liked Bo and wanted to talk to him about the accident that killed Hilton, but doubted it would happen before she had to leave. She reached into her handbag that she'd put on the floor beside her chair and took out her cell phone to call Stanton Lane.

Lane answered the phone himself. "Hello."

"Hi, it's Cait. I'd like to make an appointment to see you about the estate," she said.

"Is there a problem?"

"I don't know," she said. "It must take a lot to run the estate. I want to know how much." She pulled a pen and pad from her bag.

"Can you come by Monday, say eleven? If you need money before that—"

"I don't, and Monday is fine. I'm staying at the house now, but I haven't seen any bills."

"That's because they all come here," he said.

She sat back in her chair. "Oh. How is Marcus paid? And RT?"

"Marcus gets paid from here. What arrangements Tasha made with RT, I don't know. After she died, I asked him about it, but he dismissed the matter, said not to worry about it. I suggest you ask Rachel Cross about expenses for the festival. So far I haven't seen any statements, but there is a fund set aside for whatever is needed. Rachel knows that."

Cait wrote a note on the pad, then asked, "Same for the actors?"

"They're under contract. Their expenses were taken care of before Tasha died. After this year, we'll have to wait and see, but the money is there."

"What happens when I leave? What about that foundation for the arts you mentioned?"

Lane hesitated before answering. "I'm still hoping you'll stay, Cait."

She drew in a deep breath. The thought of being uprooted from her friends and a job she loved would hurt. How far does obligation to family go? Would investigation into Tasha and Hilton's deaths fall into the cracks?

Lane continued. "Rachel and I are coexecutors of Tasha's trust. She understands how the expenses are handled."

"Did she tell you about the recent fire at the Elizabethan Theater?"

She heard him gasp.

"Mr. Lane, we have a lot to discuss. I'll see you Monday."

CHAPTER 11

Heavy rains and high winds confined Cait to the house all weekend, and it was still raining Monday morning when she left to go downtown to Lane's office. Rain slashed against the windows; fog cloaked the vineyards like a ghost. She parked in front of the office and made it inside without getting drenched. Lane popped his head out as she hung her dripping coat on a rack by the front door.

"It was brave of you to come out in this weather," he said. "Can I offer you coffee or tea?"

"No, thanks."

He ushered her into his office and closed the door. "Well, then, have a seat." He walked behind his desk, glanced at his watch, and then tapped his finger on the intercom button. "Buzz me when those papers arrive, Sara." He sat down in his buttoned black leather chair and clasped his hands on top of a green folder.

"I've prepared copies of the Bening estate expenses that come into this office. After you've had a chance to look them over, call me and I'll come out to the house to discuss them in detail." He smiled. "I assure you, Cait, that the Bening holdings are solvent. You've nothing to worry about. You can trust me on that."

I hope so, but from where I stand everything and everyone connected with my inheritance is suspicious. "It might be different if I'd known Tasha." She shook her head to shake off her frustration. "RT said local wineries would buy the grapes." She shifted to the edge of her seat.

Lane opened the folder before him and glanced at it. "Let's talk about the vineyard, since you brought it up." He shuffled a couple of pages and pulled out a sheet. "The wineries have agreed to buy the grapes for as long as it's beneficial to everyone. You can read about the agreement here." He tapped the paper he held. "Tasha and Hilton set up separate operating funds for the vineyard and theaters. As I've said, I was not privy to any compensation for Mr. Tanner. That was strictly between him and Tasha. Marcus Singer is the only full-time employee. Volunteers were brought in for the festival last year and will come again this year. All accounts are reviewed periodically by my chief financial officer." He glanced again at the sheet of paper he held before fixing his eyes on Cait. "Once you've made your decision whether to stay, we'll sit down with the financial officer and go over everything in detail with him. Is that agreeable?"

She nodded. "Just how much are we talking about? What is the Bening estate worth?"

Lane smiled. "Should you choose to accept the responsibilities of your inheritance, you will be a wealthy young woman. The estate has been appraised into the millions."

Her chest tightened. "I had no idea."

"However," he cautioned, "if it's turned over to a foundation, you'll receive only a token amount."

She couldn't wrap her brain around so much money. The responsibility frightened her. She came from a middle-class family. Both her parents had worked. She exhaled a long breath. "I hope I don't fall prey to a bunch of vultures coming out of the woodwork. Ignorance is never bliss, so I trust you'll alert me if you receive calls about false claims or strangers who might turn up proclaiming some bogus relationship with either Bening."

"Of course." He opened a top drawer, shook out two Tums and popped them in his mouth. "Ulcers," he explained. "You're a lot like her. Nothing ever got past Tasha, which was a blessing because she was involved in many projects having to do with the arts." He leaned back in his chair. "There's more than enough money that you'll never have to worry." He smiled. "Unless, of course, you gamble it all away. Tasha would never have left you with a financial burden. I wish my other clients were so lucky."

"Where did the money come from?"

"Investments. Tasha invested wisely. Hilton was born into a wealthy cattle-ranching family in Colorado. However, none of that is part of your inheritance. His ranch in Livermore passed down through generations of Benings and will continue to do so. He did leave it to Bogard Tuck and his family, his vet and ranch manager, but should anything happen to Bo it would go back to the Bening estate. It can't be sold."

"I met Bo last week. I liked him."

"He's a good man, someone you can trust." He sat forward in his chair. "Fax your personal expenses directly to me, Cait. If you decide to stay and accept the terms of your inheritance, I'll have a personal account set up for you." He plucked a business card from a stack in a leatherette holder on his desk and handed it to her. "I'm here to help you."

She slipped the card into her handbag and then glanced out the window. The rain had tapered off and the fog had lifted. She looked back at Lane. "I'm still driving the rental."

"Use the Jaguar. It's yours anyway. Marcus has the keys and can return the rental." He checked his watch. "Anything else?"

Still confused about Rachel's position with the trust, she asked, "If Rachel is an executor, why didn't she know Tasha had passed away?"

His brow puckered; his cheeks turned red. "I can't answer that. When I talked with Ben, Rachel's husband, he said he'd let her know. She was working out of the country, but he knew how to contact her."

"Then what about me? How could she be an executor and not know about me? She thought I was an imposter."

"I didn't know about you until I drew up the trust, and Tasha and I were personal friends." He briefly glanced away as if gathering his thoughts. "I wanted Tasha to reconsider since Rachel's gone a lot, but she wouldn't hear of it. The administration and management of a trust needs attention, especially a sizeable one like the Bening estate, but extensive knowledge isn't required. Not to excuse her, but Rachel knew she could always consult with me if she had to." Lane seemed to sink into his chair, as if he wished to hide. His eyes wandered; he looked as if on a mental journey. It made Cait wonder about his personal relationship with Tasha.

When his phone buzzed, he grabbed it as if it were a lifeline. "Yes?" Pause. "All right." He rose. "Excuse me, Cait. I have papers that need to be signed. I'll only be a moment." He rushed out.

Cait stood and walked over to a wall of floor-to-ceiling shelves crammed with books. She traced her finger over a red leather-bound set of Harvard Classics, law books, and medical texts, and randomly pulled one out—*Medical Entomology: A Textbook on Public Health and Veterinary Problems*. After testifying in court on murder cases, she could appreciate the wide range of subjects attorneys had to know and understand. She slipped the book back on the shelf.

A print of the four faces of Ronald Reagan by Norman Rockwell hung on one wall. She studied it closely before moving on to an oil painting of a somber-looking gentleman.

"My grandfather," Lane said as he walked in. "He started this firm in his garage after graduating from college."

She smiled. "I know you're busy, so I won't keep you any longer. Thanks for seeing me."

He picked up the folder from his desk and handed it to her. "Tasha may have been an absent aunt, but she was a good person. You would have liked her."

She took the folder and nodded. "That's what I keep hearing. So why would someone want to kill her?"

His face turned the color of fog. "You must be mistaken. She died from a heart attack."

The lack of color on his face and the sweat on his upper lip concerned her. "Actually, the cause is undetermined." She started to reach for the door handle, and then looked back. "How well do you know Rachel Cross?"

He chuckled. "Ah. Rachel the actress or my cousin Rachel?"

Cagey lawyers had a habit of dropping bombs—little disclosures—as they saw fit. That Stanton Lane and Rachel Cross were cousins startled Cait. Fortunately for Lane, his secretary approached before Cait had a chance to comment.

CHAPTER 12

After a nap, Cait awakened with a start at four o'clock that afternoon, restless and disoriented. Instead of dreaming of castles in the air, she dreamt of grapes dying on their vines from neglect. She got up from the chaise lounge and stretched out the kinks. Dressed in jeans, pullover sweater, and a pair of old sneakers, she slipped her badge in her back pocket and went downstairs. She checked the office for Marcus, but as usual, he wasn't there.

Annoyed, she left the house and went to the garage to look for him. The rain had stopped, but a cold wind curled across the hills sending chills through her body. She rattled the doorknob at the side door of the garage as she peered in the window. Tasha's Jaguar was parked in the middle slot.

She cut between the house and garage and headed to RT's trailer. The door flew open and banged against the metal side as she approached.

Startled, she jumped back.

RT stood in the doorway, a revolver in his hand at the side of his leg.

"Well, damn," he said as he lowered his gun. "You don't look like a mountain lion." He snapped the lock on his gun and tucked it out of sight at the small of his back.

"Lucky me," she said, heart pounding.

"Where've you been?"

"Excuse me?"

"Don't get your knickers in a twist. I was looking for you. You've been gone a long time. I was worried."

"My knickers?"

He grinned. "I calls 'em like I sees 'em."

"I went to see Stanton Lane."

"Learn anything interesting?"

She shivered and clasped her arms around herself against the wind. "You really don't like him, do you? Ask me in before I freeze my butt off and I'll tell you."

A wicked smile lit his eyes. "Everything looks intact from my point of view."

She glowered at him.

He held his hands up as if in self-defense. "Okay. But if I invite you in, does that mean you've decided to trust me?"

She shifted her feet. "RT—"

"It's difficult to work with someone who doesn't trust you." His gaze slid from her eyes to her lips and slowly to her sneakers.

Cait couldn't have felt more undressed if she were posing in an art studio. "Dammit, RT."

He opened the door wide and held his hand out to help her up. "Come on. Got a fresh pot of coffee."

The trailer left little wiggle room but looked comfy. Cait glanced at an open laptop on the table as she slid into one side of the blue leatherette booth. She glimpsed a few words on the screen—silver, fish, timepieces, coins—before RT set two steaming mugs on the table and closed the laptop.

He sat down across from her. "Sorry. No sugar, no Sweet'N Low."

"Never use it." She clasped her cold hands around the hot mug. "Smells good."

They sipped coffee and watched each other like a pair of hawks.

"Is it always this windy up here?"

"Don't know, but my guess is you'll appreciate it when the summer months hit a hundred."

"I won't be here, remember." She sipped her coffee. "You make good coffee."

"I rarely poison my guests." He leaned back in his seat. "Something bugging you, Cait?"

"What do you mean?"

"Why are you here? Or are you just naturally nosey?" He tapped his laptop.

She set her coffee down. "I'm looking for Marcus."

"He's been here and gone. Tell me about your visit with Stanton Lane."

She studied him for a moment. "I was concerned about expenses. When does Marcus work? I think he's avoiding me."

"Could be. He doesn't trust many people, and you're a stranger here. So what concerns you about the expenses? Do you need money?"

She sighed. "No. Did you know Lane and Rachel Cross are cousins?"

His hand paused as he lifted his cup. "No."

"They're coexecutors of Tasha's trust. I got the impression things are not so sweet between Lane and Rachel, but she should have known about me."

RT stared into his coffee before taking a long drag of it. "One thing you have to remember about Rachel is that she's an actor. She's not always what she appears to be."

"I'm finding that out. I want to talk to her. Do you have her phone number?"

RT pulled his laptop close, opened it, and tapped a few keys. He pulled a paper napkin from a metal dispenser on the table and wrote a number on it before sliding it across the table toward Cait.

"That's efficient," she said, referring to the dispenser.

"Have to be in a trailer."

"Now where might I find Marcus?"

He shook his head. "You don't want to know."

She raised her eyebrow. "I'll ask someone else if you won't tell me."

"It's not a place for a lady. Leave him a note—"

The trailer suddenly jolted side to side. Coffee sloshed in their mugs. Terrified, Cait grasped the edge of the table. "What the—"

"Earthquake." RT grabbed Cait's hand, pulled her to her feet, and in one swift move had her around the waist and out the door. "Sometimes the ground has to let off multiple orgasms."

Laughter bubbled up in her throat. "That's a poetic way of putting it."

"You never want to be in a trailer during an earthquake." He let her go.

Velcro brushed against RT's ankles. He reached down and picked the cat up. "Scared you, huh, little fellow?"

Cait noticed a softening in RT's eyes as he ran his hand down the cat's back. She heard footsteps, turned, and there was Marcus Singer. Dressed in pressed blue jeans, white shirt opened midway down, and a black leather jacket, he could have stepped off the pages of *GQ*.

"Another shipment arrived," Marcus said. "I signed for them. Boxes are in the gift shop."

She nodded. "I'll walk back with you." She glanced at RT and raised her eyebrows before following Marcus to the house. He went into his office, turned the printer on, and sat down at the computer and began to type, ignoring Cait.

His dexterity at the keyboard amazed her. *Craftsman, cowboy, computer whiz? So what's he doing playing secretary?*

The printer hummed and spat out several sheets of paper.

Marcus handed them to her. "Copy of the order. You can check to see that everything ordered came in."

She ran her eyes down the first page. "Thanks."

"Yeah." He turned back to the computer.

"Where are the keys to the Jaguar?"

He stopped typing and stared up at her. "Why?"

"Stanton Lane said I should use the Jaguar and you could turn my rental in."

"Crap." He banged on the keyboard.

She stared at him. "Excuse me?" She wanted to hit him over the head with the keyboard, but took a deep breath and held her hand out. "May I have the keys, Marcus?"

He reached across the desk, plucked them from an in-basket, and dropped them on the desk.

Cait stared at the keys but didn't touch them. "What's our problem, Marcus?"

He stared at the computer screen. "Bullshit! Why are you here? Tasha never said anything about having a niece."

His language didn't disturb her; she'd heard far worse, but it was out of sync with the model image he tried to portray by his appearance. She reached to her back pocket and pulled her badge out. She wiped it on her sleeve and dropped it on the desk next to the Jag keys. "We need to talk about this. Soon."

Marcus stared at her badge and blanched.

She exchanged her rental keys for the Jag ones. "We're cool, right?" she said as she collected her badge.

CHAPTER 13

Tuesday morning, RT was gone. Ilia told Cait that RT had family issues in San Diego and left sometime during the middle of the night. When a police officer knocked on the front door that morning, he introduced himself as Officer Thom and said Detective Rook asked him to patrol the grounds until RT returned. Thom said he'd let her know when he came and left so she wouldn't think he was a prowler. Cait remembered his name from the night of the fire.

Restless, she settled in the bedroom with Tasha's heavy binder on her lap. The sun spilled across the bay sitting area and the pages as she read Tasha's vision statement for the festival: "To create a small, concentrated theater compound of exceptional quality in which to proceed courageously to fulfill artistic dreams." Thinking of the smaller Blackfriars Theater, Cait interpreted the statement to mean size doesn't always equate to quality.

As she continued to read, her mind began to wander and an uneasy sensation formed in the pit of her stomach. Why and when did Tasha decide to leave the Bening estate to her? Was it because she had been an English-lit major in college and understood Shakespeare? Or was the trust a way for Tasha to get her to Livermore to investigate Hilton's death? Cait didn't think it would change anything, but she intended to ask Lane when the trust had been prepared.

She set the binder on the floor by her feet, closed her eyes and drifted off to sleep for an hour when a bird slammed into the window and startled her. It took a while for Cait to remember where she was. When she stood, the room spun before her. She grabbed an arm of a chair to steady herself, blinked a couple of times until the room settled, then picked up the binder and went downstairs.

The house was silent but the sun streamed through the stained-glass window over the sink, giving the kitchen a warm glow. When her cell phone beeped, she pulled it from her belt.

"Cait, Stanton Lane. When you were here yesterday, I should have had you sign a paper that allows you to take money from the estate's account. I'll fax it to the house now. If you would sign it and fax it back, I would appreciate it."

"No problem. I'll watch for it," she said. "I'm glad you called. I'd like a security system installed at the house and theaters. Would that be okay?"

"Of course, but I think they're already in the theaters, just not connected. You might find something in Tasha's files about a security company. If so, call and ask them to come out to look at the house. The Benings should have taken care of it a long time ago, but somehow they never got around to it."

"Thanks. Another question. When was Tasha's trust written up?"

"I don't recall the exact date, but about five years ago."

"Was my name on the trust from the start or added later?"

"From the start, when the trust was prepared. Is there a problem?"

My parents died five years ago. Is that why Tasha left her estate to me? "No, just curious. I'll wait for your fax." She closed her phone and went into the office. Within minutes, she received it, read and signed it, and faxed it back to Lane.

Outside, she clutched Tasha's binder as she strolled around the meditation garden looking for inspiration or some divine influence about her inheritance. *If I was written into Tasha's trust five years ago, it wasn't because she wanted me to investigate Hilton's death as I'd thought. It had to be about the plane crash that killed her twin brother. But what did that have to do with me?*

She left the garden and walked toward the Elizabethan Theater to see what progress had been made since the fire. She sat a few rows back from the stage and watched the electricians drag cables and wires across the floor until she grew restless and opened the binder. By now, she'd practically memorized Tasha's notes.

Tongue of a Bird, the first play scheduled at the Blackfriars Theater, held Cait's interest as she reread the brief description. The play revolved around the search for an abducted girl. The characters live in varying aspects of metaphysical, spiritual, and psychological worlds. Tasha thought a smaller theater helped the audience hear the language and enter the heads of the characters. *You enter the play through your head and exit through your heart,* she'd written.

As intriguing as the play sounded, Cait wondered why Tasha would pick an emotional play like *Tongue of a Bird,* yet cut herself off from her own family.

The Royal Family, a 1927 comedic portrait of the comings, goings, phone calls, and general pandemonium of a clan of famed actors, appealed more to Cait. Tasha's footnote, "This season's bon-bon, a brandied treat," had Cait laughing.

"What's so funny?" a deep voice said.

Startled, Cait looked up and saw RT slip into the row and sit down next to her.

"Caught a flight back with a friend," he said when she remained silent.

"Phone lines were dead? No pen or paper?" she said.

"I left in the middle of the night, Cait. Family emergency."

Other than the fact that she was technically his boss, he didn't owe her an explanation for his absence. She felt foolish for making a point of it. "I'm sorry. Ilia told me."

He smiled. "Did you make friends with Officer Thom?"

"Someone must have told him I bite. He introduced himself and then I never saw him again."

He reached over and tucked a stray hair behind her ear. "I told him to keep a low profile, that you were sensitive about accepting protection from anyone."

She looked up at the stage. "Why would anyone want to burn this beautiful theater?" She shook her head in disgust. "I'd like to help put it back together—paint, hang curtains, assemble the back rooms. Just don't give me a hammer."

He grinned. "Something to remember."

RT leaned forward, elbows on his knees, and clasped his hands. "For what it's worth, I think you'd do one hell of a job for the arts in this valley. Tasha would be proud."

"I'm impatient, moody, and fly by the seat of my pants."

"But you're not afraid to speak your mind, and you can get emotional over a horse. How am I doing so far?"

"You're crazy; scary too." She closed the binder. "I told Lane I want a security system installed in both theaters and the house. He thinks there is one in the theaters, just not connected yet."

"Then let's take care of it while I'm here."

"I'll talk to Marcus," Cait said. "He should know what security firm installed the system at the theaters, and at the same time order one for the house."

"Good idea." He stood, stretched. "Ready to go back?" With a coy smile he said, "You can tell me how much you missed me."

She grinned as she stood up. "Like a migraine."

He laughed as they walked out of the theater. "I like you, Cait Pepper. Were you a good cop?"

"I'd like to think so. I worked hard at it because I loved it. Why?"

"I just wanted to see if you thought you were," he said. "Tells a lot about someone." He opened the arbor gate for her.

"Do you know where the actors will stay when they come?" she asked.

"All I know is that the Bening estate leases apartments around town for them. Last year a few were from the Bay Area and bunked with family or friends. Understudies earn extra for housing if they stay outside a fifty-mile radius of town, but you might want to confirm that with Lane or Rachel if you're worried about it."

"I don't think it's an immediate issue for me to worry about." Head down, she walked beside him. "I'm surprised how few of them there are for seven plays. Some of the names are mentioned for more than one play."

"That's because they're required to be in two or three plays at a time, even understudy a couple."

She stared at him. "You've got to be kidding. Shakespeare's difficult. How is that possible?"

"They're professionals. It's what they do." He smiled. "Much like cops and SEALs."

The back door flew open. Ilia almost ran into them. "Actors' Equity just called." He handed RT a slip of paper. "Sounded urgent."

Chapter 14

RT took the paper and glanced at the phone number. "Did they say what it's about?"

"A rumor that Tasha's death was suspicious and the fire at the Elizabethan was arson. I refused to confirm or deny anything, but they did say they're concerned for their actors' safety."

RT glanced at Cait. "Want me to make the call?"

She took the note. "No. It's my responsibility, but I'll put it on speaker. Feel free to jump in if I stumble." They went into the office where Cait sat down at the desk. She found a pen, pulled a notepad close, and dialed the number.

"This is Cait Pepper," she said when a man with an accent answered. "I'm returning a call about the Bening estate." She glanced at RT. "Yes, I'll hold."

Another man came on the line and introduced himself as Sam Cruz. She wrote his name down and listened to his concerns about their actors' welfare until his demands for extreme security became greater than were acceptable. She interrupted him. "Mr. Cruz, I appreciate your concern. However, the coroner's report indicated the cause of Tasha's death was undetermined. As for the fire, it may have been an environmentalist making a statement about destroying the view of the hills." Not too far of a stretch, she thought. "I suggest you ignore the rumors and have your actors here as scheduled. They are under contract." She rolled her eyes at RT. "Yes, security will be tight. Thank you for calling."

"Well done," RT said when she hung up.

"There will be plenty of security, right? We'll both be gone by then, back to our jobs."

"I'll talk with Rook again. And I'll tell Rachel about the call."

She tore the page from the notepad and clipped it to Tasha's binder. She stood. "I have an errand to run." An errand she'd decided on as she'd sat in the theater. She didn't want to tell RT where she was going because she knew he would try to stop her.

Cait took the binder upstairs to the bedroom and grabbed the keys to Tasha's Jaguar. It was near noon when she located Novak Investigations nestled among other small houses that had been converted into offices. A tall blonde stood in front of a file cabinet when Cait walked in. She thought the young girl looked like a sex trophy in her cropped pink sweater that barely covered her ample breasts and exposed an inch of bare midriff.

"I'm Cait Pepper. I'd like to see Mr. Novak."

"Concerning what?"

"Tasha Bening. I believe he'll remember our previous phone conversation."

The blonde picked up the receiver and punched a button on her phone with the tip of a flamingo-pink fingernail. "Cait Pepper's here to see you about Tasha Bening." She nodded and replaced the receiver. "You can go straight back," she said.

Cigar smoke hung heavy in Novak's office, burning Cait's eyes.

Karl Novak looked to be in his mid-fifties, his square face framed by heavy waves of black hair. His shirtsleeves were shoved to his elbows. Cait recognized the tattoo on his left forearm as the astronomy symbol for infinity. His tie hung loose under his collar. He stood, frowned as he crushed Cait's hand in his, and motioned toward a single wooden, straight-backed chair in front of his desk.

"I'm afraid you've made the trip for nothing. Can't tell you any more now than when you called," he said.

She expected his negative response and held up her Columbus PD badge, hoping he wouldn't look at it too closely.

His eyebrows arched. "What the hell's that for?"

Cait smiled. "I thought it might help jar your memory."

Novak stared hard at Cait, then buzzed his clerk. "Bring me the Tasha Bening file."

While they waited, Cait noticed a framed police officer's commendation on the wall behind Novak's desk. She couldn't read the date, but Karl Novak's name stood out in large gold letters. She wondered why he'd left the police force to become a PI.

The clerk handed a file to Novak and left. He opened it, gave it a quick glance. "As I said, not much here. Mrs. Bening made one appointment. Classy woman, as I recall."

"I thought you said your only contact was a phone call."

He glanced at the file. "I forgot. Her visit was brief."

She held out her hand. "May I see the file?"

Novak hesitated but handed it over.

Cait closely read the one-page description of Novak's two phone contacts with Tasha. No mention of a follow-up to her concerns. No acknowledgment whether she had purchased a gun. Simple statements that any first-year officer could have written.

Then she read the last paragraph.

She looked over the file at Novak. "You went to the Bening estate? Did she ask you to come?"

He shook his head. "No. Took a chance she'd see me."

"Did she?"

"No." He pointed to the file. "As I wrote in there, I heard voices in the garage. I didn't want to interrupt so I left."

She reread the brief description of his visit to the estate to be sure she'd read it correctly. "You thought Tasha was being threatened." She looked up at him. "And you knew she wanted to buy a gun, that she was afraid someone wanted to kill her. Why didn't you go in the garage to investigate? What kind of an investigator are you, Mr. Novak?"

His face turned red as he slapped his hands on the desk. "Don't question my credentials, lady."

She glanced at the commendation on the wall. Maybe his quick temper explained why he was no longer a cop. "Tell me what you saw and overheard. Everything, or I will report you to the authorities for negligence of duty."

"What?" They stared at each other. He leaned forward and took a deep breath. "Okay. I recognized Mrs. Bening's voice. I was standing outside the garage by the side door. It was a heated argument. I think it was a man's voice I heard, but I'm not positive."

"You didn't think you should investigate?"

Novak replied with renewed energy and smoldering indignation. "I had no business being there, all right? So I left. I did see a couple of groundskeepers and asked a few questions. You know, like had they seen Mrs. Bening. Who was she with? They were Hispanic and either reluctant to talk or didn't know English. Mine was the only car in the driveway, so I thought maybe she had a complaint with one of the groundskeepers. That's it. I left."

Cait wondered if Novak knew about the back entrance to the estate. "You didn't see anyone else around?"

He glanced away for a second. "Well, there was some skinny guy out back on a horse, but he couldn't have been the one in the garage with Mrs. Bening."

Had to be Marcus.

"Did you talk to him?"

"Nope. As I said, I left."

Frustrated, Cait knew she wouldn't get any more from Novak. She rose and dropped the file on his desk. "I suggest you complete this. The police may want to see it."

Novak jumped up. "I've been in law enforcement longer than you've been alive! Don't tell me how to do my job!"

"You didn't have a job, Mr. Novak, when you went to the Bening estate. You were trespassing."

Cait drove to the Livermore police station, hoping Detective Rook could see her. She entered the building and approached a kiosk manned by a male clerk.

Cait smiled. "Hi. I don't have an appointment, but if Detective Rook's available I'd like to see him."

"I'll see if he's working today." He rolled his stool over to a computer.

Cait's cell phone rang. She stepped away from the kiosk and pulled the phone from her purse. She checked the screen and recognized Shep's number.

"Hi, can I call you back? Thanks." She snapped the cell shut and turned back to the clerk.

"Detective Rook is scheduled to be here. I'll page him." He dialed a number. "Detective Rook, you have front-lobby traffic."

Cait heard the announcement overhead. While she waited, she glanced through a display rack of leaflets—*Hate Crimes; Identity Theft;* and *DARE, Drug Abuse Resistance Education.* She heard a door open and looked up.

Detective Rook smiled as he approached her, dressed in a gray suit, lilac shirt and tie. "Cait. Please tell me there hasn't been another incident at the Bening place. Officer Thom would feel real bad about that."

She smiled. "Not that I know of. Can you spare a few minutes?"

"Sure." He pulled out a set of keys. "Let's go in here." He unlocked a small interview room. "Have a seat." He closed the door, sat down, and laced his fingers.

"Remember that private investigator's number I found in Tasha's date book?"

He nodded.

"Are you familiar with Novak Investigations?" she asked.

"I know Karl Novak has an office downtown."

"But do you know him?"

Detective Rook leaned forward. "What's your point?"

She hesitated. Just because Novak was overbearing and negligent didn't mean he was inadequate. He *had* received a commendation when he was a cop. Still, she wondered why he left to become a PI. She'd have to admit to Rook she'd been to Novak's office if she wanted to learn more about Novak.

Rook continued. "Surely, one of Columbus's top crime analysts hasn't stepped out of line."

She stared at him. "You checked me out."

"Of course."

She nodded. "Okay. I went to his office to talk to him."

His eyebrows arched. "And why did you do that?"

"He said Tasha called him because she was afraid someone might try to hurt her and wanted to know how to purchase a gun for protection. I already told you that. But I thought he wasn't being totally honest so I went to see him." She expected Rook to rebuke her for butting in on an investigation. When he didn't, she continued, her voice rising with frustration at the thought of Novak's carelessness. "He showed me Tasha's file, what there was of it. Something not in the file was his unauthorized visit to the estate. He said he overheard a heated argument in the garage between Tasha and a man. It sounded to him like someone was threatening Tasha. Instead of investigating, he left. That's irresponsible."

Rook took a Life Saver roll from his jacket pocket and offered it to Cait. When she shook her head, he took one and left the rest in the middle of the table. "Let me get this straight. You drop into his office, ask to see the file, and he just handed it to you?"

She looked down at her fingernails. "Not exactly. I flashed my badge as encouragement."

"Your *Ohio* badge."

She swallowed. "Yes."

He crossed his arms on the table, his eyes fixed on hers. "I'll let that go for now. Since you're in the business, what I'm about to tell you remains in this room."

She nodded. "Absolutely."

He sucked on his Life Saver. "About ten years ago, Novak had been a good cop. Unfortunately, he got caught up in his own ego, his own rule book. He took chances by working outside the law. Took liberties and bribes. Then his partner got caught in the line of fire during one of their unauthorized interventions and died, leaving behind a wife and newborn. Novak was suspended and later fired on several counts of negligence."

"Fired from this department?"

"No." He laced his fingers together. "Stay away from Novak, Cait."

She nodded. "Still, he took an oath to honor his badge."

Cait returned Shep's call while still parked in front of the police station. "It's me. I just left the Livermore PD."

"Everything okay?"

"I hope so. How are you?"

"I'm okay." He hesitated. "Cait, I have to ask when you're

returning to work."

She felt a heavy lump settle in her chest. "I don't know, Shep. I want to come back, but it's complicated . . . this darn inheritance." She rolled the window down for fresh air, sensing something was off about Shep's call. "Is there a problem I need to be concerned with?"

"I'm only the messenger, Cait, but the commander wants to know your intentions, and he wants to know now."

Cait sighed. "Give it to me straight, Shep."

"He wants you here next Monday. Something about that frat case you've been working on and if it's connected to another murder. I explained your situation, but he wants you to call him. My advice is you come in, explain your situation, and ask for a leave of absence until you can figure out what to do. I'm really sorry."

"I know, and it sucks, but I'll be there."

"I'll pick you up at the airport. Let me know when."

"Thanks. They can't take my job from me, can they?"

"No, but they could transfer you out."

CHAPTER 15

Cait returned to the house and parked in front of the garage. Velcro appeared and rubbed against her leg and pawed at his whiskers.

She crouched to stroke the cat. "What have you got there?" She ran her fingers through his whiskers and attempted to remove fragments of what appeared to be pistachio shells like ones she'd seen all over the yard. The cat scampered off and Cait walked around to the back of the house.

Marcus stood in the doorway blocking her way.

She tried to sidestep him.

"I returned your rental," he said.

"That's great. I appreciate it."

"You left the Jag out. Tasha always kept it in the garage to keep it clean," he said.

"I'll keep that in mind. Now let me by." She shouldered past him and went inside.

If I didn't need his help, I'd fire his skinny ass.

RT walked in from the front hall, thumbs hooked in his jeans. "Come upstairs. I want to show you something."

Now what? She followed him through the hall and up the stairs. "What is it?"

"Don't look so worried. It's a good thing."

At the second floor, he stopped and opened the door to the stairs up to the third floor. "I want you safe while you're here so I can stop worrying about you." He stepped into the stairwell.

"Come on."

As she took a step up, their shoulders touched.

He closed the door and turned a knob.

She heard it click in place. "You installed a lock. Thank you."

"I'd like the entire top floors closed off, particularly while the gift shop is in the house. If Tasha had let me install a lock, things might have turned out differently." He handed her a key. "Lock the door every time you leave."

She clutched the key in her hand. "I will. Come on up. We have to talk."

Their footsteps echoed on the timeworn stairs as they climbed to the third floor. "You might consider getting one of those fancy red velvet cords to go across the foot of the staircase to discourage anyone from coming up here."

"You mean stanchions?"

"Yeah. Your aunt was one stubborn lady. Flatly refused when I suggested it."

Sunlight filtered through the stained-glass windows, spreading splotches of red, gold, and green across the walls. When she was settled in a chair in the bay area, RT sat down across from her, clasped his hands together, elbows on his knees. "This sounds serious."

"It could be. I have to go back home for a few days, commander's orders."

His shoulders appeared to sag as he stared at her. "You'll be back?"

"Yes." Frustration fueled her restlessness and she rose and stared out the window at the lush green hills. "I know it's rotten timing, RT, but I don't have a choice." She turned back to him.

"I understand, Cait. You want to keep your job. If I have to ask for an extension of my leave, I will."

"When I meet with my commander, I'm going to ask for a leave of absence."

He nodded. "I'll be here when you get back." He looked down at his hands for a moment. "I have news. While you were out, Sam Cruz from Actors' Equity called. That rumor about Tasha and the fire at the Elizabethan started with an anonymous phone call . . ."

Her eyes lit up. "Calls can be traced," she interrupted.

". . . from a prepaid cell phone," he continued.

"Every criminal's favorite toy. No paper trail and hassle free. Like a disposable camera."

"Yeah. The good news is Cruz called to reassure us everything would go ahead as planned. The actors for *Tongue of the Bird* should arrive on the twenty-sixth to begin rehearsals."

She felt like a weight had been lifted from her shoulders. "That's good. I'll fly out Thursday, meet with my commander Friday, and fly back Sunday. I've been staying with friends since selling my house. I'll need time to pack some of my clothes to bring back with me."

"Sounds like a lot to accomplish over a weekend," he said.

She thought how little was left after seven years of marriage. She'd sold Roger's cars, and most of their furniture went with the house. Her stomach knotted as she recalled the scene before their split.

She'd returned home after an exhausting day with a local gang member, a teenager on the verge of going to jail, to find that Roger had locked her out of the house. He'd yelled at her through an open window that she cared more about other kids rather than trying to conceive one of their own. She'd spent that night at Samantha's house and the next day in her lawyer's office.

The memory sent chills through her body.

RT jumped up. "Cait? What's wrong?"

She shook off the memory. "Just . . . nothing."

He hesitated. "Get a flight out of Oakland. Less hassle than

San Francisco. I'll take you to the airport." He flashed a smile. "And I'll pick you up if you promise to come back."

She lightly punched his arm. "Your generosity is overwhelming."

He wiggled his eyebrows. "You'd be surprised how far my generosity can go with the right incentive." Before she could respond, he continued. "Now tell me why you were in such a lousy mood when you came into the house."

Her anger with Novak still lingered. "Remember the PI's name I found in Tasha's date book? I went to his office. He's an ex-cop." She told him about Novak and what little information he had in his file about Tasha. "He's totally incompetent."

RT stared at her.

"What?" she asked.

"Are you out to make an enemy of Rook? Cait, you had no business going there. Not only are you out of your jurisdiction, but you don't know what Novak is capable of."

"I'd do it again if I thought I'd learn more from him. He's hiding something, RT. I know it."

CHAPTER 16

Cait locked the door after RT left, took her laptop and cell phone over to the desk and made online plane reservations to fly to Columbus Thursday. She printed her confirmation, and then e-mailed her commander and Shep.

The paper napkin RT had scribbled Rachel Cross's phone number on was clipped to Tasha's binder on the desk. She called and, after several rings, was about to hang up when Rachel answered.

"Hello! Hello!" Rachel snapped.

"Rachel, it's Cait, Tasha's niece. Sounds like I caught you at a bad time."

"No time's a good time. I should have called you, but I'm home so little that I tend to hide from the outside world. But that's another story."

Cait hadn't seen or heard from Rachel since the fire a week ago. "I have to leave town Thursday for a few days and wondered if we could get together before then to talk about the festival. RT said there are volunteers who work at the performances, but when I read Tasha's notes I didn't see a list of names. If you have them, I'd be glad to call and confirm they'll be here before I leave." The real problem was that she felt pretty useless.

"Don't worry about it," Rachel said. "Marcus has the names and can follow up with them. When you're back, we'll get together and decide what you can do. I'm just surprised you're still here. I expected you to go back home before now."

Cait sat upright in her chair. "Really? Why would you think that? The Bening estate *is* my inheritance, and when I decide what I'm going to do about it I'll let you know."

"I only meant that I'm capable of seeing to the festival if you decide to leave. I know the estate can't be sold."

"I never run from a problem, Rachel. There's a situation with my job I need to attend to, but be assured I'll be back by Sunday."

"Fine. I'm just saying you don't have to worry about the festival."

Geez, what's her problem? "I got it, Rachel. What I don't understand is if you and Stanton Lane are coexecutors of Tasha's trust, why were you surprised to learn she had a niece? I'm the only one named in the trust."

Rachel hesitated so long that Cait thought she'd hung up. "Someone should have told me about you. Of course Stan knew; he drew up the trust. I'm gone a lot, weeks, months at a time. I didn't want the responsibility of coexecutor, but Tasha insisted." She laughed. "I didn't have time to read the damn thing."

"Maybe you should have. Didn't Mr. Lane know how to reach you when Tasha died?"

"Of course." Then, "Well, sometimes my plans change and I'm too busy to call home. Even Ben, my husband, is occasionally left in the dark about where I am. Why is this important now?"

"It's a cop thing to ask questions," Cait said automatically. "Maybe you're right, it's not important now. What is, is my learning all I can about my inheritance and the responsibilities that go along with it."

Rachel's voice rose. "What's that mean, a cop thing?"

Wishing she hadn't mentioned it, she said, "I work in law enforcement."

"Well, aren't you full of surprises, just like Tasha."

You don't know the half of it. "Did your husband explain why he didn't tell you about Tasha?"

"Ha. You don't want to be in hearing range when I lose my temper." She hung up.

Cait smiled. "I love it when someone hangs up on me. It usually means I've touched a sensitive spot." She logged back into her laptop and e-mailed her friend, Samantha, giving her flight schedule and letting her know Shep would pick her up at the airport.

She stood and stretched, then heard a rattling noise from the stairwell. She walked over, tilted her head to listen, and then asked, "Who's there?"

Silence.

She walked down a few steps. "Who is it?"

"Cait? It's Stanton Lane."

She continued down, slid the bolt back, and pushed the door open, nearly hitting him.

He stumbled back.

"What are you doing up here?" she asked as she stepped down onto the second floor.

His face flushed, Lane ran his hand over his gray crew cut. "I didn't expect the door to be locked."

Obviously. Just how close were he and Tasha?

Cait couldn't help but say, "Maybe if Tasha had locked it, she would be alive today." Lane's attempt to get in the bedroom reminded her she hadn't asked Marcus to call about alarming the house.

He studied the floor. "Tasha was too trusting, that's true."

"Wait right here." She ran up, grabbed the key RT had given her, and went back down. Lane hadn't moved from where she'd left him.

"I own you an apology, Cait," he said. "I wasn't expecting anyone to be up here."

She closed the door, locked it, and dropped the key in her pocket. "I told you I was staying here."

"You did, but I forgot. I'm sorry."

"Let's go down. You can tell me why you're here."

No one was around when they reached the first floor.

"Tell me what you were looking for," she said when they walked into the kitchen.

"A book of poems Tasha and I shared. It meant something to us."

Was he in love with Tasha? "Did you check the sitting room on the second floor?"

"Briefly. I didn't see it."

"I'm going to make coffee. Would you like some?"

"Yes, please."

Cait prepared a pot of coffee while Lane sat quietly on a stool at the counter.

"When was the lock installed?" Lane asked.

"Just today. RT surprised me with it." She turned to him. "I didn't expect it to be tested this soon."

He chuckled. "At my expense. Sorry. I expect Mr. Tanner will be leaving soon."

She pulled a stool out and sat down next to him to wait for the coffee to perk. "I expect so."

He picked up a packet of Sweet'N Low from a basket. "Are you any closer to making a decision about your inheritance?"

She heard the coffee gurgling in the background as she processed how best to answer Lane. "After what's happened here—Tasha's death, the fire—eight days is too soon to rush into a decision."

"Of course, you're right."

"Any decision I make will affect my life," she said. "If only I'd known her . . ."

"It would be easier, I know."

The coffee slowed and stopped. She stood, filled two coffee cups, and set one in front of Lane. "Sorry I don't have cookies to offer you."

He patted his stomach. "This is the result of too many sweets," he said.

She opened a drawer from under the counter, handed him a spoon, and sat down with her own coffee. While he stirred his coffee, she said, "Every day I have to remind someone that I'm not Tasha, that I work differently. I know I said you were welcome here anytime, but this is my house now. As long as I'm here, I'd like you to restrict your visits to the grounds unless you're invited inside." She smiled to soften her words. "Please use the doorbell next time."

Lane nodded and set his the spoon down. "You're absolutely right. It won't happen again."

"I'll look around the house and let you know if I find your book." She sipped her coffee and toyed with the question she'd wanted to ask him after the shooting incident. "Do you own a rifle?"

Without reacting to the change of subject, he said, "No. I have a revolver I keep in my desk. In my business, one never knows when a disgruntled client might attack. Happens more often than you can imagine. Why do you ask?"

She pointed to the new window in the back door. "Someone shot at me through there."

He stared at Cait. "What? Why on earth . . ."

"I wasn't hurt and the window's been replaced. The police were called."

"My God, no wonder Mr. Tanner installed a lock on the bedroom door and you asked about security."

"Yes. I have a situation at work I need to attend to. I leave Thursday, but I'll be back on Sunday. I thought you should know."

He drank more of his coffee, set his cup down, and stood. "I hope they won't lock you up and toss the key away so you can't come back."

She smiled. "I am going to ask for a leave of absence."

"Good. It will give you time to make up your mind about the inheritance. Thank you for the coffee. I'm going to drop in at Rachel's to see how Ben is doing."

"Oh? I just talked to her. She didn't mention he'd been sick."

"Ben suffers from depression. It's been worse since he retired from the Livermore Labs. He's a physicist turned sheep farmer."

She walked him through to the front door, opened it, and held her hand out. "May I please have your keys to the house and theaters?"

CHAPTER 17

Cait woke Wednesday morning tangled in damp sheets, struggling to snatch onto a vanishing dream that attempted to stitch disturbing pieces of her life together like a quilt. Odd pieces she didn't recognize.

She showered and dressed, then went down to the second-floor sitting room where she did a cursory search of the shelves for Lane's poetry book. Not finding it, she went back up to the bedroom to rearrange her luggage to make room for a few of her clothes she wanted to bring back. By eleven she was downstairs looking for Marcus in the office. The computer and printer were on, but there was no sign of him. She grabbed a Post-it, wrote a note about her trip, and stuck it on the screen where he couldn't miss it. If the house burned down in her absence, at least he'd know she wasn't upstairs burnt to a crisp in the same bed where he'd found Tasha.

Coffee had already been made. She poured a cup and took it into the gift shop. To her surprise, someone had opened the rest of the boxes and placed the items on the long glass counter and shelves. She picked up a Harlequin mask, held it up to her face, and looked at herself in the mirror that sat on the counter. When she heard a laugh behind her, she turned and saw Rachel in the doorway.

"Reminds me of when I met Tasha, except then it was a lacey mantilla." Rachel walked in dressed in tight white jeans, red heels, and a cherry-red sweater. "Spooky how much you resemble her. Must be the violet eyes."

"I didn't expect to see you today." Cait set the mask back on the counter.

Rachel strolled around the room. She fingered the pins, folded T-shirts, and gypsum heads of Shakespeare and then riffled through a stack of books on Shakespeare. "I changed my mind. I was rude to you on the phone." She picked up one of the books and opened it. "Ever wonder if Shakespeare truly wrote all those plays?"

"No, but it usually came up in my college English-lit classes," Cait said. "His plays were full of mistakes, but he understood the poetry of the moment was more important than getting the geographical details right. At least, that's what the professor thought. I agreed."

Rachel put the book down and looked at Cait. "Interesting. Hypothetically speaking, what if a thousand monkeys, scrawling randomly with a quill, accidentally produced the works of Shakespeare? It would be a miracle, but one that wouldn't in any way diminish the quality of the plays. They would remain masterpieces of entertainment and literature."

Cait laughed, enjoying the supposition and this new side of Rachel. "And secure the knowledge that William Shakespeare, the Bard of Stratford-upon-Avon, *was* the literary genius who wrote those plays."

Rachel clapped her hands. "Exactly. Let's go in the kitchen to eat before the quiche I brought gets cold."

Who says there's no God, Cait thought as she followed Rachel into the kitchen.

Rachel slipped onto a stool and peeled back the foil from the quiche. "My humble attempt to apologize for my rudeness on the phone and for neglecting you." She slid a blue folder towards Cait. "I brought copies of my notes about the festival and the tea. Something to read on the plane."

"Thanks." Cait took plates from the cupboard and a knife and forks from a drawer and set them on the counter. She opened the folder while Rachel cut the spinach quiche.

"It's really not a big deal, you know. The tea. You'll enjoy it, if you're still here." She looked at Cait as she slid a plate to her.

Cait glanced at the names that had accepted the invitation to the tea.

"Tasha encouraged students from Las Positas College to get involved in the festival," Rachel said. "She never said, but I had the impression her family discouraged acting as a profession."

"I wouldn't know, but I wish I'd known her. Sometimes I feel like an intruder here."

Rachel stared at Cait. "Interesting you feel that way."

Cait closed the folder and picked up a fork. "Was Tasha a good actress?"

Rachel toyed with her quiche. "I guess you could say the true test of performing is being a character totally unlike yourself, even someone you don't like. Your walk, hand gestures, and even your thought processes change as you step into character." Her eyes glazed as she spoke. "Tasha lived her roles twenty-four/seven. A true professional." She hesitated. "You learn more being around great actors than from a dozen books. Tasha and I believed Shakespeare should be studied through stage productions, not dissected as literature. That's why she was so interested in the students."

"I thought advanced degrees for Shakespearean actors were required."

"Preferred, but not all have them. Neither Tasha nor I had a degree. But, then, we'd been in the business a long time. We learned by doing." With a bitten-back smile that bordered on arrogance, her usual brusque tone returned. "You don't know much about her, do you? Strange that she would leave her estate to you, don't you think?"

"I can't answer that," Cait said. "Maybe someday I'll find out."

"But here you are, you came not knowing what to expect," Rachel said. "That took guts, but then when money is involved—"

"Rachel." Cait slid off her stool and picked up the plates. "Thank you for the notes. I'll read them on the plane." She went to the sink as RT walked in.

Rachel slipped off her stool, her heels clicking against the tile floor as she trotted over to greet him. "Hey, big guy." She stood on tiptoes to hug him.

RT winked at Cait over Rachel's shoulder. "Something smells good."

"Spinach quiche," Rachel said. "Sit. I'll cut a slice for you."

"You doing okay, Cait?" he asked.

She nodded. "I made my reservations. It's early, six o'clock. You okay with that?"

He smiled. "I never renege on my promises."

Rachel set a plate in front of RT. Then she glanced at Cait as she took a key ring from her pocket and dropped it on the counter. "I also came to return my keys to the house and theaters. I'm not sure I should have them now that you're here."

Cait stared at the keys but didn't reach for them. She should have realized Rachel would have keys. She wondered if Stanton Lane had told Rachel that she had asked for his back. She smiled and slid the key to Rachel. "No, it's okay. You keep them for now."

Rachel's lips turned up in a subtle smile. "Well, if you're sure." She clutched the keys in her hand.

"I am." She glanced at RT. "Lane stopped by. He thinks he left a poetry book in the apartment. I looked but didn't see it."

"Probably love sonnets for Tasha," Rachel said.

"He tried to go up to the bedroom to look for it," Cait said.

RT's eyes glinted like fortified steel.

"We had a little encounter," Cait continued. "I think he understands now that rules have changed."

Rachel pursed her lips. "He wanted to marry Tasha."

Marry? That caught Cait off guard.

"I told him he was wasting his time," Rachel said. "She would never marry him. Stan likes his poker too much. Tasha disapproved."

Cait rolled that over in her mind. "He gambles?"

"Let's say he has a taste for it," Rachel said. "Along with half of California. Busloads leave the Bay Area regularly for Reno and Lake Tahoe."

"A dangerous habit that can get out of control with one roll of the dice," RT said, his eyebrow raised. "Bad stuff happens—bankruptcy, divorce, even murder."

"Does he win?" Cait asked.

Rachel teetered back and forth on her heels. "Not anymore. His credit cards are maxed out."

Cait's mind raced. "What about Marcus? Does he gamble?"

"Who knows what he does?" Rachel said. "Why the interest in gambling?"

"Money is often a motive for murder," Cait said.

Rachel grabbed the edge of the counter. "Murder? Who said anything about murder?"

RT took that moment to take his plate to the sink.

"Do you know Karl Novak, a local PI?" Cait asked.

Rachel blinked. "We've met. Why?"

"His name was in Tasha's date book. I thought she might have mentioned him to you."

RT came back and stood beside Cait.

"Well, she didn't," Rachel said. She turned and hurried out the back door.

Cait glanced at RT, shrugged, and then followed Rachel.

When she caught up with her, she said, "Mr. Lane said you're cousins."

"Not kissing cousins, by any stretch of the imagination. And drop the 'Mr.' stuff. It's annoying."

"He also said he showed the property to the Benings. I didn't realize he was a Realtor."

"He dabbles at it. The property had been on the market for about a year. I thought it suited their needs. Tasha wanted space to build her theaters. And Hilton wanted a vineyard, somewhere not too far from his ranch." She toyed with the keys Cait had returned to her, making a clinking noise. "Stan's a fair lawyer, specializing in medical malpractice." She opened the door of a relic red pickup that smelled suspiciously of dung. "Stan and I never ran in the same circles. He never married. We have little in common." She slid behind the steering wheel, closed the door, and with a wave started the motor and drove off.

Cait returned to the house where she found RT sitting at Marcus's computer. "You're in here more often than Marcus."

He looked up at her and smiled. "But he gets the work done. Check this out." He opened a folder on the desktop. "Festival files updated; phone conversations with newspapers and TV stations recorded. Even has your name listed as primary contact. Marcus is not a slacker."

"So he's efficient. The least he could do is communicate with me. I don't even know what all he's supposed to do." She sighed, crossed her arms, and leaned against the edge of the desk. "Maybe he'll be gone when I get back."

"No way. He's got ties in the area." He sat back in the chair and looked up at her. "I want to know what happened when Lane went upstairs."

She grimaced, not wanting to go into it. "It was embarrassing . . . for both of us." She reluctantly explained. "I asked for his keys."

"That's probably a good thing." RT stretched his legs out under the desk and wiggled his eyebrows. "Maybe Stan left something upstairs that could embarrass him. Like condoms."

She choked on the image. "That's disgusting."

"Yeah, but interesting if you look at the full picture: money issues, gambling, sex. What's next? Murder?"

CHAPTER 18

Cait went upstairs to see that she'd packed everything she'd need for the trip. When her cell phone vibrated in her jeans pocket, she pulled it out, glanced at the screen, and saw it was Shep calling.

"You're still picking me up at the airport, aren't you?" she said.

"Unpack your bag. Everything will be settled with a phone call," he said.

She sat down on the edge of the bed. "You've got to be joking."

"Nope. With a little persuasion, the deputy chief and Commander York agreed your leave of absence could be handled over the phone and by fax."

Cait breathed a sigh of relief. "Wow. I've underestimated your powers of persuasion, Detective Church. Whatever you did, I'm grateful."

"You're welcome. So, noon tomorrow Columbus time. Think you'll be up by nine?"

She laughed. "I can be up at five if I have to." She wondered how Shep worked his magic. Probably mentioned their budget problems. The police officers had agreed to forego a raise for the next two years instead of layoffs.

"I suggest you be prepared to ask about all those issues you want addressed while you have both of them on the phone."

"I will." Her heart thumped against her ribs. "What about

the latest murder on campus you told me about? The DC thought it might be related to my frat case."

"Ask him. I wasn't invited to participate in the phone call."

She'd tried not to let the frat case become too personal when she was asked to join the investigation, but she'd practically grown up on the Ohio State campus where her dad had been a professor. Her parents and grandparents had rooming houses for students. How could she not care? she wondered.

"Cait?"

"Sorry, just thinking. I had hoped to bring my Glock back," she said.

"Maybe not a good idea," he said, "but ask me later if you still want it and I'll see what I can do. But I doubt you'll get approval."

"Probably not. I better cancel my reservations and call Sam. Maybe she wouldn't mind sending some of my stuff since I'm going to be here for a while." She rose and walked over to the window. "Whatever you did to convince them a phone call would save time and money, it's relieved a lot of the pressure I was feeling. Thank you so much."

"I'm glad I could help. Call me."

Humming, Cait reached into her handbag for the reservations she'd printed and called the airlines to cancel. Her next call was to Samantha.

"Sam, guess what? Shep fixed it so my leave could be arranged by phone. I know, me too, but next time I'll be back for good." *I hope.* "I have a favor to ask."

After Sam agreed to send some of Cait's clothes, Cait emptied her luggage and stored it in the bottom of Hilton's wardrobe. Then she called RT.

"Change your mind about going?" he answered.

"Better. Everything will be handled over the phone tomorrow."

Twisted Vines

"That's good. Want to go out for dinner?" he asked.

"I would, but I want to be prepared when the call comes tomorrow morning. Shep told me to write down everything I want to ask while I have them on the line. A leave of absence means I'll have my job waiting for me when I go back."

He hesitated.

"RT?"

"That's good, I guess, keeping your job I mean. If it's what you want."

She read between the lines. *He's hoping I'll change my mind and stay.* "RT, one day at a time. Okay? For now, let's concentrate on Tasha's murder. Isn't that what we want?"

"You're right. Who's Shep?"

"Probably my best friend at the department. I'd trust him with my life."

"You have a good evening, then. I'll see you tomorrow."

Something was bothering RT, she thought. He sounded distant, distracted. Reminded of food, she went downstairs to fix something to eat. The refrigerator revealed the leftover quiche Rachel had brought for lunch. She slipped it in the microwave.

While she waited for it to heat, she went into the office to leave Marcus a note that her trip was canceled and to look for Lane's poetry book. She stuck another Post-it to the computer and then searched the shelves for the book but didn't see it.

She ignored the microwave when it beeped. Instead, she pulled desk drawers open to snoop in Marcus's files. Disappointed, she didn't find anything incriminating. She looked at the clean desk and saw a digital camera behind the computer. As she reached for it, she heard what sounded like leaves crunching under someone's shoes. She turned and noticed the door from the office to the outside was open a crack. She went to investigate and stepped outside. It was still light, but she saw no one. She closed and locked the door.

117

She left the camera for another time and took the quiche out of the microwave and poured a glass of apple juice. After eating, she checked that the back door was locked, turned the kitchen light off and went upstairs. But her mind lingered on the camera and what pictures might be on it and if they would reveal a clue about Marcus.

Chapter 19

Cait rose early Thursday morning—six A.M. By seven, she was in and out of the shower, dressed and downstairs in the kitchen preparing coffee. While she waited for the coffee to perk, she stepped outside and walked over to Tasha's meditation garden.

A melon color spread over the hills. Cait held her breath as she strained to see what appeared to be a golden eagle dipping high overhead. She sat on the bench and thought about the phone call from Columbus and how she would respond if forced to give a time frame for her leave. She loved her job. The last thing she wanted was to lose it.

Her mind shifted to Roger and how her dedication to her job had affected their marriage. She had once hoped that the arrival of a baby would help heal what had started as petty problems between them. The reality was their marriage had been doomed beyond healing.

She stood and strolled around the garden and smelled the lime thyme, rosemary, and lavender, and wondered what Roger would have thought about her inheritance. Would it have made a difference? Would he have been more excited about the money than having a baby?

Chilled by the morning air and annoyed that she'd allowed herself to dwell on the past, she headed back to the house. The smell of freshly brewed coffee perked her up as she entered the kitchen. Restless, she poured a cup of coffee, ate a bowl of

Cheerios, and then went into the office to wait for the phone call.

The last half hour finally ticked by, and then her cell phone rang promptly at nine.

She took a deep breath. "This is Cait," she answered.

"Morning, Cait. Commander York here. I have the deputy chief on speaker."

"Good morning. I hope you know how much I appreciate the call and saving me a trip back at this time," she said.

"Detective Church convinced us it would work in both our favors." She knew York was thinking financially. "We've approved your leave and have papers ready to fax for your signature. You have a machine ready to receive it?"

"Yes, right here in the office."

"But, first, how long you think you'll need to be away?"

Her stomach clenched. She expected the question. They couldn't hold her job forever. "Two months?" *Surely I can resolve Tasha's murder and decide what to do about my inheritance by then,* she thought.

"And what do you hope to accomplish during those two months?" the deputy chief said. "Shep hinted that your aunt's death was suspicious."

"He was being considerate, leaving it to me to explain. The autopsy report says cause is undetermined, but we think she, as well as her husband, were murdered. I didn't know Tasha, so I have a lot to catch up on. But there is a Navy SEAL here. Tasha asked him to come when she realized she was in danger. He and his family were friends of Tasha and her husband."

"I see," the DC said. "Call if there is anything you need from us."

"I appreciate that."

"What do the police say?" interrupted Commander York.

She laughed. "Not much, except to remind me I'm on their

turf. But the detective on the case seems like a decent guy."

"Good. If you need interference, I'd be glad to call him. Might help a little."

"Thanks. He's already checked my credentials," she said. "I think he'll give me a little latitude. The Bening estate *is* mine."

"Well, then. It's settled. You have two months. I'm sending the fax now," York said. "Read it, sign it, and fax it back."

"I will. Right away."

Within seconds the fax machine buzzed and began to force paper out.

"Once last thing, Cait," York said. "Don't worry about the campus case. We've discussed it with Dot. She's handling it. You keep in touch."

"Absolutely. Thank you."

She hadn't had to ask the one question she'd been concerned about. Dot, her assistant, would take over the frat case. She knew it was for the best. She had become personally involved with the case. Not a good thing.

CHAPTER 20

Cait read the fax, signed it and sent it back to Commander York. She started to leave the office when her eyes fell upon the camera behind the computer. She hesitated, then walked into the kitchen and out the back door to see if Marcus was about. When she didn't see him, she returned to the office and picked up the camera.

She leaned against the side of the desk so she could keep her eye on both doorways. Most of the pictures were of the house and every room in it, including the upstairs apartment. Some were taken of the grounds. None were of people, but two were of a horse that Cait assumed was the one she had seen Marcus on. Disappointed, she returned the camera to its hiding place behind the computer.

"Why take so many pictures of the house?" she mumbled. "Why none of the theaters?"

The door at the back of the office opened and Marcus walked in.

He froze when he saw her.

Startled, she stood up. "Oh, hi." She plucked the Post-it she'd left him yesterday from the computer and wadded it up. "I left a note yesterday that I was leaving town, but everything was handled by a phone call and fax so I didn't have to go." She dropped the note in the wastebasket. "I made coffee."

Marcus stared at her and then at the computer.

"This is ridiculous. Talk to me, Marcus."

"What about?"

"Stuff? What you *do* here would be a nice start," she said. "Let's get to know each other."

"I worked for Tasha," he said. "I do my job."

"Right. And now you work for me."

He sat down at the computer and punched some keys.

Exasperated, she walked toward the kitchen. "Think about it. We need to talk." She walked out, went through the kitchen and out the back door. She needed fresh air and she needed to talk to RT about Marcus. She was not someone to shrink from her responsibilities, but right now she wanted to walk away and keep going.

Instead, she headed for RT's trailer and knocked on the door. "RT? It's Cait. Are you in there?"

When he didn't answer, she walked all around the trailer and then peeked inside the Hummer. Puzzled, she wondered if he could be at the Elizabethan Theater checking on repairs. With a last glance at the trailer, she walked toward the theater complex. Being alone with Marcus on top of the hill and no neighbors close by freaked her out. This was one of those times she wished for her Glock.

She entered the side door of the Elizabethan Theater and went up the steps to the stage and around the side of the red velvet curtains where she found several men working. One man was sweeping the floor.

"Hi," she said. "I'm looking for RT."

The man with the long-handled broom shook his head and kept sweeping.

A tall, athletic-looking blond smiled. "Haven't seen him today. Can I help you?"

"Maybe." She glanced around the Green Room and peeked into a couple of the rooms. "If you'd like, I could help clean up in here."

He looked her up and down. "And you are?"

She grinned. "Cait Pepper." She reached out to shake his hand. "I just inherited this place so I should help clean it up."

He smiled and shook her hand. "Tad, PG and E inspector. Congratulations on your inheritance."

"Thanks, I think. So what can I do?"

"She could start in the wig room where the fire began," a rugged-looking man said as he joined them. He had a purple birthmark on his neck that extended beyond the open collar of his tan sport shirt.

"I can do that." They gave her a broom and large trash bag. She entered the wig room and got to work sweeping charcoaled hair into a huge pile in the center of the room. She stomped on burned chairs to break them down and dumped the pieces in the same pile as the wig remains. She hoped new wigs had been ordered to replace the burned ones, something to ask Marcus about. It took her longer than expected to clean up, but when she finished a couple of hours later, the room was clean, and she was happy from physical exertion. She also needed another shower.

She told the guys she was leaving but would return as soon as she could. Back at the house as she unlocked the door, Ilia ran out from between the house and garage.

"I've been looking for you," he said.

"Well, here I am. Dirty but feeling good after cleaning up the mess in the wig room."

He grinned. "You look cute, all sooty like."

She brushed at the soot on her T-shirt. "Where's RT? His trailer looks closed up but the Hummer's there."

"That's why I was looking for you. He went to San Diego again. Family emergency."

"Oh. When did he leave?"

"He caught a red-eye. Said he didn't want to disturb you so

he asked me to tell you he should be back tomorrow."

She nodded. "I should give you my cell number," she said. "It could have saved you a trip." They exchanged numbers and entered them on their cell phones.

"He wanted me to check on his trailer and Hummer, so I'll be around for a while," he said.

"What could go wrong? We're on top of a damn hill." Then she remembered the fire. "Oh, stupid me. Another fire."

Ilia laughed. "That and mountain lions."

"What?" She turned and looked behind her.

"They've been sighted around these hills, just not lately."

"Oh, that makes me feel better." She said good-bye to Ilia and went into the house and locked the door behind her. She peeked in the office. Marcus was gone but a note was stuck on the computer. His mother was sick.

She went upstairs to clean up.

After a second shower, she was back in the kitchen checking the cupboards for something to eat. She heated a can of tomato soup, toasted two slices of wheat bread, reheated the coffee, found an unopened bag of chips, put it all on a tray and carried it upstairs.

Cait ate and watched the news on the small TV in the second-floor sitting room. She fought her weariness, but finally called it a night and went upstairs to the bedroom.

She opened the window on the west side of the room to help air out the musty smell. High above, a shining star flickered then disappeared in the inky backdrop of space. She caught a flash of light, and then another, like a Morse code. She stared out the window but couldn't see anything in the black velvet night. Probably another flickering star, she thought, or cars on the road below, and went to bed.

CHAPTER 21

It had been another night of taunting and tormenting dreams for Cait. Her eyes snapped open. Sunshine spread across the room. She got out of bed and looked out the bay window at the green hills, sparkling white fences, and the vineyard below. Suddenly chilled, she felt a slight push, as if someone wanted her attention. Maybe RT was right, she thought, and the house was haunted.

She turned from the window and glanced around the bedroom. "This is crazy," she mumbled as she stripped for her shower. Beneath the pelting hot water, she thought about the strange feeling that had come over her. *Maybe the phone call from Commander York unsettled me; maybe it's a feeling of insecurity about my job,* she thought. She shut the water off and reached for a towel.

When she went downstairs, music pulsed through the halls from the back of the house. Cait recognized Kenny Chesney's voice and followed the melody into the office. She was surprised to see Marcus working, bobbing his head and shoulders to the beat as he pounded on the computer keys. When he saw her, he snapped the CD off.

"You didn't have to turn it off. I like Kenny Chesney."

He stared at the computer screen.

"I didn't expect to see you today," she said. "Will you be around for a while so we can talk?"

"Yes." His fingers flew across the keys.

"Good. Do you usually come in on weekends?"

He rolled his eyes. "Not unless Tasha asked me to."

"So you're here every weekday," she said, trying to pinpoint his work schedule.

He stopped typing and looked at her. "As long as I do my job, why does it matter when I come in? Tasha didn't care."

Enough! Cait slapped her palms on the desk. "I am not Tasha, and that won't work for me."

Marcus jumped but continued to type.

Frustrated, Cait reached over and pulled the plug on the computer.

He glared at her. "You shouldn't have done that."

"Now do I have your attention? You don't have to like me, but you do have to show respect if you want to remain working here. Even if it hurts you to do so."

He had the courtesy to blush.

She tamped her anger. "Do you have a cell phone?"

Marcus unclipped a phone from his belt and set it on the desk.

She picked up a pen, wrote her cell number on a Post-it, and stuck it on the computer. "Put my number in it. Now." She watched while he entered it, and then reached in her jeans pocket for hers. "Give me yours." She entered his number as he recited it. "I'll see you later." She walked out of the office and into the kitchen where she filled a coffee mug and grabbed a banana. *I'd like to hang an electronic tracking bracelet around his skinny ankle.*

She was in the front hallway when the house phone rang. She wondered who would be calling on a Sunday and took the call in the gift shop. "Bening estate," she answered.

"I'm looking for Rachel Cross," a gravelly voice said.

"I haven't seen her today. May I take a message?"

"This is her husband. She said she'd be there."

Cait glanced at the wall clock: nine-thirty. "This is Cait Pepper. I'll tell her you called if I see her."

He hung up.

How strange, she thought. Why would she tell her husband she was coming here?

With a lingering look at the shelves and their gifts, she left the room and went out the front door and into the sun. Half wine barrels on both sides of the steps overflowed with multiple colors of tulips. Cait sat down on the top step to drink her coffee and eat the banana. Red, orange and blue wildflowers spread among the yellow mustard on the hills. She squinted and shielded her eyes from the sun with her hand to see across the road where Rachel lived, and again wondered why Rachel's husband expected her to be here on a Sunday morning.

She stood, finished her coffee, wrapped the banana peel in a Kleenex from her pocket, and decided a walk in the sun would be nice. She cut between the house and garage, but hesitated when she noticed the door at the side of the garage was ajar and the window broken. She pushed the door the rest of the way open with her toe. Glass covered the floor. She cautiously stepped around it and into the garage and turned the lights on. Nothing appeared to be disturbed. Tools of various sorts hung in order of size on hooks on a wallboard next to the door. Small plastic containers held bits and pieces of a handyman's hobby.

Cait walked around the Jag parked in the middle of the three-car garage and shook her head in disbelief. Garden tools hung on the west wall in descending order of size, same as the tools, except for one empty space. She had never seen a garage so organized as this one. When she turned to leave, she noticed a shovel lying on top of a large blue tarp. She reached for the shovel to hang it up.

And froze.

A foot protruded from beneath the tarp.

"Oh, shit!" She backed away and reached for her cell phone.

CHAPTER 22

"You need to get over here right away," Cait said when Detective Rook answered. "There's a body in the garage."

"Who the hell is that?" a voice behind her said.

Cait spun around, saw Marcus, and snapped, "Stay back! This is a crime scene."

"Rook, get over here, now," she said and hung up.

Marcus backed away, his face ashen. "How long has . . . it been there?"

"I don't know." She glanced at the tarp as she clipped her cell phone on her belt. "Did you break the glass in the door?" But Marcus had fled.

Even after years with the police force and seeing her share of dead bodies, Cait never got used to them but had learned to accept them as part of the job. But this was different—an invasion of her space—and this death shook her on a deeper level. She stared at the foot.

"Oh, God. Please, not RT." She felt as if she'd been standing in the garage with the body for hours when she finally heard sirens in the distance. She hurried to open the garage doors and then went outside to wait for the police.

The first to arrive was an unmarked Expedition. It braked hard in front of her, kicking up gravel. Detective Rook jumped out. A crime-scene van and two black-and-whites, their lights flashing, followed. "Where's the body?" he asked.

"In here." She led him inside the garage.

"Any idea who it could be?"

"No." She swallowed, anxious to find out.

"Get this garage cordoned off," Rook hollered to someone as he reached in his trousers and pulled out a pair of latex gloves. He motioned the two crime-scene technicians to follow. He gave Cait a long look. "I thought you were out of town."

"Canceled in favor of a phone call. Body's over here," she said.

Rook stared down at the tarp. "Ruffle any feathers lately?"

She rolled her eyes. "What's that supposed to mean?"

"I'm not making light of what's happened here, but think about it. You inherited a prime piece of real estate."

She stared at Rook. "You think I was set up?"

"Don't know. Who besides me thought you were out of town?"

She thought about it. "I think most folks knew my trip was cancelled."

The CSTs stepped carefully, watching where they placed their feet. They set their black bags down near the tarp and pulled on latex gloves.

Rook and Cait watched from a distance as the technicians shot pictures from all four corners of the crime scene, then moved in for a close-up of the bloody shovel. They snapped open a large plastic bag and placed the shovel inside.

The male tech nodded to Rook.

"Let's do it," Rook said.

Cait held her breath while Rook lifted the tarp to expose the body.

Cait gasped. "Karl Novak!" He was lying on his right side, one hand out, palm up. The back of his head was covered in dried blood. She moved closer.

"Stay back," Rook said. "You know the drill."

Cait froze.

The technicians moved cautiously, taking long-distance,

medium, and close-up shots. The female tech then straddled the body, shooting pictures from her vantage point, while the other tech collected samples of hair, fiber, and body fluids.

A glint of metal at Novak's waist caught Cait's attention. "Is that a gun or a cell phone protruding from his pocket?"

Rook stooped. "Looks like a gun." He glanced at the tech standing over the body. "Get this," he pointed. A flash went off. "And bag that tarp for fingerprinting."

"You'll want to look at the side door," Cait said. "The glass has been broken out."

He rose. "Show me."

Cait led him over to where glass lay shattered on the floor.

Rook looked down at the floor, careful not to step on the glass, and then at the jagged shards of glass remaining in the frame. "Was the door open or did you open it?"

"It was ajar, Detective. I pushed it the rest of the way open with my toe."

Rook called to the techs. "Hey, guys, over here."

"Let's go outside," he said to Cait. "Anyone else here? Where's Tanner?"

"Supposedly on his way back from San Diego." An ugly thought popped into her head. Had she trusted Tanner because he was a Navy SEAL? She remembered how fast he'd turned up after the shooting in the kitchen. Then she dismissed the thought as quickly as it had appeared. Her gut told her RT was the good guy.

"What?" Rook asked. "You remembered something?"

"Marcus Singer. He saw the tarp. He took one look and fled."

"I'll talk to him."

Something nagged at her. She struggled to remember. "Last night I saw a couple of flashes of light." She looked at him. "I assumed they came from a car on the road and went to bed, but maybe someone was out here with a flashlight."

"Probably, since the road is a long way down the hill. You got a security system up here?"

"No." She shifted from one foot to the other and watched the techs and officers go about their job. "I don't suppose we can keep the media out of this." She looked hopefully at Rook. "A murder so soon after Tasha's death would be seriously bad publicity for the festival."

"Any murder in Livermore is news, but maybe we can hold off the media for a day . . . two at the most."

"Detective?" The male technician approached. He held up a revolver.

"Has it been fired?" Rook asked.

"Not recently."

"Looks like a Chief's Special, a five-shot Smith and Wesson," Cait said.

Both men stared at her. "You continue to impress me," Rook said.

She grinned. "And piss you off?"

He allowed a smile. "That, too." He nodded to the tech. "Bag it." To Cait, "Maybe you pissed Novak off and he came here to retaliate."

"And killed himself when he found I wasn't home? Come on, Detective, get real."

He arched his eyebrow. "Okay, let's hear your version. I'm sure you've got one."

She watched the cops and techs do their job. "I don't." She thought for a minute. "I assumed Novak had moved on to a more promising case when Tasha didn't hire him. Obviously, I underestimated him. Maybe he knew someone connected with the estate. Maybe he knew Hilton."

Rook peeled off his gloves and stuffed them in his back pocket. "Could be, but I still think you're it."

"Good grief! Now what?" Rachel yelled, pulling on the yellow tape. She ducked under it.

Rook's startled expression amused Cait. "Detective Rook, have you met Rachel Cross?"

Rachel jabbed her finger at the detective. "What's happened now?"

"Rachel's an actress, a neighbor, and a friend of Tasha's," Cait said to explain Rachel's theatrics.

Rook spread his legs and crossed his arms. "This is a crime scene, Ms. Cross. Step back on the other side of the tape."

Rachel planted her hands on her hips. "Not until you tell me what happened!"

"You sure about that, ma'am?"

"Absolutely."

"Well, in that case," he turned to an officer standing nearby and tipped his head. The officer approached. "Help the lady back over the tape, officer."

Rachel looked like a peanut next to the six-four, barrel-chested, seasoned officer. He placed his hand on her elbow.

"Get your hands off of me." Rachel skirted around the officer and started toward the garage, her high heels catching in the gravel.

Cait stifled a laugh.

The officer caught up with Rachel before she had a chance to go inside the garage. He picked her up at her shoulders and set her down on the other side of the yellow tape.

Rachel sputtered. "I demand to know what's going on."

Cait couldn't swallow her laugh, but she cupped her mouth to hide it. She noticed Rook struggling to keep a stern face.

"Ma'am, did you know Karl Novak?" Rook asked Rachel.

Her eyes wide, jaw opened, Rachel shook her head and ran off.

"She told me she'd met him," Cait said.

CHAPTER 23

Cait heard a rumble and turned to see the coroner's van pulling up in front of the garage. She stayed back while Rook went over to talk with the attendants.

A sudden pounding noise came from somewhere behind the garage. Cait caught a glimpse of a horse and rider.

"Who was that?" Rook asked.

"Marcus."

"I want to talk with that young man."

"Good luck." She turned to look at Rook. "I'll try to honor your jurisdiction, but you should know I am now on a leave of absence from my job. While I'm here, I intend to find who murdered Tasha and what Karl Novak had to do with it."

Rook's eyes glinted like amber nuggets. "You could end up in jail for interfering with an investigation, or worse, get yourself killed." Then with a hint of a smile, "You've got grit."

She smiled.

Attendants rolled out a cart from the back of the coroner's van.

Rook jammed his hands into his pants pockets. "Being family, you're emotionally involved. You need to step back and let me do my job. If I need your help, I'll ask for it."

Cait couldn't believe what she was hearing. Back off? Not a chance.

A commotion grabbed their attention as three uniforms ran across the yard, their guns drawn.

"Get on the ground! Get on the ground! Now!" the officers yelled.

"Cait!" Ilia panted. The winded officers grabbed him from behind and dragged him to the ground on top of the camera hanging around his neck.

Cait ran to him, dropping to her knees as his arms were pulled back and handcuffs snapped on his wrists.

Ilia lay on his stomach, his chin sprouting grass, his eyes wide in fear. "Get these clowns off my back! I'm not a criminal."

She looked at the officers. "Let him up. He's a friend." She looked at Rook for help. "You know Ilia."

Rook nodded to the officers. "Let him go." To Ilia, he said, "Sorry, they were just doing their job. You okay?"

"Oh, sure. I'm used to having guns drawn at my back. Any idea how much it's going to cost you guys to replace this camera if it's broken?" Uncuffed and back on his feet, Ilia brushed grass from his clothes. He rolled his shoulders as he looked at Rook and Cait. "When I saw a coroner's van, I thought Cait . . ."

Cait looked at Rook. "You tell him."

"There's been an unfortunate incident in the garage," Rook said.

"What kind of incident?" Ilia looked at the yellow tape. "Oh, gosh. Someone was murdered?"

"A private investigator," Rook told him. "Ever heard of Karl Novak?"

"A PI?" He looked at Cait. "Great. Just what you need for the festival. You'll need a miracle now."

Her eyes fixed on Rook's haggard face; she felt compassion for him as a fellow officer. "Then we'll just have to create one."

The coroner's van had left, a flatbed tow truck had come and gone with Novak's car, which had been found in the large parking lot, and all black-and-whites had dispersed. Detective Rook lingered long enough to encourage Cait to move into a hotel for a while, but he gave up and left. However, he refused to remove the yellow crime-scene tape as Cait had requested.

Ilia stayed close to Cait, as if to reassure himself that she was okay. They sat in Tasha's meditation garden talking about Novak and what ramifications could come from his murder on Bening property.

"I hope RT comes back today," she said.

Ilia reached down to stroke Velcro who had appeared from nowhere. "He'll be here. I may have to pick him up at the airport." He stood up. "I better check on his trailer."

Cait remained in the garden and thought about Marcus and his anger toward her. The pictures on the camera had given her no clue toward understanding him. The more she thought about Marcus, the more she knew she needed to investigate him. *He's the only salaried person who works here. He must have a clue about the murders.* If he wouldn't talk to her, then maybe some of his friends would, she thought.

Eager to find out, she went to find Ilia. If he knew where Marcus hung out, she'd go there.

As she approached RT's trailer, she saw Ilia looking into the Hummer.

"What's wrong?" he asked.

"Where does Marcus hang out?"

He frowned. "Somewhere you don't want to go to. Why?"

"Where is it?"

He hedged. "It's no place for a lady, Cait."

"I'm a seasoned officer, remember? Just give me the directions."

"Cait—"

"Ilia, where?"

"Oh, man. It's a bar, out Mines Road, past the Bening ranch, three or four miles. If you insist on going, I'll take you."

"I learned to drive when I was fifteen. I'll find it."

He shoved his hands into his jeans pockets. "Jeez, RT wouldn't . . ."

Her spine stiffened. "Well, he isn't here, is he?" Then, "Okay, let's go. Thanks."

"You've got to be kidding," Cait said as Ilia pulled his VW onto a plot of dirt in front of the Dirty Dog Saloon. They parked near the front door of an old frame building beneath a faded sign of a steer's head. A Harley and a beat-up, rusted orange pickup were the only vehicles there.

Ilia had insisted they take his bug because the Jaguar would draw the wrong kind of attention. He locked the car and joined Cait where she stood staring at a weathered and lopsided headstone. It was engraved WHO.

"That's original," she said. "I wonder who . . ." Then she laughed.

"Could be an Indian," he suggested. "Miwok, Yokut, or Ohlone."

She gave the headstone a last look and reached for the door handle.

Ilia slapped his hand on the door to stop her from opening it. "Wait. Promise you'll be on your best behavior."

She rolled her eyes. "Yeah, yeah. But I doubt you could take me someplace I haven't seen the likes of." She pulled the door open.

The bar was small, dark, and silent. No jukebox, no voices, and no dance floor. Only the smell of beer and stale cigarette smoke; the lighting barely enough to transform black shadows into human flesh.

A place for serious drinking, she thought. And a fire marshal's nightmare.

When they were settled on stools at the bar, Ilia whispered,

"Order a beer."

"I'd rather not."

"Do it, Cait. You don't have to drink it."

A six-foot Hispanic woman approached, swiping the bar in front of them with a dirty cloth that left damp streaks on the Formica top. Her baggy coveralls were worn over a red plaid flannel shirt, the sleeves to which were rolled up and shoved to her elbows. Over that she wore a patched brown leather vest pocked with what looked like cigarette burns. Her cropped silver hair contrasted against her dark skin. Cait pegged her age as over fifty.

She eyed Cait and Ilia. Her voice gravelly, she asked, "What'll it be?"

"Two beers, Corliss," Ilia ordered.

The woman glanced at Cait before turning her back on them.

"You know her?" Cait whispered.

"Everyone does."

She glanced around. "Who's everyone? The place is empty."

Prepackaged snacks hung on a metal spin-rack. She wondered how the bar passed inspection or was even allowed to remain on what appeared to be prime real estate. It was built smack in the middle of a fork in the road—one way to Del Valle Reservoir and the other to Mount Hamilton above San Jose.

Corliss set two bottles down on the bar.

Ilia picked up his bottle and swallowed some beer. Cait didn't touch hers. She studied the bartender standing silently in front of them. She smiled. "Has Marcus been in today?"

At mention of Marcus, Corliss's stare turned to a hard glare, as if putting a hex on Cait.

Seconds ticked. Then, Corliss said, "Didn't think you stopped in here because it's pretty, and we're far enough out not to attract tourists, so figured you must want something besides wettin' your lips."

Carole Price

Ilia kicked Cait's foot. She ignored him, knowing this would most likely be the last time she'd enter the saloon. People talked in bars, tongues loosened by alcohol. She glanced around the dismal bar. "What about his friends?"

Corliss's eyes turned to Ilia. "You brought a *cop* in here?"

"She's not a cop."

"She smells like one."

"Why would you assume I'm a cop?" Cait asked.

Her eyes back on Cait, she said, "You ask questions about Marcus. He don't do no drugs. No alcohol. He comes to inhale the atmosphere."

"I see," Cait said. "Have you known him long?"

That got another kick from Ilia.

"Long enough. You know where the door is." Corliss pulled a loose cigarette from her shirt pocket, lit it with a wooden match that she lit with a flick of a fingernail, and drew in hard. Then she blew smoke directly in Cait's face.

Cait refused to move away. RT had told her Marcus had been charged with drug violations in his teens, but she'd never smelled marijuana or even cigarette smoke on him since moving into the house. She did, however, smell marijuana on Corliss. She kicked Ilia's foot, nodded toward the door. It didn't take brains to know when a source wouldn't talk.

Ilia dropped a twenty on the bar as they slid off their stools.

Before they reached the door, Corliss offered a piece of advice. "When a stranger drops by nosing for answers 'bout one of us, it don't sit well. Life's been hard on Marcus. Leave him be."

"I can't do that . . . he works for me," Cait said. She saw Corliss shift her attention to someone exiting the restroom. The man pulled out a stool and straddled it. Corliss pulled bottles from a shelf, tossing a drink together with deft hands.

The man glanced over his shoulder at Cait, his weathered

140

face as lined as a map, long hair a matted mix of red and gray, his eyes as dead as a corpse.

Cait shuddered as a cold weariness crept over her.

CHAPTER 24

"Hey, there's RT," Ilia said as he eased his VW off to the side of the driveway and onto the grass. Rachel's shiny black Mercedes and an old Jeep Cait didn't recognize were parked in front of the house.

Royal Tanner stood on the front steps with Rachel and a young Asian girl. Cait's chest heaved at the sight of him, remembering the sudden panic she'd felt that it might be RT under the tarp in the garage. He looked tired in the late-afternoon light, dressed in blue jeans, a wrinkled blue shirt with sleeves rolled up, his dark aviation sunglasses perched on top of his head.

He walked toward them. "What the hell happened here?" He pointed at the yellow tape around the garage.

"Well, it doesn't mean the garage is being painted." Cait glanced over at Rachel standing on the steps watching them. "Didn't Rachel tell you?"

"I just got here. Apparently it's not something to discuss in front of a stranger."

"Wasn't I supposed to pick you up at the airport?" Ilia said.

Without taking his eyes off Cait, RT said, "Caught an earlier flight. Can you imagine what I thought when I got here and saw that tape?"

That something had happened to me? "Someone murdered Karl Novak."

He closed his eyes for a second, pursed his lips, and then

142

asked, "The PI guy?"

"Yes."

He jammed his hands in his pockets. "Jesus."

"Rook thinks whoever did it thought I was out of town. I cancelled my trip and took care of the situation over the phone. I'm on leave for two months."

A look of relief crossed his face. "That's great. Look, that girl over there with Rachel says Tasha offered her a job. Go talk to her and then come by my trailer." He took off.

Cait approached the house, thinking Rachel looked like a moneyed matron on her way to High Tea at Harrods. Her rich chocolate silk pantsuit, shimmering jeweled blouse, and brown stilettos made Cait feel dirty from her stint at the Dirty Dog Saloon. But beneath the polish and glitter, Cait sensed a coiled animal lurking to strike. She smiled at the attractive girl standing next to Rachel. "Hello."

"Cait, this is Fumié Ondo," Rachel said. "Tasha promised her a job."

Fumié's obsidian eyes sparkled. A gust of wind tossed shiny strands of black hair around her face. She held her hand out to Cait. "Hi."

Cait shook her hand. "You're looking for work?"

"Yes. Mrs. Bening said she needed help with the festival. But when she died I wondered if there would even be a festival."

Cait liked her lyrical voice and directness. "How did you know Tasha?"

"We met at Las Positas College. She was a guest speaker in the theater arts department." Fumié glanced at Ilia.

Cait hadn't noticed Ilia behind her. "I'm sorry. This is Ilia," Cait said, surprised when Ilia blushed as they shook hands.

Fumié checked her watch. "Can I come back tomorrow to discuss the possibility of working here?"

Cait saw her glance toward the garage and yellow tape and

wondered if it made her nervous. "Okay. How about noon?" She didn't know how much help was needed, but she liked the girl.

Fumié grinned. "Perfect. Thank you so much."

Cait watched her run to the old Jeep. "Her turning up like that could be a stroke of luck."

"I guess," Rachel said.

"I agree," Ilia said as he sprinted off.

"Rachel," Cait said, "I forgot to tell you your husband called earlier looking for you."

Rachel froze at the car door. "What?"

"Well, he said he was your husband."

"You must be mistaken. He never calls here."

Cait watched Rachel climb behind the wheel of her Mercedes and drive off. She wondered where she had been all dressed up like she was. She headed to RT's trailer and tapped on the door.

He held the door open for her. "Have a seat. Want a beer?"

"No, thanks," she said.

He slid into the booth across from her. "Tell me how you found the body."

"Novak." She didn't admit her fear that he might have been under the tarp. "Marcus walked in while I was talking to Rook, freaked out when he saw a foot sticking out, and ran like a scared rabbit." Then she told him about the flashes she'd seen last night. "Rook thinks whatever happened had to be about me, that someone still thought I had gone out of town."

RT ran his hand over his hair. "Damn. Maybe they knew I was gone too."

Someone rapped on the door. "Hey, anyone in there?"

RT slipped out of the booth and opened the door.

"I'm going to be around taking pictures," Ilia said. "Didn't want you to think I'm some prowler and shoot me."

"I'll try to control my trigger finger." RT shut the door.

Cait slid out of the booth. "That's all I know, RT."

"Stay. Please. I'll make coffee. We have to talk this out."

It had been a long day and she was exhausted, but she sat back down and watched RT pour water into the coffeepot.

RT looked at her from under heavy eyebrows. "Where did you and Ilia go today?"

Oh, dear. She hesitated. "I wanted to talk to Marcus's friends."

"Why?"

"It's not working with Marcus and me, RT. Maybe if I understood him . . ."

"So where did you go?"

"A place he hangs out," she said.

"The Dirty Dog Saloon." He sat on the edge of the booth. "Christ, Cait, that's no place—"

"For a lady. Stop. It's that or fire him. This can't go on."

He rubbed his jaw where black hairs had begun to sprout. "Even if you end up dead?"

"I've been a cop; I'm not naive. I know the chances I'm taking."

He rose, checked the coffee, and took two mugs from a shelf. "I wonder if you do." He poured the coffee and set one mug before Cait.

"My only fear was that the place would burn down while we were inside. How does it pass inspection?"

"Some things you don't ask. You talked with Corliss?"

She nodded. "Does she own it?"

"Her common-law husband left it to her when he died . . . from a bullet to the head." He raised his eyebrows.

She shifted position in the tight booth. "Do you think Marcus is capable of murder?"

"Under the right circumstances most of us are."

"We can expect to hear from Actors' Equity when news of

145

Novak's murder gets out," she said. "When you do, assure them there will be plenty of security and their actors will be safe."

RT's cell rang. He picked it up from the table and checked the screen. "Hey, Rook," he answered. "Yes, I know. Already? I'll tell her." He closed his cell phone and looked at Cait. "AE knows."

CHAPTER 25

Monday morning broke hazy and warm. Cait wondered what Actors' Equity would do now—tell their actors not to come even though they were under contract? This was so out of her area of expertise. She glanced at the clock on the bedside table: 7:45. Too early to call Rachel for advice.

She went over to the desk and picked up a notepad. She wrote: See Dr. Crider (Tasha's doctor), Alameda County coroner's office, Livermore Heritage Center. Call Rachel.

After showering, she dressed in black slacks and a blue sweater and went downstairs where she found coffee already made and a bag of bagels. As she filled a mug, Marcus came into the kitchen from the office.

"Cream cheese is in the fridge," he said.

His unexpected attempt to be friendly so surprised Cait that all she could do was stare at him for a few seconds. "Thanks." She reached into the bag for a bagel. "A young girl's coming at noon today. Her name's Fumié." She went to the refrigerator and found the cream cheese and then opened a drawer for a knife. "She said she'd met Tasha at the local college and was offered work. Did Tasha mention her to you?" She pulled out a stool and sat down.

"No, but I'm not surprised. Tasha was always helping someone."

Cait watched Marcus fill a cup with water and set it in the microwave. When it was ready, he dropped a teabag in and sat

147

down beside her.

"Who was that dead guy in the garage?" He dipped the tea-bag up and down in the hot water.

"A private investigator—Karl Novak."

"Why would a PI come here?"

"I think Tasha was afraid. She contacted him before RT was here."

He stared into his tea. "I'm in and out of that garage all the time. Must have happened late."

She tore off a piece of her bagel and spread cream cheese on it. "Probably." She studied Marcus, his drooped shoulders, spiked hair, pasty face, his almost defeatist tone of voice. Was he afraid? "Ever hear anyone threaten Tasha or Hilton?"

"Never." He hesitated. "She did seem preoccupied and abrupt lately, even with me."

"How so?"

"Confused. Lost her sense of humor. That's what I liked most about her. Her humor." His direct look at her spoke volumes. He *was* afraid. "You think she was murdered."

"I can't rule it out." Carefully weighing her words, Cait asked, "How did you happen to find Tasha?"

He hunched over his tea. "She was always downstairs by eight-thirty. When she didn't show by ten, I got curious. If she wanted to go out and needed me to drive her, she'd call early in the morning or the night before. Since I hadn't heard from her, I thought I should check to see if she was okay."

"She was a person of habit."

"Yeah." He drank his tea.

"How often did you go upstairs?"

"Never, unless she needed something done, like those shelves built in the sitting room. Something just didn't feel right that morning so I went up."

She nodded as encouragement for him to continue.

Marcus dragged his hand across his hair. "It was real quiet up there. I checked the second floor; sometimes she'd read on the sofa. I called her name as I went up. Then I knocked on the door before going up to the bedroom. She kept the door open because she had a thing about closed spaces."

Something Cait shared with her.

"I called her name a couple more times as I went up the stairs."

She noticed his hand around his tea shake. "Go on," she urged.

He took a deep breath and let it out. "I almost turned around and went back down. The shutters were closed. That surprised me because she liked waking up to sunlight coming in windows. I didn't see her; blankets were piled high on the bed." His voice quivered. "I walked over and saw she was on her back, like she was sleeping. I said her name. She didn't answer." He finished his tea.

Cait wanted to console him, put her arm around him, but knew he'd bolt. "I know this is difficult, but I need to know everything. Was it then you called nine-one-one?"

He raised his head, his eyes pained. "No. Not until I was back in the office."

"Why not use the phone in the bedroom?"

"I was scared, not stupid. I have a record. I thought I'd be blamed if caught there." He looked at Cait, anguish in his eyes. "I didn't kill her."

She nodded. "Did you call RT?"

"Yes. After I called nine-one-one." He slid off his stool. "I gotta go."

"Wait," she said. "I've been meaning to ask you about having an alarm system installed in the house. Lane tells me the theaters are alarmed, just not activated. Would you take care of calling someone to see that it's taken care of?"

He nodded. "Okay."

"Thanks, Marcus." She took their cups to the sink, rinsed them, and put them in the dishwasher. It was now nine o'clock. If she left now, she might be able to catch Dr. Crider before he got backed up with patients.

Cait waited twenty minutes before a nurse showed her into Dr. Crider's office. He sat behind a gray metal desk tapping on a keyboard, his eyes glued to the computer screen when she walked in.

Dr. Crider stood when he saw her and introduced himself. "Sorry to keep you waiting. I understand you're here about Mrs. Bening." He motioned to the chair in front of the desk.

"Yes. She was my aunt." Sun spilled through open shutters, across the uncluttered desk, the doctor's unlined face, and his salt-and-pepper hair. "You were Tasha's primary care physician?"

"Yes."

"Does doctor-patient confidentiality extend beyond death?"

"It does."

She took her police ID from her handbag and showed it to him. "Even in a homicide investigation?"

He looked closely at her ID. "Ohio?"

She smiled and nodded. "I'm a crime analyst. Her lawyer called me."

"What is it you want to know?"

She tucked her ID back in her handbag. "There are reasons to believe Tasha was murdered. I was told she died in her sleep from a heart attack, but since she'd recently been to see you for a checkup, I wondered if you suspected heart problems."

He turned to the computer screen. "I reviewed Mrs. Bening's records when I was told you were here. She *had* been in for a cursory exam. Other than high blood pressure, for which I added another blood-pressure medication, she appeared in good health." He glanced at Cait. "Sometimes there's no explanation why a healthy heart suddenly stops. Sometimes it simply tires out." He ticked off other possibilities on his fingers. "Depression. Family tragedy. A sudden shock. Any of those could trigger a heart attack, particularly in someone her age."

Cait thought he looked as if he had something else to say. She waited.

"The police called me to come to the house," he continued. "I examined her record before going. When I got there, she was dead, for no apparent reason that I could see. But the man who was there—"

"Royal Tanner?"

"Yes, I think that's his name. He seemed surprised when I mentioned a heart attack."

"So what did you do?" Cait asked.

"After a cursory view of the body, I refused to sign the death certificate based on her health as I know it and Mr. Tanner's suspicions."

"Why?"

"To cause an autopsy to be done. That's normal when a death is sudden and unexplained. It takes six to eight weeks for toxicology results to determine cause of death."

"I read the autopsy report. The cause—undetermined death."

"I see," he said.

"Had she been your patient long?"

"Off and on for about five years. She explained that she and her husband had bought property several years ago before actually moving in."

"How was Hilton's health?"

He hit more keys and looked at the screen. "Nothing more than a virus. Unfortunately, a horseback riding accident took his life. After that, Mrs. Bening consulted with me over the phone about depression, but when I offered medication for it, she refused." He rested his hand on his watch. "I'm afraid that's all I know."

"The report mentioned cardiac arrest as a possibility even though there was no evidence of heart trouble, but it did indicate very high potassium. Does that surprise you?"

He frowned, looked back at the screen and hit a few keys. "All bodies have elevated potassium at autopsy, which is why we don't test for it in the blood. Potassium occurs naturally in the body; my records show her blood tests were normal." He looked at Cait.

She'd learned what she'd come for and saw no reason to detain him any longer. She rose. "I won't keep you. I appreciate your seeing me. I wanted confirmation that nothing was wrong with Tasha's heart. I wish there had been."

He stood and shook her hand. "I understand. Mrs. Bening's tests indicate she was in good shape for a woman in her sixties. If she'd shared concerns about personal problems, I would have noted them in her record. You might call the sheriff's department and talk with Jonas Mills, the county coroner. He may be able to answer any questions you might still have."

"I'll do that. Thank you."

When Cait returned to the house, RT was on his knees in the kitchen patching the side of the counter where birdshot had punched holes in it. He stood when he saw her. "Where've you been?"

"When was it established that I check in and out?" she snapped, and immediately regretted it.

"Aren't we testy? I was worried about you, okay?"

She swallowed the anger that had come from nowhere. She filled a mug with coffee. "Sorry. I was at Tasha's doctor's office. She had a healthy heart."

He nodded. "I've been on the phone with Rook. He'd talked with Sheriff Jonas Mills. He's also the Alameda County coroner. After I reread the autopsy report, I called Rook because I'm still not satisfied about Tasha's elevated potassium."

She sat down. "What did he find out?"

"Excessive potassium is toxic and stops the heart almost immediately if a person is given a lethal injection. The coroner would have had to get to the body immediately after death to determine if the person died naturally or from some other cause." Cait caught a warning of suspicion in the quick twitch of his eyebrow. "She could have been given a sedative, making it easier for someone to overpower her."

"Like succinylcholine," she said.

Her words carried a somber tone.

He nodded. "Yeah. But elevated levels might not have been found even if she'd been given a substantial IV dose." RT massaged his neck. "According to the coroner, everyone, as they're dying, has an increase in potassium."

Cait ran her finger around the rim of her cup. "Someone with medical knowledge could have stolen the drugs from a hospital ER or operating room, but why would Tasha let anyone near enough to administer an IV, and in her own house? I forgot to ask Marcus if he noticed signs of a struggle in the bedroom."

RT leaned against the counter. "There weren't any. I'm surprised Marcus talked to you about finding Tasha."

"He asked about the PI." Her hand stilled on her cup. "Succinylcholine can be used to paralyze the muscles."

They stared at each other for a few moments, each in their own thoughts.

"It would be easy to give an injection into the muscular tissue," RT said, "the arm or hip, like a penicillin shot. But it would sure hurt like hell. Onset is rapid—less than a minute after injection."

She looked at him. "Wouldn't it show up during the autopsy, in toxicology tests?"

He shook his head. "Nope. Dissipates from the bloodstream. Can't be traced postmortem. And no pathologist would suspect succinylcholine as a cause of death based on elevated vitreous potassium."

She thought about that. "But without the autopsy, we wouldn't have much of a chance to prove succinylcholine was the cause of death within reasonable medical certainty. I wonder if this would affect my inheritance."

CHAPTER 26

Cait and RT lingered over coffee while they waited for Fumié. "I keep coming back to Hilton," Cait said. "Maybe it really was a freak accident that killed him."

RT shook his head. "No way. I wasn't here at the time, but it's too coincidental that both Tasha and Hilton, apparently in good health, would die within months of each other under the circumstances they did."

"So what have we got in the way of evidence?"

"That's the problem. Hilton was an excellent horseman. He and Faro had been together a long time."

"Hmm. Maybe someone or something frightened Faro. Or maybe someone strung a wire across the path to trip him. Did anyone check?"

"I don't know about a wire, but Rook said by the time he got there the ground had been trampled over by Bo, his staff, and EMTs." He raised his eyebrow. "I suppose you want to have a look."

"Absolutely. Neither one of us was here at the time. What else have we got?" As the lone female officer in her unit, Cait had to work a hundred times harder than a man to prove herself. A couple of male officers still begrudged her the accolades she'd received from her perseverance into uncovering evidence, which was one reason she still missed being a cop—to prove female officers had a place in law enforcement.

The doorbell chimed.

She glanced at the wall clock. It was noon. "That'll be Fumié—right on time." Cait slipped off her stool and went to the front door. Fumié's fresh appearance, porcelain skin, and shimmering black hair made Cait feel old, weathered, and out of shape.

"Hi." Cait held the door open for her and then started to close it after her.

"There's a box on the porch," Fumié said.

Cait stepped out on the porch. She picked up the large box, glanced at the mailing label, and saw Samantha had sent it. She set it down near the stairs to take upstairs. "Come on to the back," she said to Fumié.

RT stood in the middle of the kitchen, his cell phone in his hand as if about to make a call. "It's Fumié, right?"

She grinned. "Yes."

"You're brave. Seeing that yellow tape might have kept you from coming back. I'm going to take it down now." He went out the back door.

"What would you like? Coffee, tea, Dr Pepper?" Cait said.

"Dr Pepper would be great."

Cait grabbed a can from the fridge and a glass from the cupboard and filled it with ice. "Sorry about that tape around the garage."

"I know what it means."

Cait set the can and glass on the counter in front of Fumié. "Have a seat." She pulled out two stools and sat down. The youth of today seemed to accept and shrug off whatever they were dealt, and that made it easier for Cait to explain the situation. She made it brief and then asked if Fumié had questions.

Fumié poured Dr Pepper into her glass. "No, but it must have been hard finding a body like that."

"I've been a cop, seen many bodies, just not in my own house."

Fumié shrugged her hair back from her face. "I have a degree in urban forestry from UC-Davis and a minor in English lit, but I want to be a park ranger. They find bodies in parks."

So maybe the crime tape didn't freak her out, Cait thought. "Park ranger?"

She grinned. "Sure. There's an academy in Santa Rosa, a nine-week basic law enforcement training program I want to attend, but that's on hold until my mom gets better."

"Oh, what's wrong with your mom?"

"Cancer," Fumié responded. "But she's getting better."

"That's good. So you want to work here until then?"

Fumié nodded. "You're not a police officer now?"

"No, but I'm still in law enforcement. What's a ranger's primary responsibility?"

Fumié crossed her arms on the counter and smiled. "Protecting our natural resources."

"Tasha knew about your goal?"

"She encouraged me, said everyone should follow their dreams."

"What about dreams?" RT asked as he walked in the back door.

"Fumié wants to be a park ranger," Cait said.

RT eyed her petite frame. "A ranger's work can be strenuous and dangerous. Can you shoot?"

"I grew up on a ranch and learned how to shoot when I was ten," Fumié said.

Way to go, Fumié, Cait thought.

"Tasha wanted to use the new theater for rehearsals and thought I could help if the actors needed anything."

This was news to Cait. "You mean the Elizabethan?"

"No, the new one, farther out back."

Cait looked at RT. "Do you know what she's talking about?"

He nodded. "When Hilton died, Tasha put the idea of another

theater on hold. It's been staked out, but that's all."

"Show me sometime," Cait said, and slid off her stool. "I want to show Fumié around, particularly the gift shop and Elizabethan Theater."

Fumié grabbed her glass and followed Cait.

"I'll be in my trailer," RT said.

"The gift shop is where I'm going to need the most help," Cait said when they walked into one of the rooms. "Boxes keep coming. Everything needs to be tagged and set on the shelves. There is a price list Tasha prepared. Does this sound like something you'd be interested in?"

"I'd love it."

"Great. Arrange the shelves however you'd like; it's not something I'm good at. Would you be able to work in the evenings when the theaters are open?"

Fumié grinned. "Oh, yes."

"You've no idea how happy that makes me." Cait checked her watch: one o'clock. "Let's see how the Elizabethan is coming along."

Two workers relaxing against a wall back stage straightened up when they saw Cait. The green room, surrounded by smaller ones, was intended for the actors to relax in when not on stage. "The furniture's still in storage," Cait said, "until the remodeling is finished."

"This is so cool," Fumié said as she walked about the room.

Cait pointed to two monitors mounted on the wall. "Those are so the actors can watch and listen to what's happening on stage and know when to make their entrance." Whiteboards ran around three of the walls, and were labeled PLAYS, ACTORS, REHEARSALS, and NOTICES. A wall phone, first-aid kit, and fire extinguisher hung on another wall.

Cait went into every room and was satisfied with results from the cleanup. In the PROPS room, large crates were stored beneath long tables that had been set up in the middle of the room.

In the COSTUMES room, freestanding racks on wheels were scattered about with size tags clipped to their rails. Fumié walked about with a grin on her face. "Wouldn't it be fun to dress up in period costumes?"

Cait laughed. "I don't think I'd like to make my living at it."

In the WIG & MAKEUP room, shelves lined the walls, interspersed with makeup tables and mirrors. Fumié sat in one of the chairs and made faces at herself in the mirror. "I wonder if actors feel more secure hidden behind all that makeup. They could hide their true feelings and no one would know." She swung the chair around. "When the makeup comes off, they're themselves again. That might be hard, changing back and forth like that."

She's sharp, Cait thought. She glanced around the room where she'd spent a few hours cleaning and sweeping fragments of burned synthetic wigs. Thinking of Rachel, she said, "I'm told that sometimes Shakespearean actors immerse themselves so deeply into their roles, they can't turn it off when they're not on stage." *Is that how it was for Tasha? Maybe I'm finally beginning to understand her dedication to the theater.*

They left the room. Cait waved to the men still hanging about.

"When do you think you'd like to start work?" Cait said. "I'm sure, as it gets closer to when the festival opens, I will need more help, but right now the gift shop is a priority."

"I can come in the morning," Fumié said.

"Okay. We can discuss your salary then."

Spring bloom was at its peak. Lupine ranged from blue to red-purple, California poppies from pale yellow to deep orange.

Cait walked Fumié to her car, thinking that now she could spend more time finding a murderer.

★ ★ ★ ★ ★

That afternoon Cait carried the box from Samantha upstairs to the bedroom. She opened it and found her favorite jogging shorts, T-shirts, and socks, along with cotton slacks, a Buckeye sweatshirt, and a jeans skirt. Beneath the clothing was the blue-and-black-silk jewelry box her dad bought for her mom on a trip to Japan.

Cait swallowed hard. Her eyes welled with memories. A note from Sam was in the box, wishing Cait a happy stay in California. She took the jewelry box to the front window and sat down with it on her lap. She pulled out two small black pins and raised the lid. Inside were birthday and holiday cards her mom had saved.

On the bottom of the box was a pale blue onionskin envelope addressed to her dad, postmarked New York 1976. She turned it over. No return address. A piece of crusty yellowed tape crumbled when Cait pulled the flap back. She peeked inside and removed a note written on plain blue tissue-thin notepaper and read:

Randy—I called but hung up when Sally answered. I'm pregnant. A baby would interfere with my acting career. I left home to pursue my dreams as an actress. You and Sally always wanted a child. Would you please consider adopting my baby as your own? And promise to keep it a secret from our parents? I need an answer soon. The baby is due in September. I'll call next Tuesday morning. The father is not a consideration. T

Cait felt as if the air had been sucked out of her. The autopsy report indicated Tasha had given birth. September? Her hand shook as her mind registered what that meant. She looked at the postmark again—1976. The month too faded to read, but she knew. She was born in September, 1976.

Tasha wasn't her aunt. She was her birth mother.

Her life as she'd known it—a lie.

Her eyes dry, she slumped back in her seat, a dull pain in her chest. The box slipped to the floor. "I don't want to believe it. My mom, my dad, kept my birth a secret all these years. Why?"

She moaned. "The inheritance. The mysterious aunt." Everything became crystal clear for Cait. She thought about her parents who'd raised her, the happy life she'd known. They'd shown their love in every way possible, no hint that she wasn't their child. How could she resent that? Her mind reeled with visions of living a different life, a life on the road with Tasha, and appreciated the decision Tasha had made. Still, she should have been told.

It was dusk when Cait finally rose. She had to move, do something. She went to the twin wardrobes still full of Tasha's clothes. Hangers of dresses in ripe eggplant, melon, turquoise, and plum were wedged together on one side. Cait touched the soft fabrics and let them drift through her fingers and then gathered armfuls and piled them on the floor in one corner of the room to be donated later. She cleared shelves of belts, scarves, and handbags and dropped them next to the dresses. She located two book bags under the bed and filled them with shoes and lingerie.

She looked at Tasha's belongings and felt a tinge of guilt for putting them in a heap on the floor. A bronze metallic raincoat on top of the pile caught Cait's eye. She picked it up and tried it on in front of the mirror that hung on the inside of the wardrobe door. It fell to mid-calf. She decided to keep it.

When she hung the coat back up in the wardrobe, she noticed a small box on the floor in the corner. She picked it up, carried it over to the bed, sat down and opened it.

It wasn't the lacey cover and pink satin ribbon that caught

her attention, but her baby picture that had been inserted into an oval cutout in the middle of the album.

CHAPTER 27

With a lump in her throat, Cait pulled the bedside lamp closer. She untied the ribbon and opened the album. Page after page with pictures of Cait at all stages of growing up: baby pictures, high-school prom, college graduation, police academy graduation, and, last, her wedding picture.

Her cell phone beeped. She ignored it.

Then the house phone rang. She ignored that also.

She closed the album and retied the ribbons.

All these years her parents had corresponded with Tasha, but never said a word to Cait about her. Or was it Stanton Lane who'd acted on behalf of Tasha to keep her updated on Cait?

She found her cell phone and called Lane.

He answered immediately. "I have a very important question to ask, and I want an honest answer," she said without giving him a chance to say a word. "Did you obtain pictures of me for Tasha?"

"Cait, what are you talking about?"

"Pictures of me, during important phases of my life. I found an album filled with pictures from when I was a newborn until my marriage."

"I only learned about you when I made up Tasha's trust, about ten years ago. That's as long as I knew her."

She bit back tears that clouded her eyes. "Okay. Sorry, but I had to know." She sighed. "While I have you on the phone, whose idea was it to have Tasha cremated?"

"It was her wish. She was very specific about that."

"What happened to her ashes?"

"They were spread over the vineyard, also her wish."

Cait set the album on the bed, stood, and went over to the bay window and stared down at the moonlit vineyard. "Who attended?"

"Bo Tuck and his family, Royal Tanner, and myself," he said. "Marcus was a basket case and didn't attend. Rachel was out of the country."

"Was Hilton also cremated?"

"Yes. His ashes were released at his ranch. Tasha, Rachel, Bo and his family, ranch hands and several neighbors and I were present. I think there was also a family member from Colorado."

"You're not in your office this late, are you?" she said.

"No. Your call was transferred to my cell phone. Cait, are you all right?"

She jumped at the sudden pounding on the bedroom door.

"Cait! Open the door! I know you're up there!"

"Mr. Lane, I'm sorry to bother you." She disconnected the call, set her cell phone down, and went down the stairs to open the door for RT.

RT stared at her. "What's wrong? Are you sick?"

She headed back upstairs. "No. Come on up. I want to show you something." She picked up the album from the bed. "Did Tasha ever show this to you?"

He glanced at the album. "No. What is it?"

She sat on the edge of the bed. "My life." She gestured for him to sit beside her.

She handed the album to him. "It was in Tasha's wardrobe. Go ahead, open it."

Before he opened it, he frowned at the baby picture on the cover. "Is that you?"

She nodded.

"Real cute," he said, and turned the cover.

While he looked through the album, Cait stood and paced in front of him.

RT closed the album and looked up at her. "How did Tasha get your pictures?"

"She must have communicated with my parents," she said. "I just talked with Lane, and he said he knew nothing about it. What about your mom? She knew Tasha."

"Yes, and she knew of you, that Tasha had a niece."

Tension clamped around Cait's neck and shoulders. "I'm not her niece, RT. I'm her daughter."

He frowned; confusion flickered across his face. "What?" He set the album aside.

She took a deep breath. "Tasha was my birth mother. I got a box of my clothes from my friend and inside was this." She showed him the jewelry box that was still on the bed. "Inside is a letter from Tasha to my dad. She was pregnant and asked my parents to adopt the baby. That would be me."

He reached out for her hand and pulled her down on the bed beside him. "This is the first you knew?"

She nodded. "Yes. It changes everything. I'm more determined than ever to find who killed her."

"We will, believe me we will. I'm so sorry you had to learn about your adoption this way."

"Yeah, me too. They were twins, my dad and Tasha. Maybe that's why my birth was kept secret. At least it clears up any confusion about my inheritance."

"Will this influence your decision to stay?"

She bowed her head. "I honestly don't know."

"Did the letter say who her lover was?"

"No, and I don't care to know." Cait stood up.

"Oh, damn." He rose. "Rook called. That's why I was trying to call you. He'd like us to meet him at Novak's office. An alarm was tripped and his office trashed."

"Are you sure he wants me there too?"

"That's what he said. Ready to go?"

She grabbed a jacket from the back of a chair, her handbag and keys. After she locked the bedroom door, she followed RT on down to the first floor. They left by the back door, almost running into Marcus. His face contorted in anger when he saw Cait. He appeared disheveled, dirty fingerprints smeared around the buttons on his white shirt and rolled sleeves. "Did you think I wouldn't find out?"

She instantly knew what he was referring to.

"You went to the Dirty Dog Saloon and talked to Corliss about me. What I do on my own time is none of your business."

Cait saw his hands fisted at his side and stepped back from him. "It would be a stretch to call it talking."

Marcus spat pistachio shells on the ground at her feet. "What did you think? I'd go there and spill my guts to whoever listened? Confess I killed Tasha and that guy in the garage? I'm not a murderer. I thought you believed me. I respected Tasha. She was the only one who cared a damn and gave me a chance when I got out of prison. I owe her." He glanced off as he choked up.

"Marcus—" she said.

He stepped closer and thrust his finger in her face. "Next time you want to know something, ask."

RT reached out and grabbed a fistful of Marcus's shirt and lifted him up off the ground like he was a sheet of paper. "Listen to me, butthead, or I'll tear every one of those spiked hairs out of your skull!"

Cait's throat felt like a gravel pit. She put a hand on RT's arm. "RT—"

He brushed her off with a ferocious look. "Butt out, Cait. You were warned not to go to that dirt hole. This is the consequence." He set Marcus down and shoved him away. "You ever threaten her again, I'll have your ass back in jail. You hear me?"

Marcus squared his shoulders, straightened his shirt, turned and walked away.

RT charged after him, grabbed his shoulder, and spun him around. "Answer me!"

"Yeah, I hear you." He backed off, but not before Cait saw his quivering mouth.

RT stormed off toward his trailer, leaving Cait to stare at his back.

Swearing under her breath, she trotted after him. "RT—"

He kept walking, his long strides forcing her to jog to catch up.

"Damn it, RT! Stop! That was not your business. I can handle Marcus."

He stopped at his Hummer. "Like hell you can." He opened the door. "Get in."

Standing in the threshold of Novak Investigations, a combination of guilt and sadness flowed through Cait. She reflected on her last visit to Novak's office when she accused him of negligence. She glanced around the office and again wondered if his murder in her garage had been intended as a warning for her. Why else did it happen there?

Detective Rook greeted RT and Cait at the door with latex gloves. "Put these on." Lights flashed as a uniformed officer snapped pictures of the destruction.

"Sweet Jesus," RT said. "Looks like hell on wheels rolled through here."

"Close enough," Rook agreed.

Like others in the neighborhood, the small house had been converted into offices. Desk drawers and filing cabinets had been tossed, computers smashed, magazines strewn across the floor.

Cait stared at the mess. "I'm curious why you asked me to come."

"You said you wanted to be involved." He led them back to Novak's office next to the kitchen.

Aside from the stale cigar odor clinging to the room, Cait noticed Novak's commendation dismantled on his desk. "This was hanging on the wall. It's how I knew he'd been a cop."

"I found a couple things taped to the back." Rook picked up a sheet of paper, unfolded it and handed it to her.

She glanced at it. "Why would he have a list of the actors who will be at the festival?"

"I thought you might know. When you were here, did Novak ask about anyone on that list?"

Her eyes ran down the list again. "No."

"Odd it was hidden like that," he said.

"Did you ask his deputy?"

Rook stared at her. "What deputy?"

"The receptionist said he had a part-time deputy."

"I'll ask her about him." Rook picked up a strip of black-and-white photos and handed it to RT. "That was also taped on the back. Look familiar?"

Cait shrugged. "No, should it? A couple of teenagers taken in one of those old photo booths."

RT shook his head. "Sorry, I haven't a clue." He returned the picture to Rook.

"Worth a try." Rook picked up a blank business envelope off the floor and slipped the sheet and photo strip inside. "People hide things in the strangest places. Appreciate your coming out."

Puzzled, Cait said, "That's it?"

"Correct me if I'm wrong, but did you not say this investigation was stuck in mediocrity? That I needed your help?"

Cait felt heat flush her cheeks. "Maybe I was a little quick to judge."

RT chuckled, then ducked his head as Cait pretended to swat him.

"Did you check for Tasha's folder in the file cabinet?" Cait pointed at the papers tossed on the floor. "Or on the floor?"

"Not yet," Rook said.

"Can I ask a favor—" Cait said.

"Is it legal?"

She rolled her eyes. "I'd like to see Marcus Singer's file sometime soon."

Rook frowned. "Cait—"

She smiled. She wouldn't force the issue, because she knew she could take the long way around and call her commander for interference.

"You already know Singer served time," Rook said. "What are you looking for?"

"Maybe more information about him, since he now works for me. Wouldn't you?"

Rook raised his hands in the air as if he gave up. "I'll see what I can do."

She smiled. "I would appreciate it."

"Don't thank me yet."

She started toward the door but then turned back. "Oh. One more thing. RT removed that tape from the perimeter of the garage. It tends to intimidate people."

"You're as persistent as a dog after a pork chop. Karl Novak was probably silenced because he snooped where he wasn't wanted. He was an ex-cop, like you. So don't think you're safe from getting whacked on the head. I don't want to be around when *that* call comes in."

CHAPTER 28

It was close to nine when Cait and RT left Novak's office. "I'm starved," RT said. "Want to stop for a bite to eat?"

She hadn't eaten since breakfast. "Sounds good."

He unlocked the Hummer and opened the door for her. "You seemed uncomfortable in there."

She fastened her seat belt. "That's because I'd recently been there and because Novak was murdered in my garage. I think his murder was meant as a warning to me, but darned if I can figure out why."

He drove a few blocks and parked behind Casa Orozco.

"Rook's a cautious guy. I'm sure he had reason to want us there, if only to connect the actors on that list to those teenagers in that picture. Let's go in."

They were seated and handed menus. The place was crowded for a Monday night. A birthday party was in full swing at a long table not far from where they were seated.

Cait took one look at her menu and closed it.

"A woman who knows her mind," RT said. "I like that."

"I always get the same thing. Chile rellenos and a margarita."

"Good choice," he said, and ordered two of each when the waiter returned.

"Why would Rook think we might know those kids in the photo? We're not from here."

"Maybe it's as simple as him inviting you into the investigation."

After the waiter brought their drinks, RT raised his glass to Cait's. "Let's not waste the Valley's best margaritas on the devil's dirty deeds."

They tapped glasses.

RT tasted the salt along the rim of his glass. "I'm a salt addict."

Cait thought about the photo album while she tasted her drink. "Tasha had pictures of me, but I haven't seen any of her or Hilton. I'd like to know what she looked like."

He sipped his drink and looked at Cait. "Dark hair like yours when she was younger. You're taller and more serious. She had a sense of humor. Maybe you do too when you're not under so much stress."

She stared into her glass. "I like to think I have a sense of humor."

The waiter set their chile rellenos before them. Cait found she was hungrier than she'd thought.

"Does Lane know you're Tasha's daughter?"

"No, but I told him about the album." She wondered how it might affect Lane if she told him, and if it would change anything about her inheritance.

The celebration at the other table grew louder, making it hard for them to hear each other. Cait concentrated on her dinner.

"Want another margarita?" RT asked when they finished their meal.

She toyed with the stem of her glass. "Not unless you're willing to carry me to the car and put me to bed." Her cheeks flushed when she realized how that sounded.

RT met her eyes as he licked the last of the salt from the rim of his glass. "I could manage that."

Her heart fluttered with the speed of a hummingbird as she watched him lick his lips. *I'll bet you could,* she thought. She'd never been sloshed in her life and had no intentions of starting now. She hadn't even had a date since her marriage ended.

He smiled. "For the record, I'd never take advantage of you . . . not unless you wanted me to."

"I appreciate that," she said, then wished it hadn't sounded so stiff.

The sky had gone from plum to inky black by the time Cait and RT left the restaurant. The temperature had dropped sharply. She slipped her jacket on as they walked to the parking lot. Three teenagers circled RT's Hummer. The vehicle definitely spoke of ego and money, enough to attract the attention of kids on the prowl, she thought.

When the streetlight glanced off a blade in one kid's hand, Cait said, "RT—"

"I saw it." He held his arm out to hold her back.

She assumed RT had his gun but hoped he wouldn't draw it to scare the kids, yet when she saw their intention was to run the knife along the driver's side of the Hummer, she yelled, "Hey!" and ran toward them before RT could stop her.

The kids froze and then dispersed in different directions.

"Well, that taught them a lesson," he said.

"They were going to run a knife along the driver's door," she snapped. "What did you think I should do? Applaud?"

He unlocked the Hummer. "I had another idea. Call the police. Have them talk to their parents."

"Wait until you're a parent. See how that works." She climbed into the passenger seat and slammed the door shut.

RT got behind the wheel but didn't start the engine. "Are you speaking from experience?"

She shrank back in her seat and stared out the windshield. She drew a deep breath and slowly let it out before she answered him. "I'm not very patient about some things, like those kids. They should be home doing their school assignments."

RT took her hand in his and stroked her palm. "Yes, they should. Cait, does this anger have anything to do with your marriage?"

She took her hand back, aware of her racing pulse. His touch almost had her out of her seat and into his lap. She shook her head in frustration. "Roger was an introspective man. He seldom took action before thinking things through thoroughly. He spent his leisure time waxing his thirty-two Ruxton and reading. And he prayed a lot. I suppose most chaplains do." She closed her eyes briefly. Even now the memories were painful. "I couldn't conceive. That was the final straw for him."

"I'm so sorry, Cait. What an insensitive jerk."

"Not to those he prayed with. To them he was God."

RT turned the ignition and drove out of the parking lot. As they put the town behind them, Cait stared out into the black velvety night. There was little traffic. The moon lit the long stretch of road before them and played upon the vineyards.

"Owning a vineyard is a good business," RT said. "You'd love it once you got the hang of it and met other growers in the area."

"I'd have a better chance making a go of the theaters. At least I know something about Shakespeare."

"Not as profitable as growing grapes. And you can't beat the rewards. Think of it, your own label."

As RT turned up their driveway, Cait looked across the rows of grapevines. The moon seemed to taunt her as it spread its ghostly light over the vineyard.

They were silent while RT parked his Hummer behind his trailer.

"Thanks for dinner. I enjoyed it." She stepped out of the Hummer and started toward the house when RT grabbed her hand and pulled her close.

"All I'm saying is Tasha and Hilton got a lot of pleasure from watching their vineyard grow. Give it a chance. I could introduce you to some of the vintners I've come in contact with."

She was grateful for the dark. It helped hide her flushed face. She stepped away from him. "Rachel said I should expect a few to show for the tea just to see what I intend to do with the vineyard."

"She's probably right." With his hand on her back, he said, "Come over here." He led her to the nearest rows of vines. "Look close; you'll see six inches of new growth. It's called bud swell."

Cait leaned in to see what he was talking about.

"Hilton was smart to plant on the hill. You won't have to be concerned about frost protection since you're above the cold air that settles in the valley at this time of year."

"Maybe Tasha should have left the vineyard to you."

He laughed. "I live in San Diego, remember? I'll see that what needs to be done is done before I leave. I've sent the March pesticide-use report to the Department of Agriculture. April's is almost finished."

She groaned. "Pesticide reports?"

"Goes with the territory, like the bad guys we both deal with at our jobs."

"The last I knew, operating a vineyard or running a Shakespeare festival didn't fall into my job description."

He chuckled.

"Or, for that matter, that of a Navy SEAL who writes children's books," she continued.

He froze. "What did you say?"

"I saw on your laptop . . . uh . . . something about treasures from the bottom of the sea. I assumed it was a children's story. I wasn't snooping."

The moon played tag across his face, his jaw knotted. "It's a hobby."

"An honorable hobby," she said to cover her embarrassment of peeking at his laptop. "Mine is working with stained glass."

"No wonder you like the windows in the house." He fell silent for a moment. "I have another hobby, a small vineyard. A crew manages it when I'm away."

She studied his serious face. "Oh. So that's the emergency that takes you away? I assumed you had a wife waiting at home. Or do you? I mean, you've never said."

His tone flat, he said, "Never been married. Never intend to. I'll walk you to the house."

She quickened her step and followed him, the house key in her fist.

He followed her in. "I'll look around."

Cait turned the lights on all the way back to the kitchen, then stopped when RT grabbed her arm. He reached under his Gore-Tex Windbreaker, removed his gun, and held it along the side of his right leg.

A hushed murmur came from the office. They inched across the kitchen and flattened themselves against the wall on either side of the door.

RT peeked around the corner and stepped into the doorway, his gun at arm's length.

Cait caught the last words of a recorded message left on the answering machine: "Marcus, a good son never forgets to visit his mother."

The red message light flickered.

CHAPTER 29

Tuesday morning sunlight flickered through the open shutters, across the walls and onto the bed. Cait pulled the sheet over her eyes until Velcro pounced on her. The time on the bedside clock read eight-fifty, unusually late for her to get up.

She hurried through the process of showering and dressing and went downstairs. Finding coffee and donuts or bagels each morning had become a ritual, one that she appreciated since she seldom ate breakfast. She took a clean mug from the cupboard and filled it. When she heard voices in the office, she peered in. Marcus looked up at her but continued to listen to the answering machine play back its message.

"Marky, it's Mom. You said you'd visit. You must have forgotten. A good son never forgets—" He turned the machine off before it finished.

Cait recognized sorrow in Marcus's eyes when he looked at her. "I'm sorry. I didn't mean to intrude."

He shrugged.

"Does your mom live nearby?"

"She's in Tracy, in a nursing home."

"I'll leave so you can return her call."

"Doesn't matter. She won't remember she called, just like she doesn't remember that I saw her yesterday."

Cait hesitated. "I'm sorry—"

"I deal with it." He sat down at the computer.

"Thank you for the coffee and donuts." She left him, grabbed a donut, and went outside. Without purpose, she walked off the path and cut through the grass, her senses filled with the soft perfume of wildflowers. A meadowlark trilled. A cool breeze stirred the California poppies, royal larkspur, and blue lupines. She passed through the arched gate and went around the Black-friars Theater to her favorite place where she could view Mount Diablo, majestic and alluring, to the northwest. She sat on the damp ground, her coffee already cooling.

She wanted to enjoy the morning peace and quiet, not think about Tasha and the album or Karl Novak and his murder. Or RT. She finished her breakfast, lay back on the grass and stared up at the blue sky. She stayed like that until a voice interrupted her thoughts.

"Cait? Are you out here?"

She sat up and looked over her shoulder. Detective Rook stood on the grass, an envelope in his hand, not yet seeing her.

She stood up. "Over here. How'd you find me?"

"Marcus pointed me in this direction. Said you often come here. You've worked magic on him. He was polite and even offered me a donut and coffee."

Cait laughed. "Probably his way of apologizing for his behavior yesterday."

Rook's face darkened. "What happened?"

She told him she'd been to the Dirty Dog Saloon and about Marcus's reaction when he learned of it. "I've seen worse places and met more difficult people than Corliss, but usually, with enough provocation, I learn something." She looked over Rook's shoulder as if expecting to see Marcus. "Not this time."

"It's a motorcycle hangout. Mostly old guys trying to be cool."

"Only one old guy. That place should be condemned." She pointed to the envelope in his hand. "Is that for me?"

He handed it to her. "A copy of Marcus's file. In principle, you are involved and, therefore, can have a copy."

She had asked to see the file last night while at Karl Novak's office, but hadn't expected to get one. She grinned. "Thanks."

"Maybe it will help answer some of your questions. I'm on my way to court."

That explained his crisp dark suit and lavender shirt and tie. "I'll walk back with you," she said.

"I located Karl Novak's deputy. Name's Aaron Kapp."

Cait logged the name into her memory bank. "You talked to him?"

"Yes, but he didn't have much to say. Worked part time for Novak. He's a night security guard in Brentwood where he lives. The security company confirmed he was working the night Novak was killed."

Cait nodded. "Worth a try."

"His opinion of PIs is that they have their challenges and that's probably what did Novak in. I may talk with him again." He smiled. "I wouldn't have known about him if you hadn't mentioned a deputy. So thank you." Gravel crunched beneath their feet as they cut between the house and garage. "I still haven't been able to contact his secretary."

They had reached Rook's unmarked Expedition. "She's probably too scared to go back to the office." Cait tapped the envelope. "I appreciate this. Thanks again."

Rook nodded, got behind the wheel and drove off.

Cait tucked the envelope under her arm and wandered over to look at the gnarled trunks of vines, their arms outstretched as if waiting for buds to blossom, when she heard a sputtering noise, like a vehicle that couldn't quite decide to either run or stall. As Fumié drove into view, her Jeep coughed, jumped to the left and died in the middle of the driveway.

Fumié climbed out of the Jeep. "It's temperamental. Wish I could afford a new one."

RT materialized like a phantom.

"Everyone okay?"

"We are, but not sure about Fumié's Jeep," Cait said.

RT stared at the Jeep sitting at an angle across the driveway. "That took work parking like that. Where'd you learn to drive?"

Fumié grinned. "In a cemetery. My dad didn't think I could hurt anyone there."

Cait laughed at RT's expression. Then his blue eyes twinkled, the corners of his lips turned up as he fought to look serious.

"Keys?" he asked.

"They're in the ignition."

They left RT to deal with the Jeep and walked the rest of the way up.

"He's cute when he's annoyed," Fumié said.

"You think? Come inside. There's someone you should meet."

They went around to the back door. Cait took Fumié to the office to meet Marcus. His hands froze on the keyboard when he saw them.

"Marcus Singer, meet Fumié Ondo, our new helper I told you about."

He jumped up, ran his palms down the sides of his jeans, and adjusted his shirt at the waist.

By the grace of God, the guy's got manners, Cait thought.

Fumié held out her hand. "Hi. It's nice to meet you."

They shook hands. Marcus said, "Same here." Red crept around his shirt collar.

"I'll be right back," Cait said. "Help yourself to donuts and coffee." She set her coffee mug in the sink. Upstairs, she got on her knees at the side of the bed, pulled out her carry-on bag, unzipped it, shoved in the envelope Rook had given her, and pushed the bag back under the bed. When she returned downstairs, she found Fumié munching on a donut and looking through *The Independent,* the weekly local newspaper.

"Before you start organizing the gift shop, I'd like to go to the Elizabethan Theater to see if there's anything we can do to help there," Cait said.

Budding roses the color of aged piano keys trailed over the trellis at the gate to the theater complex. RT was standing in the orchestra pit watching the crew when they walked in. "Are you on stage manager duty?" she teased.

He shook his head. "Do I look like it? You'll find the real manager backstage."

"Good. I'd like to meet him."

"Oh, you will," he said. "But if you get gnarly with him, you may regret it," he said as a voice from behind the curtains boomed.

"Hells bells! Where's the crew? Jesus H. Christ! It's nine-thirty!"

Cait looked at RT with raised eyebrows.

RT grinned. "That would be Ray Stoltz, stage manager extraordinaire."

"They'll be here," a second voice said.

Cait tossed RT a wry look as she and Fumié went up the stage steps, pushed the heavy red velvet curtain aside, and came upon a tall man built like a football lineman.

He eyed them skeptically. "Which union do you two belong to? Disney?"

Cait regained her balance and stared at him. "Who's asking?"

The man glared at her. "Cut the attitude. I'm Ray Stoltz, stage manager." He cocked his eyebrow, his eyes roving up and down Cait and Fumié. "Hope you're tougher than you look or you won't last long. Lots of lifting to do."

"Oh, we're up to it." Cait winked at Fumié.

"Work starts eight sharp. No second warning." He led them back to the green room.

It amused Cait that he didn't know who she was, and she

decided to have a little fun with Mr. Stoltz. "Ummm . . . I'm really not at my best before nine."

Ray stopped in his tracks and turned to her. Veins popped out in his thick neck, his hard jaw locked.

"Hey, Ray. Which room's the wig room?" a voice said.

A smaller version of Ray stood in the middle of the room with a large cardboard box balanced on his shoulder.

Ray scowled. "Read the damn signs above the doors, Jay."

Ray and Jay? Cait studied their faces. *Have to be brothers.*

RT came around the curtains. "Good, you've met."

"Broad's got an attitude," Ray said pointing to Cait.

"Yes, she does," RT said. "Cait Pepper also carries a badge, so maybe you should watch your mouth."

Ray's eyes hooked on Cait. "This is *her?*"

RT chuckled. "Oh, yeah. I guess she didn't introduce herself. Stay on her sunny side and you'll be okay. I hear she's a real sharpshooter. And her friend here wants to be a park ranger and knows which end of a rifle to use, too."

Cait rolled her eyes.

RT crossed his arms, a grin spread across his face. "Ms. Pepper is the new proprietor of this lovely estate. You two should get along real fine, Ray. Maybe as well as you did with Tasha."

Jay slapped his brother on the back. "See you, big mouth," he said and hurried off.

Ray coughed into his dirty fist. "Seems I owe you ladies an apology." He looked at Cait. "My condolences. Mrs. Bening was a fine lady. Knew her a long time."

"Thank you," Cait said.

"Anyone other than Tasha, I wouldn't be here now. Got lots of work, but we had a deal and I respected her. Promised I'd have her theaters in mint condition for the start of the season. That was before the fire that put us behind schedule." He narrowed his eyes and glanced around the green room.

"Mr. Stoltz, we are here to help," Cait said. "What can we do?"

"You can start by calling me Ray." He picked up one of many boxes and placed it in Cait's hands. "This goes upstairs. Unpack the gels and go-bows and stack them up somewhere."

"Go-bows? Gels?" Cait said.

He stared at her. "You don't know about go-bows and gels?"

RT snickered. "Go easy, Ray. You might explain them to her."

Cait shot RT a look that could blister paint. *Yeah, like you know all about it.*

Ray scratched his beard. "Go-bows are metal disks used to add designs to stage floors. Gels are colored gelatin sheets that change colors in the scenes and costumes." He picked up another box and forced it at Fumié. "When you're finished unpacking, go to the prop room."

Cait glanced around the room. She hadn't even known there was an upstairs.

Ray sighed as if he'd read her mind and pointed to a far corner across from where they were standing. "Over there."

"Got it." Cait and Fumié headed to the door marked Loft.

Tiny slits of windows emitted little light in the loft. Cait shifted her box on her hip while she felt along the wall for a light switch. When she found it, bright overhead lights reached all corners of the loft, exposing bare walls, beams and rafters. Pieces of Victorian furniture were set against the walls. Naked dress forms and racks of draped period costumes were aligned along one wall.

"Oh, wow," Fumié said as she set her box on the floor.

Cait sniffed and was relieved not to smell remains of smoke damage. "These things must have been brought in after the fire." She noticed a modern sewing machine set up on a long table, and a rolled up rug under it. She dragged the rug out to the center of the loft and unrolled it. "Let's empty the boxes on here." They carefully lifted the tin go-bows and large colorful gels out of the boxes and set them on the rug, occasionally holding one up to the sliver of sun from the windows. After they finished, they went down to the prop room where RT was busy prying lids from crates. Long tables were covered with black drop cloths.

Ray walked in and tossed the cloths back, revealing orange chalked outlines in multiple shapes and sizes. "All props—guns, swords, knives, hatchets, and others—have to be placed on the outline that perfectly fits them. This has to be repeated before and after every performance." He stared hard at them as if to see they understood. "It's a daunting task, but has to be done. I'm doing it now to make sure everything that should be here is here. All props have a corresponding number that matches the outlines on the table. Different play, different tools, of course." He picked up a knife, opened and closed it, and then located its exact spot and set it on the outline. "That's what I want you to do. Most of the guns are real but unloaded. A few are made of foam but appear real from where the audience sits. When an actor is finished using a prop, it's critical that it be returned to the appropriate outline. That's how they're accounted for. Questions?"

Cait and Fumié exchanged glances and shook their heads.

Ray handed RT a clipboard. "All props are listed here. Check each prop off as they're placed on the table. Let me know if there's a problem." He turned and left the room.

"Whoa. I'm impressed," Cait said.

They worked in unison for two hours. RT examined each prop as he removed it from a crate, called out the number written on the prop, and handed it off to Cait or Fumié. Many of the weapons were similar in size and shape, and some of the orange numbers had begun to wear off.

"Okay, we're done," RT said as he handed a sword to Cait.

They walked around the tables admiring their work.

Fumié pointed to an empty outline. "Shouldn't there be a shotgun for here?"

Cait and RT looked where she pointed. RT checked the clipboard, flipping pages back and forth.

"Right. Let's check the crates."

CHAPTER 30

They checked all of the crates and the entire room before yelling for Ray. He stuck his head around the doorway. "I can hear you already."

RT gestured at the chalked outline on the table. "Come over here."

Ray sputtered something unintelligible as he walked into the room. When he realized what the problem was, he froze. "Damnation! Where the hell's the shotgun?" He looked at the others standing at the table as if expecting one of them to produce it. "Stuff like this happens way too often when we're packing up and heading out of town. Now you understand why it's important to check the props before the show."

"Everything has to be in place on my watch or someone's head rolls," RT said.

Ray glared at RT. "And what watch is that?"

I guess RT neglected to explain to Ray what he did for a living, Cait thought.

RT mumbled, "Navy business."

"Huh, that explains it." He scowled. "Problem is, that particular shotgun's the real McCoy." He pursed his lips. "Still works."

RT looked at him. "How do you know? Have you tried it?"

Red crept up Ray's neck. "Once, to shoot quail."

"Isn't there some code of ethics that says props aren't for personal use?" RT asked.

Cait understood RT's accusation, but the look RT gave her meant there was more to his question than a problem of ethics. Something he wasn't telling the brothers.

Ray bristled. "You accusing me of dereliction of duty? Maybe you took the damn thing."

RT shrugged. "Search my trailer. All I'm saying is it's reckless to use a prop for anything but what it's intended for. Accidents happen."

Cait stepped in to quell the argument. "Lighten up, guys. No one's accusing anyone of anything." But she knew what was stirring in RT's head: the birdshot through the kitchen window.

The strained silence between RT and Ray was shattered by a sound like nails being hammered into wood. All heads turned toward the doorway.

"Look who I found snooping around outside," Ilia said.

"I wasn't snooping." Rachel grinned. "Hey, Ray."

"Rachel." Ray grimaced at her shoes. "Don't you ever tire of tromping around in six-inch heels?"

"Four-inch," she corrected him. She turned to Cait. "What would you think about donating Tasha's clothes to the theaters?"

"Perfect. I emptied her wardrobe. Everything's on the floor in the bedroom," Cait said.

Ilia pointed his camera at the prop tables. "Okay if I take a picture?" He snapped a couple before Ray could object.

No one heard Marcus until he tripped over an empty packing crate just inside the door. His face flushed, he looked at Cait. "Detective Rook wants you to meet him at the library café."

Cait found Detective Rook talking on his cell phone in the café. He motioned her to a seat and concluded his conversation.

"Thanks for coming. Would you like coffee?"

"No, thanks. I thought you were supposed to be in court."

"Postponed." He folded his hands on the table. "Have you

read Marcus's file?"

"Not yet."

"That call was someone who knew his parents. An ex-neighbor. I'd been trying to get hold of her and she just called me back."

Cait searched his eyes for answers. "Oh?"

"She confirmed some new information I'd received about Marcus, something I thought you should know if he's to work for you. His father died in Folsom Prison. That's in the file I gave you. He was in for money laundering. Loved horse racing; unfortunately, it didn't love him." He drank his coffee. "The wife hung onto the house as long as she could, then had to let it go."

"His mother's in a care center in Tracy," Cait said, wondering where this was going.

Rook nodded from beneath bushy eyebrows. "You mentioned you were interested in the background of the Bening estate." He glanced up at her.

She blinked. It took a while for his words to register. "Are you saying the Bening estate is where Marcus grew up?"

"Yes. It wasn't named, and there wasn't a vineyard or the theaters, but I thought it might explain his attachment to the place and why Tasha let him work there after he was released from prison."

"Whoa." She didn't know how she felt about that. "You're sure about this?"

"I've no reason to doubt the ex-neighbor. The Benings remodeled the kitchen and made other changes, like turning the upstairs into their apartment."

"Who's the neighbor?"

"Just someone who used to live across the road, but she lives out of state now."

"I wonder why Rachel or Stanton Lane never mentioned

this." Cait glanced out the patio doors at the people sitting at tables enjoying the sun while they ate.

"Would it have changed anything had you known?"

She thought about it. "Probably not."

"Being a boy, I'd guess Marcus would know all the hiding places on the property."

"I suppose so." She frowned. "Why? What are you implying?"

"Some of the things Marcus was accused of stealing have never turned up."

"You think they're hidden in the house?" Before he could answer, she said, "A shotgun, a prop actually, is missing from the Elizabethan Theater. That's where I was when you called." She explained about placing props on the tables and not finding the shotgun. "I wonder if Marcus took it."

"I assumed weapons used as props were fakes."

"Not all of them, as Ray Stoltz explained. He's the stage manager. He and RT almost got into it when Ray said he'd used the shotgun to track quail."

Rook pulled a pad and pen from a pocket inside his jacket. "Ray Stoltz?"

"Yes. And there's Jay, his brother."

Rook wrote on his pad and slipped it back in his pocket. "I could use another cup of coffee. You want one?"

She nodded. "Please. Black."

While Rook went for coffee, Cait thought about Marcus. Did he borrow the shotgun from the theater and then take those birdshots to scare her? Possible, but was he capable of murder? With a bit of soul searching, she decided Marcus lacked the killer instinct.

Rook returned with two steaming cups of coffee and set one down in front of Cait.

"Thanks. I only met the Stoltz brothers this morning so I don't know what they're capable of, but I thought Ray was pretty quick to admit he'd used the gun."

"You think he was defending someone?" Rook asked.

"Maybe." She changed the subject. "You and RT act like old buddies. Did you know him before he came here?" Cait sipped her coffee.

Rook smiled. "Very perceptive of you. My younger brother was also a SEAL; he talked about RT."

"They knew each other?"

A glazed look crossed his face. "Yes. They were on a clandestine mission in the Gulf. While rappelling down a cliff, someone cut the rope. That's how RT injured his back. My brother wasn't so lucky. He cracked his skull on a boulder when he fell. Killed him instantly."

Cait felt a stab of pain in her chest. "Oh, God. I'm so sorry."

"Yeah, me too."

They were silent for a while. Cait watched steam swirl above her coffee.

"RT's lucky he survived." Rook pushed his chair back and stood. "He might tell you about it someday, when he's ready, but for now I'd appreciate it if you would keep what I've told you to yourself. Thanks for coming."

"Thank you for telling me about Marcus." Cait stayed in the café after Rook left. She bought a chicken-salad sandwich, took it to an outside table, and thought about RT. She didn't think their relationship had progressed to the point of his sharing personal experiences like the accident in the Gulf, but what Rook told her answered concerns she had about RT.

CHAPTER 31

Almost two weeks had passed since RT had taken Cait to meet Bo Tuck, the vet who'd inherited the Bening ranch from Hilton. Maybe by now, she thought, he would open up and talk to her about Hilton's fatal accident. She drove through the tall metal arch, and then only a short distance before pulling off to the side and parking next to a grove of eucalyptus trees. She shut the engine off, climbed out of the Jag and crossed to the white fence that extended further than she could see. A small plane circled overhead and headed west as it started its descent toward the Livermore Airport. She raised her hand to block the sun from her eyes. Off in the distance she caught the glimmer of a pond and a cabin backed up against the hills.

A faint vibration in the ground interrupted the sense of peace she felt, and then Bo Tuck appeared around the bend on horseback, closing in on Cait in a smooth, rhythmic canter, the personification of a cowboy. His tan Stetson shaded his eyes; his chambray work shirt was smudged with dirt.

He reined in his horse in front of Cait and tipped his hat. "I thought I recognized the Jag when I saw you turn in here. You here for a riding lesson?"

She clung to the fence to get away from the horse. "Haven't found the nerve yet, Bo." She eyed the black stallion, which also had her in his sight. "That's a big horse."

Bo laughed, his blue eyes sparkling as he rubbed his hand along the horse's mane. "Relax, Cait. This is Cash. He senses your fear. If you want, leave the car here and ride the rest of the way with us."

She shook her head. "Not a chance. He looks too full of fire and spirit."

"That he is. We'll see you at the barn then."

Cait watched Bo and Cash until they disappeared around the next bend in a cloud of dust, and then she got back in the Jag. She drove slowly so she wouldn't kick up more dust. Bo stood in front of the barn when she pulled up and parked. "He looks calm now," she said as she stepped out.

"Every horse has its own personality. In my book, they're smarter than most people. We communicate, don't we, Cash?" The horse snorted, his head bobbing up and down as if in agreement. Bo gave Cash a gentle smack on his withers before turning him over to a stable hand who stood waiting by the barn door.

"We've just come from a vet visit across the road. I got Cash from the rancher in exchange for my services. I think he's sorry he let me have Cash."

With eyes on the backside of the horse as he was led away, Cait said, "That's actually done? A horse in exchange for vet fees?"

Bo removed his dusty hat, slapped it against his chaps, and wiped his brow with his sleeve. "Not often, but in this case I made an exception." His eyes followed the horse and stable hand. "Cash is a fine horse, a Morgan, full of vinegar and then some. But he proved too much for his owner to handle. He thought him too wild and not trainable for their purposes, so I ride Cash over there sometimes just for the hell of it to show off how well his horse and I understand each other."

Cait laughed. That was something she would do. She liked Bo. She thought he had a good soul.

"Come on up to the house. Time you met the family."

They crossed a footbridge over a dry creek bed to what appeared to Cait more like a small lodge than a house, with a pencil-reed balcony that ran across the entire front.

"So, if you didn't come to ride, what brought you here?" Bo asked.

"To visit Faro," she said, which was a half lie.

He held the screen door open for her without commenting.

She absorbed the rustic feel of the interior with its knotty pine tongue-and-groove floors, cathedral ceiling, and immense, soot-blackened fireplace and felt instantly at home. The open space and spectacular view of the hills and pasture through tall windows gave Cait a fresh appreciation for minimal furnishings. A chocolate-brown leather sofa and chairs fronted the fireplace. An older upright piano stood between the windows. Dozens of photos sat on top of the piano, most of a grinning child straddling a horse's back, jumping barriers, and accepting trophy ribbons.

"Hilton rebuilt this house," Bo said, "and then surprised us by giving it to us to live in. A more generous man I've never known." He gave Cait a look she couldn't interpret. "To be honest, I don't think he ever intended to live in it. He loved the barn, his horses, and the pastures more than any house. Including the Bening estate." He smiled. "He did like his wine."

"I wish I'd known both of them," Cait said.

"Our daughter adored him."

An asthmatic whooshing sound caught Cait's attention. The young girl in the photos, about ten years old, rolled into the room in a wheelchair. Her tousled smoky black hair and crackling deep-set violet eyes created a vision that touched Cait's heart.

She grinned. "Hi, Daddy. Who's this?"

Bo leaned down to kiss the top of his daughter's curly head.

"Hey, Princess. This is Cait Pepper. She inherited the Bening estate."

The girl's violet eyes studied Cait with intensity far beyond her years. Cait felt like a horse on the auction block.

"Your name's not Bening," the girl said.

Bo laughed. "Cait, this precocious child is my daughter Joy, who usually brings joy into our house, except when she's embarrassing us."

Cait smiled, walked up to Joy and held her hand out. "Hi, Joy. Your dad shouldn't be embarrassed. Directness is a virtue." The girl's hand in hers was small but strong.

"I like to think so." Joy tilted her head up. "So how are you related to Tasha?"

Oh, boy.

"Joy," Bo cautioned.

"No, it's okay," Cait said, answering with half-truth. "Tasha was my aunt. You see, Tasha and my dad were brother and sister—twins. Tilson was their last name."

"Tasha Tilson Bening," Joy said. "I like it. But yours is Pepper."

"That's because I used to be married."

"I should have warned you, Cait. Enough, Princess, or she won't come visit us again."

Cait grinned. "Sure I will."

A young woman walked into the room and slipped her arm across Joy's shoulders. She smiled at Cait, her dimples flashing.

Bo's face lit up. "Honey, this is Cait Pepper. Remember I told you we met when RT brought her here a week or so ago?" He looked at Cait. "This is Khandi, my wife."

"Mom," Joy said, "Cait owns the Bening estate. We have to teach her to ride."

"It's nice to meet you, Khandi," Cait said as they shook hands.

Khandi's soft voice had a faint accent, possibly South African, Cait thought, remembering her favorite college professor. She wore jeans and a red low-cut T-shirt that accentuated her trim figure and cocoa complexion. Her sable hair hung in a thick braid halfway down her back.

"Welcome to our home, Cait. We love company, don't we, Joy?"

Joy's curls bobbed as she nodded. "Mom, maybe she could stay for dinner and tell us about her dad and Tasha. They were twins. Tilson was their name. Isn't that pretty?"

"Oh, I couldn't impose. Thank you, Joy, maybe another time," Cait said.

"But you're already here," Joy said.

Bo saved Cait from embarrassment. "I think she has other things to do today, Princess."

Khandi's shy smile touched Cait. "Joy, honey, we'll fix your favorite dinner for Cait when she comes—pork chops with macaroni and cheese."

The cholesterol count boggled Cait's mind.

"Your daughter's beautiful, Bo. And smart," Cait said after they left the house.

He set his hat on his head. "So damn smart, sometimes it's scary."

They were quiet for a while as they walked, until Cait got the nerve to bring up the accident. "Bo, can we talk about Hilton's accident?"

He glanced at her. "What do you want to know?"

"When I was here before, I got the impression you thought it might not have been an accident. Was I wrong?" She stopped and waited for Bo to say something. When he didn't, she said, "Come on, Bo. Talk to me. Tasha and Hilton were family."

He turned to her. "Hilton and his horse were like one, each a component of the other. Which explains, in part, Faro's behavior. He misses Hilton."

"That's sad." Her heart ached for the horse. They walked together in comfortable silence.

Bo smiled at Cait. "There's been improvement lately. He makes eye contact and approaches the fence when I walk up, not distancing himself like he had been doing."

"That's good."

They walked a little farther and then Bo said, "I heard what happened at your place. What was a PI doing there?"

"I don't know, but Actors' Equity is after us to increase security before the actors arrive. I hope it won't affect attendance at the festival. Bo, there have been three deaths in a relatively short period of time. I can't believe they're not somehow related."

He nodded; his stride lengthened.

"Does it bother you sometimes, the accident, when you look at Faro?"

He stopped abruptly and exhaled as if suddenly exhausted. Reaching up and rubbing the back of his neck, he glanced off in the distance. "Sometimes when I look at that horse, it all comes back to me. I try telling myself there was nothing I could have done to prevent what happened. I just hope the neighboring ranchers don't think I had something to do with Hilton's death. That worries me."

"Was there any indication something was off that day?"

He snapped his head around and blinked at her. "You sound like a cop."

She smiled. "I assumed you knew. I used to be one; I'm a crime analyst now."

"Somehow that doesn't surprise me." He walked ahead.

"How else am I going to get answers, Bo? I didn't know the Benings. I wasn't here when they died."

"I wish I could be more helpful."

"You can start by letting me see Faro."

"Now that I can do. But first, we'll stop by the clinic for treats."

They circled around to the back of the barn where a large gray metal building stood off to the side, the open doorway high enough to accommodate a horse and carriage. She inhaled the smell of fresh hay as they walked past a few empty stalls where a stable hand was sweeping the floor.

Bo glanced at Cait, a subtle smile on his face. "In case you're wondering, no patients are staying with us today."

Cait followed him through the building to a door at the rear. He dug into his jeans pocket and removed a ring of keys, unlocked the door, and flipped a switch. Bright fluorescent lights flooded a large sterile room.

She blinked several times before adjusting to the sharp glare. Everywhere she looked she saw stainless steel—counters, sinks, shelves, cupboards, refrigerator, and a couple of small cages. She stared in amazement at the spotlessly clean room, white walls and white tile flooring with drains. Hoses hung from stainless steel trolleys.

She made a slow turn around the room. "Wow. You could eat off the floor."

Bo laughed. "Not if you knew what's been on it. Hilton wanted everything top of the line. I just wanted a sterile environment for the horses."

Cait glanced at Bo. His steady blue eyes and facial features softened when he spoke of his patients—like they did when he talked to Joy. Or about Hilton.

"You love what you do, don't you?"

"I wouldn't be a vet if I didn't." He opened a tin sitting on a shelf. "Before Hilton died, we talked about setting up an equestrian foundation to bring together troubled youths and abandoned horses. That's the first thing I did after he died." He removed his hat, holding it down at his side. A faraway look came into his eyes. "The bond between animals and children can be a powerful and healing medicine."

Cait wondered if Joy being wheelchair bound had anything to do with establishing the foundation.

"Faro's in the pasture," he said as he locked the clinic behind them.

Beyond the barn and clinic were fenced fields, a small group of paddocks, and some animals Cait thought she recognized as llamas. A couple of golden retrievers barked menacingly at a flock of ducks crossing behind a flatbed loaded with bales of hay.

The last time she'd seen Faro, he wouldn't venture close enough for Cait to see his silky bay color and sleek, long extended neck. Today he approached the railing when he saw them. A compact horse with massive muscles, he took a cautious step closer to them, his big liquid eyes bright with curiosity. As he inched toward the railing, he stretched his head. Bo held out his hand. A Butter mint quickly disappeared into Faro's mouth.

"You're right. I see a change in his behavior," Cait said. She wanted to reach her hand out to Faro, but didn't want to scare him.

"Joy visits him every day. His eyes are brighter, and he's responding to her voice. He allows her to stroke him like she used to." He sighed. "I think he knows she's hurting too. I lift Joy onto the fence. She rubs his ears and whispers sweet nothings to him." He hooked his heel over a rail.

"How long has Joy been in a wheelchair?"

"Three years now—since she was seven."

Cait thought about the pictures on the piano of a smiling little girl sitting atop her horse.

Bo pushed off the fence. "If there's nothing else, I'll walk you to your car."

She collected her thoughts as they walked, searching for the best way to ask the question she'd come here to ask, a way that wouldn't offend him. "Bo, please don't take this the wrong way, but I'd like to know about the drugs you keep in your clinic."

"I have lots of drugs."

"Potassium chloride or succinylcholine?"

He stopped. "Now we've come to the crux of your visit."

Her gut told her if Hilton's death wasn't an accident, it must have been premeditated, but she hadn't yet figured out how, because, as Detective Rook had pointed out, no killer was good enough to predict Faro would dump Hilton on a rock that would kill him. Cait's exceptional knack of observation had more often than not put her at odds with a few of her fellow officers—until she'd been proven right time and time again. She liked Bo and thought him to be the good guy, but she'd learned to never allow her personal feelings to interfere with her investigations.

"Bo, please. Are those drugs in your clinic?"

He walked the rest of the way to the Jag and plucked a leaf off the windshield. "Tasha loved this car, but Hilton refused to drive it. Thought it was a sissy car."

Cait dug her hands into her jeans pockets in frustration.

Bo's blue eyes riveted on her face, he said, "Let's be clear. *Joy* invited you to dinner, but we'd all take pleasure in having you at our table. And, yes, I have both drugs in my clinic. Am I being accused of something?"

"Of course not. Tasha's autopsy revealed elevated levels of potassium. Potassium chloride, as I understand it, could have been used as a lethal injection. But someone would need to control the victim in order to inject it." She watched for a reaction. When she saw none, she continued. "Succinylcholine paralyzes the body's muscles, incapacitating the person. The drugs could have been stolen from your clinic."

Bo frowned and crossed his arms. Cait waited while he digested the information.

"I know what the drugs are for," he said, "and the harm they can cause. Do you know that this is how Tasha died?"

She shook her head. "I'm saying it's a possibility. Who has access to the drugs besides yourself?"

"A retired vet comes in when I need assistance. Sometimes a student helps out, but I have the only set of keys and I don't leave them sitting around to be stolen."

"What about Khandi?"

Bo jerked, his mouth tight with barely suppressed anger. "Are you accusing my wife?"

For a terrifying second, she was afraid she'd pushed the wrong button. Bo's face reddened dangerously. "God, no, of course not. I'm only trying to account for everyone with access to your clinic. The door could have been left open innocently, or pried open."

"It wasn't. Khandi does the bookkeeping, scheduling, office stuff, but mostly works from the house in case Joy needs her."

She nodded. "Would you tell me if either of those drugs were used recently on any of your patients?"

"I don't see the relevance, but I wouldn't give you that information."

"I understand a person's record is private, but a horse's? Come on, Bo. I don't care about a horse or whatever, only who knew you had those drugs. Was someone angry when their horse had to be put down around the time Hilton died?"

"I will not implicate anyone I service. It's a legal issue, and a personal issue for me. If the police bring a warrant, I will show them my records. Not until then." Cait grabbed his arm as he turned away.

"Bo, Hilton's death may have been an accident, but Tasha's wasn't. Or Karl Novak's, the PI. A killer's on the loose." She took a deep breath. "Bo, think about the fires at the Elizabethan Theater." She struggled to restrain her frustration with Bo. "Talk with Detective Rook. I can read it in your face, hear it in the catch in your voice every time Hilton's name comes up. Even Faro's. Who's next, Bo? You? Your family?"

"Christ, Cait! Don't you ever let up?"

She opened her car door. "I'm sorry, Bo. That's what I've been trained to do." She climbed behind the wheel and rolled the window down and forced a smile. "I'd love it if you and your family would attend the tea Friday . . . in keeping with Tasha's tradition."

Bo tipped his hat without a word, turned and walked in the barn. Cait watched until he was out of sight and then backed the Jag around and drove off.

Whenever Cait found herself in a quagmire, she called Shep. Back at the house, she went upstairs to the bedroom, took out her cell phone, and punched in his number.

"Talk to me, partner," Shep answered.

How good it felt to hear him still refer to her as his partner, even though their partnership had ended a long time ago, when she became a crime analyst. She sat on the edge of the bed.

"Hey," she said, "how's it going?"

"Are you whispering because you're in the middle of one of California's famous wine parties or just plain tired?"

"I need to talk some stuff out with you if you have time."

"I'll take the time. What's happening?"

She kicked her shoes off. "I found a dead guy in my garage. A PI."

She explained how she found Novak and about his office being trashed.

"You've been set up," Shep said, "by someone who thought you were out of town."

"I think so, and Detective Rook agrees. I just don't know why."

"Maybe you've been asking too many questions in the right place. You've probably ruffled a few feathers. Try to identify the couple in that photo the police found in Novak's office and then look for a common denominator between them and those you think might be involved in the murders. Sounds simplistic, but that's often how it goes."

"Maybe Rook and I can track down the teenagers from school yearbooks. It's possible they're still living in the Bay Area."

"Good place to start," he said.

"There's more. The vet who inherited the Benings' ranch has potassium chloride and succinylcholine in his clinic. I don't think Bo's responsible for Hilton's accident, if it was that, or Tasha's death, but I'm thinking someone who works for him or knows he has those drugs may have stolen them."

"He could have been set up, too, Cait. Maybe by someone who resents his getting the ranch after Hilton died."

She rubbed her temple. "I hadn't thought of that angle. Thanks." Her eyes lit on the photo album on the bed. "Shep, there's something else."

He waited.

"Tasha wasn't my aunt; she was my birth mother. I found a letter and an album . . ."

"Oh, Cait. I'm sorry."

"It's okay. I'm coming to terms with it. It helps explain my inheritance."

"You were never told?"

"No, and I don't think I'll ever understand. There's no one alive to ask."

"And now you're supposed to give up the life you've known and carry out your aunt's . . . mother's dream? That sucks."

CHAPTER 32

Cait and Roger were driving south on Coastal Highway One to spend their honeymoon in Carmel. With the ceremony behind them and a promising future before them, life looked good. Low-flying shorebirds and gulls drifted in and out along the coast. Pink and orange glowed in the setting sun, merging with the blue Pacific along the vast expanse of beaches.

She smiled at Roger just as waves pounded over them and swept their car out to sea. Cait screamed. Roger laughed. A fog bank of faces drifted by—her parents, Roger, Karl Novak, dark shadows for Tasha and Hilton Bening. And then Cait's.

She jolted upright on the bed, her throat constricted as she struggled to get out of the semiconscious dream. She covered her face with both hands and squeezed her eyes tight to block out the nightmare.

Those faces, she thought. All dead.

Except me.

She sat in the dark on the edge of the bed fully clothed, gripped by a vague feeling she couldn't quite identify. Not fear—there was no rush of adrenaline. More like grief. A loss. She focused on the clock on the bedside table. Its red LED glowed back at her: 11:00 P.M. She reached over and switched the lamp on. Sleep wouldn't come easily now.

Cait slipped her feet into the same dusty shoes she'd worn to the ranch and went in the bathroom. A quick glance in the mirror told all—dark circles beneath watery eyes, deep frown lines, pale skin, and markings along one cheek from the comforter. She raked her fingers through her hair, grabbed her keys and Windbreaker and slipped it on.

If she was to get any sleep at all, she needed fresh air to clear her mind. She went downstairs and out the back door, rattling the doorknob to check that it was locked. Black and gray shadows cloaked the yard. She hesitated, sensed a supernatural spirit pulling her toward Tasha's meditation garden, something ethereal. She ignored it and cut across the yard. When she came to the gate and opened it, it screeched like nails on a blackboard, sending shudders through her in the cold night air.

She felt as vulnerable as a turtle without its shell as a sudden gust of wind ripped through the trees. She pulled her hood over her head, crossed the courtyard, which was as still as a cemetery. As she ran along the path to her favorite place behind the Black-friars Theater, a place so undisturbed it felt surreal, sensors monitored the walkway in soft golden lights beneath the subtle shifting moonlight.

A bird shrieked and burst out of a nearby tree and into the night.

A twig snapped.

Cait froze. She pushed her hood back to listen.

Another twig snapped.

"Who's there?"

Silence.

She held her arms out in shooting stance, as if she were armed. "Show yourself now."

"Cait! It's me!" RT stepped from behind a large bottlebrush shrub, its red flowers flapping in the wind, his gun at his side. "What the hell are you doing out here?"

She dropped her arms. "I *live* here, remember? You scared the crap out of me!"

"Sorry, but you know I make my rounds about this time

every night."

How could she have forgotten? She waited for her heart rate to slow.

He cautiously approached; his eyes squinted. "You have a gun?"

"I wish." She wrapped her arms around her body against the cold night air.

"Maybe you should buy one." He tucked his revolver under his Windbreaker at the small of his back. "You're shivering." He stepped closer, zipped her jacket up to her chin and pulled the hood back over her head. His hands gripped her shoulders. For a second, his eyes lingered on her lips. Then he backed away, his voice gruff. "I'll walk you back."

She sensed he wanted to kiss her. To avoid embarrassment for both of them, she said the first thing that came to mind. "I met Bo's family today. Joy's going to be a heartbreaker when she grows up."

"Yeah, she certainly will be."

"Bo wouldn't say what happened. Was it a riding accident?"

He nodded. "She was six or seven when she fell during preparations for a rodeo demonstration and injured her spinal cord. She's paralyzed from the waist down. Bo blames himself for giving in to let her ride in the rodeo. He thought the demonstration was too advanced for her age."

"Seems Bo shoulders guilt about a lot of things."

They walked the rest of the way in silence until they reached the back door. Cait was reluctant to go in. She didn't want to be alone. *Must be that miserable nightmare,* she thought.

Suddenly, RT grabbed her arm and stepped in front of her. She stiffened. "What'll it take to convince you to stay? A chance in a lifetime's been handed to you. Don't toss it away like garbage."

She stared at him then over at the meditation garden and

wondered why she'd ever thought she had a choice. She'd only been delaying the inevitable. Her breath wedged in her throat for several seconds, and then she said, "Maybe the wheel has come full circle."

He arched his eyebrows. "Meaning?"

She shrugged. "I'll wait and see. I have two months to decide."

RT dropped a kiss on her cold lips. "Sounds positive. Thank you."

She stood there speechless; the sensation from his lips on hers still lingered.

"You don't know it yet, Cait Pepper, but you're perfect for this place—the theaters, even the vineyard. This community's going to love you."

"How do you know?"

He grinned. "I heard it on the grapevine."

Or from the hills, she thought, thinking of Bo's comment.

He pushed his sleeve back to look at his watch. The face glowed green in the dark. "You going to be okay? I have a book deadline."

"Please don't jump to conclusions. I said I'll wait and see what happens," she said, but she knew the decision had been made for her. "Nice watch," she said to change the subject. "I think my husband had one like it."

"Doubt it. Luminox Titanium. Developed specifically for the unit."

"Probably with lots of cool stuff I wouldn't understand."

He laughed. "Cait, I doubt there's much you couldn't learn if you set your mind to it." He rattled the doorknob. "Keys?"

She reached in her pocket and handed them to him.

He unlocked the door and returned her keys. "Sleep tight."

But an hour later, lying in bed, Cait had trouble getting to sleep. A decision to remain at the estate weighed heavily on her mind, but RT's feather-like kiss triggered a deeper sensation that caught her off guard.

CHAPTER 33

Brilliant colors danced across the walls Wednesday morning as the sun filtered through the stained-glass windows. Cait fixed toast and coffee in the apartment's tiny kitchen and then reviewed the estate papers from Stanton Lane and Marcus's criminal record Detective Rook had given her.

She glanced over the estate papers, highlighted her concerns, and put it aside. Her concentration as high as if she were taking a college final exam, she read every word in Marcus's file. In his teens, he had the usual list of offenses—graffiti, vandalism, and petty theft. He'd broken into Livermore's History Center, but apparently nothing had been stolen. Cait expected to see drug and alcohol abuse, but there was no mention of either.

In his twenties, Marcus spent time in Folsom Prison, a prison known to confine hardened criminals. Small spatters of his blood had been found at a house where Indian relics and small electronic items had been stolen; pry marks on a window frame matched a thin metal tool—a "slim Jim," designed to work a car-door lock from the outside—found in his car. Cait didn't think the crime fit the punishment for Folsom. When she saw a Stevens shotgun had been found in his car, her heart sank with disappointment. She returned the file to the duffle bag, pushed it under the bed, picked up her jacket, handbag, and keys and went downstairs.

The doorbell chimed just as she reached the first floor. She opened the door and was handed a package from the mailman.

Assuming it was something for the gift shop, she carried it into the kitchen and slit the tape with a small knife from the wooden block on the counter. Nestled inside was a slim book of poems between layers of blue tissue and a hand-written note from Stanton Lane:

Cait, please accept my apologies again for any misunderstanding I may have caused you. I located the book of poems Tasha and I shared. I hope you'll enjoy it as well. SL

Cait recalled the day Lane alluded to and the embarrassment it had caused both of them.

She set the book aside and picked up a large Shakespeare brochure dated twenty years earlier. A blue Post-it bookmarked a page. She turned to the page and saw Tasha's name highlighted in yellow beneath a black-and-white picture of a woman dressed as Lady Macbeth. She stared at the first picture she'd seen of Tasha and tried to picture her without makeup and costume.

Cait touched Tasha's face with her fingertip. *This woman gave birth to me,* she thought. She looked through the rest of the brochure for another picture of Tasha, but found nothing. She gathered the wrappings, tossed them in the trash, and called RT.

"Hi," he said. "Please don't tell me you changed your mind."

She thought he sounded sleepy, even a little sexy. "I said I'd see," she said, knowing she had no choice but to accept her inheritance and all the accoutrements that went with it. The decision was too final to admit out loud. "When you come to the house, check out the poetry book and Shakespeare brochure Stanton Lane sent. I'm going out for a while, but I'll leave them on the kitchen counter."

"Not the infamous poetry book."

"That's the one. There's a picture of Tasha as Lady Macbeth in the brochure, but it's difficult to see what she really looks like." She slipped into her jacket. "Which house across the street is Rachel's?"

"The one with Bauer on the mailbox," he said. "Why are you going over there?"

"To see Rachel, of course." She dropped her cell phone in her handbag and locked the back door behind her. She backed the Jag out of the garage, drove down the hill, and found the Bauer mailbox. She pulled onto a gravel lane, drove through a grove of trees and up a rise to Rachel's house. Its mossy green roof appeared to rise organically from the ground. The house followed the natural curve of the hill to create a space with what appeared to be many levels. Cait parked in front and walked up the flagstone steps to the double front doors and rang the bell.

Rachel seemed taken aback when she saw Cait. "What brings you here?"

Cait smiled. "I thought we should talk."

"Well, if it's about the tea, we've been through that. Unless something's happened to change it, I don't see what's left to discuss, unless you've decided to go back home to Ohio."

Do I really want to work with this woman? "May I come in?"

Rachel opened the door wider and stepped aside to allow Cait to enter.

Cait followed her back to the heart of the house—a great room with a stone fireplace almost as large as the one in Bo Tuck's house. The ceiling soared at least thirty feet. "What a remarkable room."

Rachel crossed her arms. "Yes, it is."

"Did you build the house?"

"No. We added this room after I inherited the house from my grandparents." She glanced around as if seeing the room for the first time. "It's constantly evolving, but it keeps Ben busy while I'm away. Have a seat."

Cait sank into a lush maroon leather sofa.

Rachel curled up across from Cait in a big leather chair, one leg tucked beneath her. "So is there something in particular you want to discuss?"

Cait reined in her annoyance. "I've decided—"

"The tea's not a big deal. I have it covered, so you can relax and meet and greet your neighbors, if you're still here for it, that is."

Cait rubbed her temples with her fingertips, trying to massage the headache blossoming behind her eyes. "I have a two-month leave from my job."

Rachel stared at Cait for a few moments. "I see. Two months, huh? Why?"

"Family responsibilities, Rachel. The estate will go to a foundation if I don't live here. I need more time." She wasn't ready to tell Rachel that Tasha was her birth mother. She noticed the deep furrow in Rachel's brow and the tightening in her lips.

"If you give up your inheritance, I could talk to Stan about my taking over the festival."

"It states clearly in the trust that it would go to a foundation," Cait said.

"Stan might be able to work around that."

Cait doubted it, but she didn't want to debate it with Rachel. "For now, I want to make sure you'll stay on and help me with the festival . . . do what you did for Tasha."

"I told you I would when I learned of her death," Rachel said, her hazel eyes hard as marbles.

Cait nodded. "And I appreciate it. Do you know if Tasha left an endowment to Las Positas College?"

Rachel shifted in her seat. "She talked about it, but since I wasn't privy to her personal business, I don't know if she followed through with it. I didn't even know about you, remember?"

Wait until you hear the rest of it. Cait's head began to pound. "What about Marcus? Did she mention providing for him in some way?" She wondered if lack of some kind of inheritance could have something to do with his attitude toward her.

Rachel moved to the edge of her seat. "Ask him. If that's all, I'll see you Friday."

Cait took that as a hint to leave. She rose. "Could I bother you for some aspirin?"

Rachel led Cait down the hall to a bathroom. "In there," she pointed with her flawlessly manicured hand.

Cait locked the door. After using the facilities and washing her hands, she opened the medicine cabinet. Everything from Pepto-Bismol, Mercurochrome, Williams Shaving Soap, to Baby Magic powder and—Viagra?—filled the shelves. She suppressed a grin, reached for the Aleve, filled a paper cup from a dispenser with water, and swallowed two pills. When she returned to the room, she expected to find Rachel waiting for her. She glanced around and then called, "Rachel?" When there wasn't a response, Cait let herself out the front door. She glanced back before getting into the Jag and then drove off. She sighed. *Between Rachel's attitude and narcissistic theatrics—*

She located the town's history center in central Livermore. Inside, she approached a woman sitting behind the front desk. Her years of police work had taught Cait to sustain a network of contacts, which was critical in law enforcement. Since she would be in Livermore for a while, she wanted to learn about the property she'd inherited and where Marcus grew up.

The woman's name tag read Mildred. "May I help you?"

Cait smiled. "I recently acquired a piece of property and am interested in knowing its history."

Mildred's milky-white skin, silver hair, and cornflower-blue eyes reminded Cait of her grandmother. "Where is your property?"

When Cait told her, Mildred beamed. "Oh, *that* property. I met Mrs. Bening last year. Are you a relative?"

"I'm her niece."

Her eyes sparkled. "What are you looking for?"

Cait laughed. "I don't know exactly, but I am interested in geology."

"We're closed today. I'm here now because someone called to say they left a box of old photos on the porch. Come back Thursday and we'll see what we have, but for now try Sunrise Mountain Sports on Railroad Avenue. They sell USGS topographic maps."

"I might do that. Thank you."

"There's a magical area in Livermore with rock outcroppings and shallow sandstone caves. Some call Brushy Peak a garden of stones—where Miwok, Yokut, and Ohlone once lived. They considered it sacred, a place where gods dwelt."

Cait smiled. "Well, if there happens to be a cave on my property, I'll just let it rest in peace." She shivered at the thought of entering a cave.

Mildred was on a roll. "There's an early settler buried up there. Brushy Peak was an outpost for nineteenth-century outlaws. Joaquin Murrieta and his gang used the area as a hideout after they stole gold from the miners. Bandits hid in the Altamont Pass to prey on travelers coming from the Sierra with gold dust and from San Francisco with cash. LARPD rangers give tours in the spring. Maybe you'd like to book one."

Cait liked the idea of gold in the hills rather than a bunch of bandits. "Thanks, but I'll pass." She noticed a basket of business cards. She dropped one of hers in and added a couple dollars to the donation jar and left.

At Sunrise Mountain Sports, she bought a map and was given a copy of USGS symbols to help interpret it and then drove home.

Fumié's Jeep, Rachel's red pickup, and a silver Volvo were parked in the driveway in front of the house. She drove past the cars and parked the Jag in front of the garage. On her walk back, she heard a child's voice.

"Daddy, Daddy! Who's that?"

Cait's heart tripped when she saw RT holding the hand of a small child about five years old and shrouded in a mass of curly blonde hair.

He smiled. "Cait, this is Mindy, my daughter."

CHAPTER 34

Reality reared its complex head.

His daughter? This vision of charm clutching RT's hand? Pieces of the puzzle began to fall into place for Cait. His sudden absences, the children's books.

Envy and sorrow pulsed through her body. Her throat constricted, making it hard for her to breathe. She'd stuffed the painful memories of her sorry marriage deep inside, locked in the farthest corner of her mind. Until now.

She felt Mindy's soft touch on her hand.

"You're pretty," the child said.

Cait crouched in front of RT's daughter.

"Thank you, Mindy. I think you're pretty, too. How old are you?"

Her big blue eyes filled with curiosity, she said, "Five. Is this your house?"

"Yes, it is. Have you been here before?"

Mindy shook her head, blonde curls flopping.

"My folks are here, too," RT said.

Cait stood, her eyes focused on an older couple approaching.

"Mom, Dad, this is Cait Pepper. Cait, Ron and Meg Tanner."

Mr. Tanner's erect stance bespoke of a career military man. Cait tried to visualize RT in thirty years—gray fringe of hair, sharp eyes. Mrs. Tanner's warm smile and crinkling blue eyes put Cait at ease.

"Cait," Meg Tanner said, taking Cait's hand in hers. "I've

been so eager to meet you."

Mindy tugged on her grandmother's jacket. "Can I play with the kitty?" She pointed to Velcro sitting on the front step.

"Okay, but be careful. He doesn't know you."

As Mindy ran off, Cait studied RT's mother: Five-three, streaked ash-blonde hair, a contented smile.

"RT mentioned you didn't have a picture of Tasha, so I brought one for you. It's in his trailer."

"I'll bring it over later," RT said.

Meg studied Cait. "Your resemblance to Tasha is uncanny—tall, beautiful, same dark curly hair, and those beautiful eyes."

Cait felt her cheeks flush and glanced at RT and saw him shake his head. Apparently, he hadn't told Mrs. Tanner about her birth. "That's so thoughtful of you, Mrs. Tanner. I couldn't find a picture of her anywhere in the house."

"Call me Meg, please. Tasha had a thing about having her picture taken. Odd when you consider how famous she was, but I guess we all have our little quirks."

RT's dad glanced at his watch. "We should be going."

Surprised, Cait said, "So soon?" She glanced over at Mindy sitting on the steps beside Velcro. The late afternoon sun had cast a pink-orange glow over the house, the cat's white fur, and Mindy's golden locks. She thought her heart would break. She wanted time with Mindy.

"Dad wants to be on the other side of Sacramento by nightfall. They're headed to Utah," RT said.

Meg laughed. "We still run on military time—punctual." She touched Cait's arm. "We'll stop by on our way back to San Diego and have a nice long talk." She hugged her son.

Mr. Tanner called, "Hop to, Mindy Sue. Come say good-bye to your dad."

Mindy ran over and leaped into RT's waiting arms, hugged him and planted noisy kisses all over his face and neck.

To Cait's surprise, Mindy scrambled out of RT's arms and ran over and took her hand. She pulled Cait down to her level.

"My daddy likes you," Mindy whispered and giggled.

"I like him, too," Cait whispered and gave her a hug.

The Tanners piled into their late-model Volvo. Mindy waved out the back window until the car disappeared from sight.

Cait wanted to run and hide somewhere private before she cried. An unexpected emptiness filled her. *RT has a daughter. This house really needs a family, a dog, kids rollicking on the lawn.*

RT stood beside Cait. "I've never seen Mindy react to another woman the way she did to you, except for my mom."

Cait looked at RT and saw a hungry look in his eyes that were still glued to the driveway, and sensed deep emotion churning within him. "She's adorable. I'm sorry they had to leave so soon."

"Yeah, me too. They're off to Sundance, Robert Redford's place near Provo."

"Nice. I've been there, to the outdoor theater."

As they walked up the steps to the front door, RT stopped and put his hand on her arm. "Cait, I'm sorry seeing Mindy upset you. I didn't know they were coming."

Cait looked to where the Volvo had been parked. "Go home, RT. You need to be with Mindy."

He shook his head. "Not yet. I made a promise to Tasha, and I mean to keep it. I'm sorry you've inherited more than you bargained for when you came here."

A half smile crossed her face with remembrance. "Shakespeare wrote something about stars shining darkly over some of us."

"You think?"

"RT, where's Mindy's mother?"

"She's not in the picture."

Ilia was showing his camera to Fumié when Cait and RT walked into the kitchen.

They looked up, smiled, and continued their conversation. Cait heard clicking sounds coming from the office and expected to see Marcus when she peeked in. Instead, it was Rachel.

"I'm updating the agenda for the tea," Rachel said.

So that's how it's going to be. Carry on as usual, no apology.

Cait refused to comment. "I left something in the car," she told RT. Her cell phone rang when she was outside. She glanced at the tiny screen. "Hi, Detective Rook."

"I was reviewing Marcus's record with the detective in charge at the time of his arrest. Those Indian artifacts he'd been accused of stealing?"

"You think they could be in the house," she said. She opened the car door and reached across the butter-soft seats for the map.

"I have to consider the possibility. An expensive camera stolen from the same house was found in his apartment. Naturally it was assumed he'd taken the carvings, but he denied it at the time."

She sat sideways on the seat behind the wheel. "I read his file. I'm interested in the Stevens shotgun he had. You think it was used to take those shots at me instead of the one from the theater?"

"I checked. It's still in the evidence room. Cait, I'd like you to look—"

"Of course I will. If it's in the house, it's likely to be in the office because that's where he usually is. If he catches me, I'm toast. Does he still report to a parole officer?"

"No. He was a good boy, released early from prison."

"Really? Even when the police think he's still good for the stolen artifacts? I've heard of Folsom Prison. It has a reputation for housing hard-core inmates."

"It also houses medium-security inmates. Marcus took advantage of their educational training and self-help program. He read lots of books in their library and took college courses while incarcerated. Walked out of prison clean. Stayed that way, as far as I know."

"Let's hope he's still clean. Must have been hard for him, knowing his dad died while incarcerated at the same prison. How did he die?"

"Lung cancer. A three-pack-a-day smoker. Let me know if you turn up anything from the search."

She slid out of the car with the USGS map in hand and closed the door.

A soft footstep fell on the other side of the car.

She whirled.

A figure stepped from the shadows.

CHAPTER 35

"Marcus!" Cait slumped against the Jag, heart pumping wildly. She looked across the roof of the car at him. "How long have you been standing there?"

He plucked a leaf from the windshield. "Long enough. You were talking to Detective Rook."

She frowned. His words sounded slurred. "I was."

"I'm not going back to prison for something I didn't do." He polished the side mirror with his shirtsleeve.

She nodded as her heart rate settled down. "He said you worked on a college degree while you were there. You're ambitious. So why are you here when you could find work somewhere else and make a lot more money?"

"Leave and let people assume I'm guilty of murdering Tasha? I'm an ex-con. I'm not going anywhere until I know who killed her and Hilton. And it damn sure wasn't me."

Cait caught her breath. "You think Hilton was murdered, don't you?"

"Damn straight! I grew up with horses. Faro would *never* toss Hilton unless provoked." He slapped his palm on the roof of the car and glared across at her as if daring her to contradict him.

"Did someone have a grudge against them? A business deal gone bad? A promise they failed to keep?"

"Not that I know of," he said. "They weren't like that. They were decent, honest people."

She moved around the car, closer to him. "Marcus, I want you to trust me. Would you tell me if there was someone you suspected?"

"Trust you? Ha. Been there, done that. Look where it got me. In prison."

Was this mere bravado? "Tell me about the Indian artifacts."

He smirked. "I knew you'd get around to that sooner or later. I like them. Is that a crime?"

"Not that I know of, unless you stole them." She noticed a sudden tick around his left eye.

He glared at her.

She took in his body language—his suddenly stiffened torso, the perspiration on his upper lip—and knew his answer was only half true. She knew little about Indian artifacts and dropped the subject for now. "If you change your mind and want to talk, I'll be around."

He stumbled as he backed away from her.

Cait wondered if he'd been drinking. It was a shot in the dark, but she wanted to keep him talking. Since he'd spent time in the prison's library and taken college courses, she asked, "Marcus, if you could be anything you wanted to be, what would that be?"

He nudged a bucket near the door with his toe. "What do you care?"

"Maybe I can help you achieve your goal. Tasha obviously believed in you."

He hesitated in confusion. "Licensed carpenter . . . or a print-maker."

Now that's interesting. She'd considered commercial printing and etching while in high school until she realized she had no real talent for it. Then she fell in love with stained glass. "You have talent. You built those beautiful shelves in the gift shop and I'm told the ones in the apartment also. Hobbies turn into lucrative jobs."

Marcus shrugged and started to walk away.

"Wait. You didn't say when a security company will come to install an alarm in the house," she said.

"They said a week. Put the Jag in the garage." He walked away.

She watched him go, conflicted. Cait had noted a spark of interest, but it had quickly petered out. She climbed behind the wheel, pressed the garage opener, and pulled the Jag into the center slot.

"What took you so long?" RT said when she walked in the back door.

"Rook called." She glanced around the kitchen. "Where'd everyone go?"

"Ilia and Fumié went for a walk." He eyed the rolled-up paper in her hand.

"Want to help me decipher a map?"

"Sure, if can we do it in my trailer. I left my cell phone there."

She assumed he didn't want to miss a call from Mindy. "No problem."

On the way to RT's trailer, she told him what Rook wanted her to do. "I almost hope I don't find anything."

"I can help you look," he said.

"Maybe you could search the garage. I'll do the house."

RT cleared the table in his trailer and held the corners of the map with boxes of crayons and pencils. "What exactly are we looking for?"

She leaned over the map. "A woman at the Heritage Center suggested I could pinpoint this property on this map and maybe even find a cave."

He smiled. "You thinking of hiding out?"

She rolled her eyes. "Too late for that."

It only took RT seconds to find the quad that encompassed

the Bening estate. He stabbed his finger on it. "Here."

She blinked. "How did you do that? And don't you dare laugh at me."

RT wiggled his eyebrows. "I'd never risk laughing at you, darlin'. I've studied thousands of maps. They're fun, once you get the hang of it."

Fascinated, Cait watched and listened as RT explained the markings on the map.

He opened a drawer and removed a roll of paper held with a rubber band. He opened it and spread it on top of her map. "Here's San Diego." He stabbed his finger on it. "And here's where I live."

But her attention was on his tight T-shirt and the rippled muscles beneath it.

A ghost of a smile crossed his face. "Pay attention." Then he leaned over and brushed his lips against hers.

Her pulse spiked with a need she hadn't felt in years. She'd been in an emotional state since seeing Mindy.

"Cait—"

Someone pounded on the door. "RT! You in there?"

RT muttered, "Who the hell . . ." and walked to the door and opened it.

Ray Stoltz stood outside holding a bloody handkerchief to his nose. "Ray? What's going on?"

"You gotta get over there! I swear, Marcus has gone stark mad!"

Cait leaned over RT's shoulder. "But I just left him," Cait said. "He seemed okay." Then she remembered a smell she'd detected on Marcus.

"Shit," RT said. He and Cait left the trailer and followed Ray.

At the Elizabethan Theater they found Marcus slumped in one of the front rows guzzling down a bottle of tequila.

"I'll handle it," Cait said.

RT pulled her back. "Not when he's drunk."

Marcus raised the bottle to RT. "Hey, RT."

RT grabbed his arm. "Let's go, Marcus."

Marcus pulled away. "I like it here."

RT held out his hand. "Give me the bottle."

"Want some?" Marcus took a drink and then cradled the bottle to his chest.

Cait whispered, "Where'd he get tequila?"

RT shook his head. "How about you and me go to my trailer. I'll brew a pot of coffee and you tell me what's bothering you. If you don't want to talk, that's okay, too."

Marcus seemed to consider the suggestion. "I like you, RT. Don't like many people, but you're okay." He held the bottle at arm's length and stared at it with blurry eyes. "Never liked the damn stuff anyway." He thrust it at RT with a shaky hand.

RT handed it off to Cait while saying, "Good decision. Let me help you up. It's going to be a long trek back."

The day had been long and difficult. Seeing RT's daughter had shaken Cait to the core and left her feeling empty inside. Even if she'd had a child, her marriage wouldn't have lasted. Sometimes there's a blessing in all that darkness. Without Shep's consolation, she might not have survived the pain of not being able to conceive.

After RT had taken Marcus to his trailer, Cait returned to the house and settled into a corner of the sofa in the apartment's sitting room with her laptop and a mug of chamomile tea. Who am I kidding? she thought. There never was a choice. She drafted her letter of resignation to the Columbus Police Department, swallowing her emotions with every sip of tea.

The sound of music caught her ear, soft, smoky, floating through the open window in the kitchenette. She set her laptop

on the coffee table and went to see where the singing was coming from. Fumié was perched on the bench in Tasha's meditation garden, a guitar cradled across her. Ilia sat on the ground
at her feet. A gust of wind whipped through Fumié's long hair,
floating it out like a raven's wing as she plucked poignant bars
from a song Cait didn't recognize but didn't want to end.

The hills had fallen silent as if in appreciation of the notes
swelling into a haunting poetic melody. While Fumié segued
from one song to another, Cait wondered how someone so
young could understand and interpret so much into music. She
leaned against the window frame, closed her eyes, and listened
until overwhelmed with a longing she couldn't face.

CHAPTER 36

Thursday dawned with a fierce clap of thunder that jerked Cait out of a sound sleep. She felt her heart thumping as she tossed the covers back and ran to the window. Putty-colored clouds hovered over the valley. She shivered and grabbed her robe off the back of a chair. As she tightened the belt around her waist, her eyes fell on the picture of Tasha that RT's mother had brought.

She picked up the three-by-five black-and-white photo of Tasha as a young girl. She wore a long dress with a sash, her head tossed back as if laughing. Cait studied the picture but couldn't see the resemblance, just like she couldn't see it in the grainy photo of Tasha in the Shakespeare brochure Stanton Lane had sent her.

She propped the photo against a book on the table. It reminded her of another black-and-white photo, the one of the teenaged couple found in Karl Novak's office. If Detective Rook was available, maybe they could go to one of the high schools and look at yearbooks, she thought.

Cait located her cell phone and called Rook.

"How old was Karl Novak?" she asked when he answered.

"Assuming you have good reason to ask, he was in his mid-fifties."

"What are the chances the boy in that picture is Karl Novak?" She thought she heard him chuckle.

"It's a good possibility since it was found in his office."

"If Novak and the girlfriend went to a local high school, maybe we could find them in one of the yearbooks."

"Now why didn't I think of that?" he said.

"You must be a crock of fun to work with, Detective."

"It so happens I have a little time, so if you want I'll meet you in front of Livermore High at ten. Think you can find it?"

"I'll be there." She showered and dressed and was downstairs in thirty minutes. She opened the back door to let the cat out, then heard what she thought was a rush of Spanish and laughter coming from the front of the house. Rain threatened as she walked around the house to the front where she saw two trucks hitched to trailers in the driveway. Burlap bags filled with leaves and debris lay on the ground at the end of rows in the vineyard. A half dozen men worked the vineyard on each side of the driveway with knives and rakes.

"Morning, Cait."

She turned. RT looked as if he'd been up half the night. He rubbed his eyes as he approached her.

"Rough night?" she said.

"You could say that." He ran his hands over his face.

Cait glanced back at the workers. She didn't understand the rapid-fire Spanish they spoke. "They actually sound like they're enjoying the work."

"They're just happy to *have* work."

She looked back at RT, at the circles beneath his eyes, his unshaven face. "What happened with Marcus last night?"

"I took his keys until he sobered up and let him sleep it off in my trailer while I bunked in the Hummer."

If she'd known, she thought, he could have slept on the sofa in the apartment. Then decided that may not be a good idea. "Where is he now?"

He yawned. "Left about six this morning, sober and ashamed. We drank coffee and talked a little before he left. You shouldn't count on seeing him today, but when you do, cut him a little slack. He's remorseful and afraid you'll can him. It may not seem like it, but he does respect you."

"Could have fooled me. Where did he get the bottle?"

"Don't know and didn't ask. If he wants to tell me, communication's open. He understands that." His eyes slid over her khakis and black V-neck sweater. "Going somewhere?"

She nodded. "I'm meeting Detective Rook at Livermore High School to look at yearbooks. With a little luck, maybe we'll find that teenage couple in the picture from Novak's office. They'd be in their fifties now, Rook said."

"Needle in a haystack," he said, "but I wish you luck."

"You got a better suggestion?"

"Maybe Rook's taking you along to keep tabs on you."

She stared hard at him. "I do this sort of thing for a living, in case you forgot." She turned to go.

RT caught up and grabbed her arm. "Look, we've all experienced what you're going through at one time or another when we're in another officer's territory. Sometimes it gets unpleasant."

"Is that how it is for you when you're working out of the country?"

He pursed his lips and nodded. "Worse."

The phone was ringing when they walked in the back door. Cait grabbed it. "Bening estate."

"Is Rachel there?" a male voice said.

"I don't think so. I haven't seen her. May I take a message?"

"It's Ben, her husband. Tell her I'll see her later."

"Ben—" she said, but he'd hung up. *What a strange man.*

Cait parked across from Livermore High. Detective Rook was parked in a no-parking zone in front of the school. He stepped out of his car when he saw her.

"I know this is a long shot," Cait said as they walked up to the door, "but I've worked with less."

"You have good instincts or I wouldn't be here."

At the administration office, Rook identified himself and was handed four yearbooks.

"That was quick," Cait said.

"I called ahead. Told them to pull nineteen seventy-one through seventy-four. If Novak graduated from here, he would be in one of those books."

They were directed down the hall to a small room. Rook set the black-and-white snapshot on the table between them and slid two books toward Cait. "You take seventy-one and seventy-two. I'll do the other two."

Occasionally, Cait or Rook picked up the snapshot and held it against a face in the book. It was slow going. An hour passed. Cait began to worry her instincts had let her down. Then she turned a page in the 1972 yearbook and saw a picture of a pyramid of smiling cheerleaders. She held the snapshot against each face as she worked her way up the pyramid.

The instant she saw the girl at the top, she knew she'd found her. She confirmed it with the name beneath the picture. "Check this out."

He glanced over. "You got something?"

She slid the book toward him and pointed to the girl and then the name.

"Rachel Cross? Sounds familiar." Then, "Wait. Isn't she the one who tried to mess with my crime scene at your place?"

"The same."

"Why am I not surprised?" He checked his watch and then smiled at Cait. "Good job. Now let's find the boyfriend."

A phone rang somewhere; laughter echoed through the halls. Cait finished the 1972 yearbook and then started to work backwards to see if she'd missed the boy. Boys' faces began to blur together, but she refused to give up until she'd been through both yearbooks again.

About forty minutes later, Rook tapped his pencil eraser on a picture. "Are you sure you don't want a job with the LPD?"

Cait tore her eyes from the yearbook and saw the smile on Rook's face. "You found him?"

"Yep. Seventy-three."

"Thank you, God," she said. Cait thought back to a similar situation she'd worked as a rookie cop. Then it was four decks of cards all missing the ace of hearts. The aces were found in the bras of four bodies in a strip motel known for illegal gambling. Cait had convinced Shep, her mentor at the time, that they'd have the killer if they located those decks of cards without their aces. Took five weeks and earned Cait her first recognition.

Cait and Detective Rook studied the black-and-white picture of Rachel and Karl as teenagers. Rachel's arms were possessively wrapped around the boy's neck, her cheek pressed against his, the same impish grin on her face. Rook pulled out a notepad from his jacket pocket, noted which yearbook and page number each picture was found on and then pushed his chair back and stood. "Let's get out of here."

"Now that we know Karl Novak and Rachel Cross knew each other and live in Livermore, what do we do about it?"

"I have an appointment," he said, "and you're going home."

CHAPTER 37

A light mist coated the windshield. Cait started the engine, flipped the wipers on, and sat in the car. If not for her, Rook might never have discovered the relationship between Rachel and Karl Novak.

As she pulled away from the curb, she thought about Rachel's odd behavior at the scene of Novak's murder. She knew most high-school romances broke up within weeks, but wondered if Rachel and Novak had resumed their relationship and if her husband, Ben, knew Novak.

When she returned home, the crew was still working in the vineyard, oblivious to the rain. She activated the door opener and pulled into the garage just as Ilia and Fumié ran in to meet her.

"You are not going to believe it," Ilia said.

"What?" Cait stepped out of the car and closed the door.

Ilia glanced at her Sketchers and Windbreaker. "You're dressed okay, but you'll want a flashlight."

She looked at their damp jackets and hair. "Why on earth would I need a flashlight? The electricity's on or I couldn't have opened the garage door."

"We're going for a walk. Come on," he urged.

"Has something happened?"

"Not exactly," he said, "but you have to come with us. Please."

She looked at his earnest face, then Fumié's, and opened the car door and reached in for the flashlight between the seats.

"Okay." She closed the garage door and followed them out the side door.

Fumié's ponytail bobbed up and down as she jogged beside them. "It's not far, Cait, just past the stakes where the new theater was going to be built."

Cait hadn't strayed far from the house and theater complex, and definitely hadn't been out there. They walked under scudding clouds and through tall wind-rustled grasses on the hill. She pulled the hood over her head, zipped her jacket up, and jammed her free hand into a pocket. They crossed over a crest and past a massive weeping willow; its elegant foliage cascaded over a weathered bench. "What brought you out here on a day like this?"

He grinned at Cait and zipped up his jacket. "I just signed a contract for a big book project. A coffee-table-size book of my pictures. I figured pictures of wildflowers covered with dew and a cloudy backdrop with velvety shadows of eucalyptus trees would make a terrific spread."

Cait stopped and grabbed his arm. "Ilia! That's terrific. Congratulations."

"Thanks. I've waited a long time for an opportunity like this." They continued to walk. "If it wasn't for Tasha giving me access to the property and the house, it might not have happened. I used pictures of the stained-glass windows in the house as a backdrop for some of the flowers."

It pleased Cait to see a twenty-nine-year-old man openly express enthusiasm for his work. She knew Ilia had the patience to wait however long it took to capture the elusiveness of light in the photos she'd seen. "That's awesome, Ilia." The hills were covered with a mix of wildflowers, lilies of the valley, camellias, and azaleas. A partial sun found its way across them. Half oak barrels of budding tulips and yellow-gold daffodils anchored the four corners where stakes had been pounded in the ground.

Their petals glistened like tiny mirrors.

"Almost there," Fumié said as she led them over a rise. She skirted around a few sandstone outcroppings and then came to a stop.

Oak trees were clustered in a small grove, their branches bent and gnarled, their leaves gray with mist and dust. Overhead, the wind stirred the clouds into swirls of shadow and light.

Cait caught sight of a metal grille at the mouth of a cave where Fumié stood. "You've got to be kidding."

The entrance lay partially hidden in the deepest cleft of the knoll. "The grass has been freshly trampled around it with what looks like hoofprints," Fumié said. "That's what caught our attention."

"Let's go in," Ilia said as he set the grille off to the side.

Cait shivered. "If this is what we came out here to see, I'd rather not go in." That woman at the history center couldn't possibly have known there was a cave here, she thought.

"But you have to see what's inside," Ilia said. "There's nothing to be frightened of."

She leaned over to peek in the dark opening and immediately felt stirrings of claustrophobia. She'd never admitted her fear of tight places to anyone, afraid her fellow officers would make fun of her. She took a deep breath. "Okay, let's get this over with." She turned her flashlight on.

Ilia and Fumié turned theirs on as well and led the way in, their lights fanning across the ground in front of them. The cave opened up once they were inside, with intermittent space to stand without bumping their heads on the ceiling.

With trepidation, Cait took several steps before catching her foot on an object and stumbling. She turned her light to her feet. A lantern lay on its side, a candle stub, and a book of matches nearby.

"Cait." Ilia swung his flashlight over the ceiling and walls.

"Check this out."

Figures danced across the walls in muted shades of red, blue, and yellow—pictographs of horses, dogs, and warriors told stories she couldn't decipher.

"There are laws to protect national treasures like this," Fumié said.

Cait moved her light over the walls, more fearful of bats than California codes. Then her light revealed a shotgun propped against the wall. She stared at it with apprehension. "Oh, no."

"Yeah, we saw it too," Ilia said. "Think it could be the missing gun from the Elizabethan Theater?"

Or the one used to take shots at me. "I'll take it back to the house. Is the gun what you wanted to show me?"

"No. That's just ahead. Cait, Ohlone Indians once inhabited this cave," Ilia said, "just like at Brushy Peak." His laugh echoed against the walls. "Except there's no body buried here."

Cait shivered. *Thank God for small favors.*

"Almost there," he said.

She squinted into what appeared to be an endless hole.

Ilia trained his flashlight beam on a small boulder. "It's behind there."

Anxious, Cait wanted to get out of there. She stepped on something crunchy, jerked her foot back, and tapped her flashlight against her arm until it brightened. She aimed the beam on the ground at her feet and saw pistachio shells like those caught in Velcro's whiskers.

Ilia disappeared for a second. "That's it." He flashed his light on a wooden chest no bigger than a large hatbox. Two weathered leather straps crossed over the curved top and buckled at the front; leather handles were on either side.

Cait stared at the chest. "My God. Do you know what's in it?"

"Nope. It's locked. We thought we'd wait for you to pry it

open." He removed a screwdriver from his pocket. "Brought this back with me. Do you want to open it here or wait until we take it back to the house?"

"Let's open it at the house," she said, anxious to leave the cave.

A noise from behind caused them to jump.

Cait's first thought was bats.

Ilia swung his flashlight up. "Marcus!"

Cait banged her head on the ceiling as she turned.

Dressed in a rumpled blue shirt and jeans, Marcus squinted in the light. Raw tension lined his face; fear shook his voice when he spoke. "I *wanted* to turn it over to the police, but after so much time had passed, I didn't know how." He looked at Cait, a haggard expression on his face. "I'm not going back to prison."

Cait's heartbeat slowed as she stared at Marcus. "Why didn't you tell me yesterday when I asked about Indian artifacts? I assume that's what's in the chest."

He stared at the chest. "I wanted to."

She wondered if this was why he'd been drinking yesterday. "I assume you have a key that will open it."

He jammed his hand in his jeans pocket and removed a key.

"Unlock it," she said.

He walked around her, crouched in front of the chest, and struggled a bit with the lock. After a couple of tries the key slid into place. He opened the lid and then glanced up at her.

Cait tightened her grip on her flashlight. "Let's see what's in there."

He spread a large red plaid handkerchief on the ground and then removed a handful of arrowheads and set them out.

Cait heard a heavy sigh escape as his shoulders rose and fell. Arrowheads were common enough that she ignored them and peered over his shoulder expecting to see authentic treasures.

Marcus removed two bundles wrapped in maroon cloths and placed them on the handkerchief. He unrolled them.

"Oh." Fumié's hand flew to her mouth.

Ilia snapped a picture before Cait could stop him.

Marcus flinched at the flash of light.

Cait crouched beside him, her flashlight tucked under her arm. "What am I looking at?"

"Carved Elk Horn purses." Marcus offered one to her.

Cait held the purse in the palm of her hand. She studied the simple engraved lines, the carving, and the abalone accents. It was half an inch wide, maybe two inches long, and hung by a leather string. She held it up to show Ilia and Fumié and then returned it to Marcus.

Marcus picked up the second purse and offered it to Cait.

Eagle feathers were carved on both sides of the purse in a contemporary design, and it also hung by a leather string. "What are these worth?" Cait asked.

Fumié crouched on her heels beside Cait. "They're new. Probably cost anywhere from one to five hundred dollars."

Cait looked at her. "How do you know that?"

"I've seen advertisements on the Internet."

Cait returned the purse to Marcus. "These can be bought on the Internet?"

Fumié smiled. "You can buy almost anything on eBay."

Marcus unrolled another cloth. "This is an Elk Horn medicine pouch."

Confused, Cait took it from him. The pouch had a flying-geese design with black cowhide sewn on the top.

"Oh, gosh," Fumié said. "It does look familiar. I may have seen it or one like it in one of my books. If I'm right, the artist belongs to the Hoopa Valley Tribe, somewhere here in Northern California."

Impressed, Cait said, "How do you know so much about

Indian art?"

Fumié grinned. "I have tons of books at home on it."

Cait turned the pouch around in her hands, running her finger over the design, and then handed it back to Marcus. "Why steal these and risk going to prison? Why not buy them online?"

He unrolled a bull loon carved out of red alder with a baby on his back. Fumié held her hand out. "May I?"

He handed it to her. "Be careful. The top comes off. There's a compartment inside."

"I've never seen this." She turned it around in her hands and then returned it. "It's beautifully done."

Everything in the trunk appeared in pristine condition, not what Cait expected, and definitely not the type of Indian treasures Rook said Marcus had been accused of stealing.

Marcus started to unwrap another cloth, but Cait had seen enough and her legs were cramped. She wanted to take the chest back to the house and call Detective Rook. She stood. "There's nothing of historical value in there?"

"I never said there was." He unwrapped a multistrand neck-lace.

She caught her breath. "I have a single-strand fetish necklace from Albuquerque." The multistrand bird-and-animal fetish felt warm to the touch, with carvings of bears, foxes, mountain lions, rabbits, moles, and many more in as many colors.

"What's a fetish?" Ilia asked.

"A rock carving of an animal that's supposed to capture its spirit," Fumié said. "This one looks like it's been done in the old style. See the mother-of-pearl spreader bars between them? Either Zuni or Navajo."

Cait wove her fingers through the strands of coral, turquoise, pink, brown and black figures. "Mine is modern, ornate and detailed." She sensed Ilia focusing his camera. Although she hadn't detected alcohol on Marcus's breath, she feared another click of the camera could trigger his recent erratic behavior. She nudged Ilia with her foot and shook her head.

He lowered his camera.

"I expected something of archaeological interest," Cait said as she returned the necklace to him.

"Then you were wrong," Marcus said.

"What about the chest? Where did it come from?"

"I found it in the house, under the stairs. Been there since I was a kid."

Ilia flashed his light inside the chest. "There's something on the bottom."

Marcus reached in and pulled it out. "Just some old rug I found stuck between the beams under the stairs." He unrolled the rug and a small mask. "This was inside it."

"Cool," Ilia said. "Can I see it?"

Marcus gave him the mask.

Ilia flashed his light on it. "Doesn't look old."

"I don't think this is a rug; I think it's a Navajo child's blanket," Fumié said.

Cait ran her light over the muted orange and blue diamond shapes. "This might be authentic."

Marcus tossed the rug over the chest and set the mask on top of it. "Take it. I only care about preserving this cave and the tribal symbols on these walls. Strangers coming in here could ruin it." He turned, ducked, and headed toward the entrance.

"Put everything back into the chest and bring it out with you," Cait told Ilia as she followed Marcus. The mist had turned to a steady drizzle. She drew deep breaths of fresh air into her lungs, relieved to be out in the open. "Marcus! Wait!" She ran after him. "I understand now. A theater out here would be too close to the cave. You didn't want that." She stopped. "Marcus!"

He stopped, his breathing hard and fast. His hands clenched at his side.

Cait walked toward him. "You set those fires at the Elizabethan, didn't you?"

A flash of uneasiness crossed his face when he turned.

"I saw the shotgun. Did you think you could scare me so I'd leave?"

Rain ran down his face but he ignored it.

"It is the gun from the theater, isn't it?"

He jammed his fists in his pockets.

"Talk to me, damn it."

His shoulders sagged, his chest heaved with a deep sigh. He removed his hands from his pockets, as if resigned to the outcome. "If I'd wanted to kill you, I could have."

"I know. But you didn't."

His face scrunched as if in pain. "I'm a thief, okay? I served time for it. But I have *never* killed anyone. I am *not* a murderer! I am *not* like my dad!"

Whoa. His dad murdered someone? That announcement fell like a hammer blow to Cait's chest. *Oh, Jesus.* She had to talk with Rook, but now was not the time to ask Marcus about his dad. "You're scared, aren't you? You know something about Tasha and Hilton's murders. What about the PI?"

"I'm only scared of going back to prison." He darted around the outcroppings and out of sight.

Cait caught up with him as he was mounting his horse. "Marcus! Wait!"

He ignored her, grabbed his cowboy hat from the horn and slapped it on his head.

"Marcus! Please! Call Detective Rook."

He looked down at her from atop his horse, grabbed the reins and backed the horse around, too close to Cait for comfort. Then he turned and rode off as if ghosts of the Native Americans were hot on his trail.

CHAPTER 38

RT's gaze locked on the shotgun in Cait's hand when she walked in the back door. "What's going on?"

Fumié grabbed a newspaper from a chair and spread it on the counter for Ilia to set the chest on. "We found this chest in a cave."

"And the shotgun," Cait said. "Possibly the one missing from the theater."

He took it from her, checked the chamber, found it empty, and slammed it back together. "What the hell was it doing in a cave?" Then he raised his eyebrow. "So that's why you wanted a map."

"Don't be ridiculous," she said.

RT rested the gun against the counter. "Okay. I'm all ears."

Cait unzipped her Windbreaker and reached in her pocket for the cell phone. "Ilia can explain. I'm calling Detective Rook." She flipped it open and punched in the number.

While Ilia explained about finding the cave, RT yanked on the padlock dangling from the chest. "Was it unlocked?"

"No. Marcus had the key," Ilia said as he placed his screwdriver on the counter. "We were going to bring it back here and then open it, but that was before Marcus showed up."

Cait was put on hold while they located Rook. When he came on the line, she said, "It's Cait. You might want to come to the house sometime soon. There's something you should see. What?

Okay." She closed her cell and set it on the counter. "He'll be here."

RT removed the lock, raised the lid and peered inside. "Indian artifacts?"

Cait wiggled out of her damp jacket and draped it over the back of a chair. "More like nice imitations."

RT removed everything from the chest and set them on the counter. With the chest emptied and all items exposed, he said, "The rug and mask look authentic, but where are the historical treasures he's supposed to have stolen?"

"Apparently, there aren't any," Cait said. "The chest, rug, and mask he found in the house under the stairway, so he can't be accused of stealing them. Been there since he was a kid he said." She thought about Marcus's dad, but didn't want to bring him up in front of Ilia and Fumié.

"Any idea how long this has been in the cave?"

"No," Cait said, "but I've read over his record. Has to be at least five years. He went to prison for stealing electronic stuff and Indian artifacts, even though he said he never stole any of real historic value. The officer who wrote the record might have wrongly interpreted the term artifacts. Let's wait for Rook. He talked with the officer in charge at the time of Marcus's arrest."

"So where's Marcus now?" RT asked.

Cait shrugged. "Disappeared."

The doorbell chimed.

"Rook was already headed here when I called but didn't say why," Cait said.

"I'll get it," RT said. He returned a few seconds later with Detective Rook.

Rook nodded to everyone and then glanced around the kitchen. "Where's Marcus?"

Confused, Cait said, "Marcus?"

He nodded. "He called just before you did. He asked me to

come here." His eyes lit on the shotgun propped against the counter and picked it up. He checked the chamber and then set it back.

"Then you know about the chest?" Cait said.

He glanced at the items on the counter. "No, just that he'd meet me here to fix a wrong." He picked up the mask and turned it around in his hands. "Is this what I think it is?"

"I don't know. What do you think it is?" she asked.

He looked at her and raised his eyebrow. "The artifacts?"

"As you can see, none of these things are authentic Indian artifacts," Cait said, "except for the rug and maybe the mask."

"Looks like some kind of warrior mask. Not sure I'd hang it on my wall." He set it down.

Sounds of a door opening and closing came from the office. Marcus walked in. "I'm here."

Detective Rook walked over to Marcus and, to Cait's surprise, offered his hand. "I appreciate the call, Marcus."

Marcus hesitated before taking the detective's hand. He glanced at Cait over Rook's shoulder. "I thought about what you said, Cait. It's time to move on."

She wondered if he meant he was leaving or setting things straight in his life.

Rook directed Marcus to the counter. "Tell me about these."

Marcus tugged on his earlobe. "I didn't steal the mask or the rug. They've been in the house since I was a kid."

Rook picked up the loon carving. "Okay. What about the rest of these things?"

Marcus stared at the carvings and arrowheads as if they were insignificant bugs. "I stole them. All I thought about in prison were these stupid carvings hidden away in the cave. Hell, I could have made ones just like them." He ran his finger over the fetish necklace. "Except this. I don't even remember why I stole any of this stuff. Maybe because they were just there along with the camera and other electronic gadgets." When he touched the Elk Horn medicine pouch with the flying-geese design, he appeared to become unsettled. His face scrunched with emotion. Cait recognized anguish in his eyes and wondered why that particular pouch bothered him. Could it be the black cowhide sown on the top?

Cait knew the law could come down hard on Marcus for lying, but wondered if time already served would be enough to allow him to remain free. She watched him with a mix of sadness and pride. With a little prodding from her, he had done the right thing and called Detective Rook, knowing he could be sent back to prison.

She shifted her eyes from Marcus to Detective Rook. "I understand it's your duty to take him in, but he deserves consideration. He called you." From her peripheral vision, she saw Marcus's head turn toward her, but she kept her eyes steady on Rook. "The cave, where the chest and gun were found, and the tribal drawings covering the walls are what interest him. He wants to preserve it." A ghost of a smile prickled her lips. "The cave *is* on my property. He wasn't trespassing."

There was a flicker of amusement in Rook's eyes as he reached under his jacket for handcuffs. "I'll keep that in mind." He turned to Marcus. "You know the routine. Hands behind your back."

Marcus did as Rook said, his face expressionless, his eyes hollow, the sharpness of his facial bones more pronounced than ever.

Cait drew a deep breath when she saw the handcuffs. "Is that necessary?"

"You know the procedure, Cait. I have to take him in for questioning. I will take into consideration that he called me." He snapped the cuffs on Marcus's wrists. "If someone would put those things back in the chest, I'll take them with me." He picked up the gun. "I'll come back to see this mysterious cave."

Cait and Fumié rewrapped the carvings as best they could and returned them to the chest, along with the arrowheads, rug and mask.

RT picked up the chest. "I'll take it out to Rook."

"This looks bad for Marcus," Ilia said.

"I hate that he's going to jail," Fumié said. "Did you see his face? He looked as if the whole world was against him."

Cait had heavier worries. *What happens if Marcus does return? Do I take him back or give him walking papers?*

CHAPTER 39

When Cait went upstairs to the apartment, the last thing on her mind was tomorrow's tea. She sat at the desk, her laptop in front of her, and opened the file she'd created to document everything that had happened since Stanton Lane first called to say she'd inherited the estate.

Her fingers flew over the keys as she recalled her visit to Livermore High School with Detective Rook, the cave, the shotgun, the chest of Indian carvings, and Marcus's arrest. After all that had happened, she was still clueless as to who murdered Tasha and Karl Novak.

She sat back in her chair, steepled her fingers, and stared at the dust motes floating in the shaft of light from the lamp. Tasha's date book sat on the desk next to the laptop. Cait picked it up, leafed through the pages and hesitated when she saw the name June Hart. She remembered the name because of the familiar Oregon area code. She reached in her pocket for her cell phone and then remembered she'd left it downstairs in the kitchen. She used the desk phone to call the number written beneath the name.

After several rings, a woman answered. "Hello?"

"Is this June Hart?"

"Yes."

"My name is Cait Pepper. I found your number in Tasha Bening's date book and wondered if you'd mind if I asked you a few questions about her."

The woman hesitated. "Are you a relative?"

"Yes, I'm Tasha's niece." Easier to keep it that way, she thought.

"Oh. I knew she had a brother, but I don't recall her mentioning a niece."

Stirrings of adrenaline pulsed through her. "That would be my dad. They were twins. By any chance, are you with the Oregon Shakespeare Festival?"

"Yes, but I work behind the scenes now. Not many roles for older actors, but I've found I like it on the other side of curtains."

"So you don't mind talking to me about Tasha?"

"I'm not sure I'm the best one to talk to. We'd been friends a long time, but as you probably know, Tasha was a very private person."

"That's what I hear." Cait paused to encourage June to talk.

"Didn't you know her?"

"Unfortunately, no," Cait said.

"Well, you must be calling from her house because I recognized the phone number." She cleared her throat. "Tasha's sudden death shocked everyone here at the festival," June said. "Now we're all wondering what's to become of her beloved theaters."

"I inherited the estate, and would like to continue with what she started, but I live in Ohio."

"Maybe you'll change your mind. Her husband Hilton Bening and I were related by marriage. He was my husband's cousin. I introduced Tasha and Hilton, but it took years for her to agree to marry him. She thought marriage would interfere with her career."

Just like raising a baby would interrupt her career, Cait thought. "When did you last talk to her?"

"Not more than a week or so before her death."

Cait caught her breath. "Was she worried about anything?"

"How do you mean?"

"Financial or other personal concerns?"

"Not financial." She hesitated. "However, I did notice her usual sense of humor was missing, like something was weighing on her mind. Is there a problem?"

"I was curious about her frame of mind at the time of her death." Cait wondered how far she could push June. She hadn't learned much she didn't already know. "Have you been here to visit?"

"I intended to when Hilton died, but Tasha wanted to be alone. She shut herself off from everyone for a while, like she'd lost her way. Hilton meant the world to her and she to him. Eventually, she got back to business and threw herself into her theaters. She wanted my husband and me to come work for her to help with the festival. We were interested, but the time just wasn't right for us."

"June, there's no good way to say this so I'll just ask. Did Tasha have any enemies, maybe someone who thought she might be a threat to them?"

A small gasp came through the line. "A threat? Are you suggesting Tasha didn't die of a heart attack? That she was murdered?"

She's quick, Cait thought. "I'm saying sometimes things are not always as they appear."

June hesitated. "Oh, dear. I wonder . . ."

Cait sat up straighter in anticipation. "What? If you know something, please tell me."

"I guess it's all right. It's an open secret anyway." A sigh slipped through the phone. "Everyone knows the theater's a hotbed of gossip and at times brutal jealousy. With so much heated passion on stage, sometimes it's difficult to shake it off afterwards. Shakespeare does that to you; it draws you into the role until you feel you're that person. Nothing else compares to it. I'm not saying it's an excuse or insinuating someone harmed Tasha because she landed that envious position with OSF."

Cait grabbed a pen and pad. "What position?" Cait pressed.

"As the AAD, associate artistic director for the production of *Hamlet*. I guess if you didn't know Tasha, you wouldn't know about that."

I didn't know about a lot of things, Cait thought. Could this be a motive for killing Tasha? "Why would she leave her own theaters and return to Ashland?"

"My dear, for the opportunity to direct *Hamlet.*"

Cait jotted notes on the pad. "When exactly was she offered this position?"

"Shortly before she died. Everyone assumed she'd be the board's choice. She was a brilliant actress but had designs on directing, although she never thought it would happen as she got older."

"So this was a temporary position? Just for *Hamlet*?"

June chuckled. "My dear, are you familiar with *Hamlet,* the ultimate ghost story?"

"Of course, who isn't?"

"It's the greatest play ever written. A mystery. Tasha wouldn't have been considered for such a daunting task if she'd not been equal to it. She knew her stuff almost better than anyone in the business. She devoted her life to Shakespeare. When this opportunity was presented to her, she grabbed it."

But did it get her murdered? "She was that good?"

"Absolutely. Working with Tasha was like watching a Bentley purr on the road; you knew if you put your foot down, there was going to be a lot of elegant power. Her strength, vitality, and understanding of *Hamlet* would have added new dimension to the already loved play."

Cait smiled at the simile, but couldn't help wonder about Hilton, and how his death entered into the equation. He was a rancher, not an actor. Maybe his death really was an accident.

June cut into her thoughts. "There aren't enough opportunities for aging Shakespearean actresses. Costumes and makeup can only go so far to make us look younger than we are."

"How many others were considered for this position?"

"I don't know exactly, but a few names were rumored about before Tasha died, and they've resurfaced since then."

"Anyone that stands out?"

June hesitated. "Maybe you should talk to the director Tasha would have been working with. As far as I know, the position is still open."

Cait understood June's reluctance to gossip, particularly to someone she didn't know. "Who would that be?"

"Kenneth Alt. He's busy acting in a couple of productions, but if you leave your number he'll get back to you." She gave Cait his phone number and Cait wrote it on her pad. "You can tell him I gave it to you."

"Have you considered the position?"

June laughed. "Heavens, no. I know my limits."

"Did Tasha tell you the job had been offered to her?"

"Yes, but the board approached me beforehand. They knew we'd been longtime friends and wanted to know if I thought she'd be interested. I told them there was no doubt about it. Later, I heard a letter confirming the appointment had been sent to Tasha after the board made their initial phone call to her and that she had accepted." June hesitated. "I think I see what you mean. The timing of her death does appear suspicious."

A letter?

June continued. "*Hamlet* is heroic, intelligent, and philosophical, all qualities that are part of his undoing. Tasha would have sunk her teeth into the challenge." Her voice cracked a little. "It breaks my heart she never got the chance."

Cait wondered if those same qualities were part of Tasha's

undoing. She thanked June and hung up but remained sitting at the desk thinking about *Hamlet*. After a while, she turned back to her laptop and entered what she remembered about the play and her own conclusion:

Virtually all playgoers know his journey and ultimate fate, but I will not adopt the disposition of a fool as he did to get to the truth behind Tasha's murder.

CHAPTER 40

After identifying Rachel Cross and Karl Novak in the snapshot from Novak's office, recovering the chest of carvings, Marcus's arrest, and then the phone call to June Hart, Cait was too wired to sleep. However, she forced herself to stay in bed so she wouldn't be a basket case by the time for the tea rolled around at four.

Friday morning arrived, and Cait wanted to search the apartment for Tasha's confirmation letter from the OSF board before calling Kenneth Alt.

She thought the desk would be the obvious place to start looking. The belly drawer held the usual pens, pencils, and notepads, a tin of Oregon mints, and a small soapstone dish of loose crystals and stones Cait didn't recognize. She opened the large file drawer and found colorful hanging folders crammed together. After a cursory look at the labels, her hopes rose when she found one labeled OSF, and then fell when she saw it was empty.

Disappointed that it was still only seven o'clock, too early to call Kenneth Alt in Oregon, she went into the bathroom and stood under a hot shower until her skin almost turned red. Wrapped in a large bath towel, she blow-dried her hair, applied her makeup, and then dressed in blue jeans and a white cotton sweater.

By eight-thirty, she was back at the desk and ready to call Kenneth Alt.

"Hello?"

"Mr. Alt?"

"Yes."

"My name is Cait Pepper. I apologize for calling so early. June Hart suggested I talk to you about a play you're going to direct: *Hamlet.*"

"What about it?"

"Tasha Bening was my aunt, and—"

"Oh. I'm terribly sorry for your loss. I was devastated when I heard she'd died. What did you say your name was?"

"Cait Pepper. Is it true Tasha was to be your associate artistic director for the play?"

"Yes."

"Is that position still open?"

He hesitated. "Yes."

Cait picked up a pen. "I assume you know everyone who has applied."

His voice cool, he said, "Of course."

"May I have those names?" she asked.

"Absolutely not. Why would you ask?"

Cait wasn't surprised by his refusal, but thought it was worth a try. "I inherited the Bening estate in California. You can confirm that and my identity if you wish with the Livermore police. I work in law enforcement."

"Police? Why on earth would the police be involved in Tasha's death? And what does any of this have to do with me?"

She detected impatience in his rapid tone of voice. "Tasha's sudden demise is under investigation. The director's position in Ashland may be relevant."

"Relevant? You can't be serious."

"I couldn't be more so," she said, knowing she should have talked to Rook before calling Alt.

After a pause, he cleared his throat. "Well. Give me a number to call to verify your identification. If I'm satisfied, I'll call you back."

Cait gave him Detective Rook's number and her own cell number, and prayed Rook wouldn't blindside her, since she hadn't been entirely honest with Alt about where she worked. While she waited for his call, she read the notes she'd taken while talking to June.

When ten minutes passed and then fifteen, she began to worry. She'd given him Rook's cell phone number in case Rook was out of the office. Her cell phone beeped twenty minutes later.

"Ms. Pepper? Kenneth Alt. I spoke with Detective Rook, but I still don't understand how anyone at the Oregon Shakespeare Festival could possibly have anything to do with Tasha's death."

"I don't either. But as I'm sure Detective Rook confirmed, her death is under investigation. I would like to know who stood to gain from Tasha's death. I would like to have those names to eliminate possible suspects."

Apparently that got his attention because Cait heard a distinct gasp.

"Good Lord. You don't think she was murdered, do you?"

"I'm saying her death is suspicious."

"Christ. Well, there is a short list of three, though I'd swear on the Bard's head that none are capable of killing anyone. Especially Tasha."

"I can appreciate your concern."

Still he hedged. "Have you any idea what this means for me? I *know* these people. I've worked with them over many years. They're professionals. If they ever learn I passed their names on to the police in a murder investigation, they'd never work for me again."

Cait recognized anguish in his voice and felt sorry for him. But sometimes you have to do what you have to do. "Mr. Alt, I promise they won't hear about our conversation from me." With a last effort to convince him, she said, "Wouldn't you rather know if you're working with a criminal?"

"Oh, dear. Well, put that way . . . James Durbin, Kit Marx, and Rachel Cross." He rushed the names together as if one. "Not necessarily in order of choice, you understand."

Rachel? Cait's hand gripped the pen hard as she wrote the names in her notebook. "Perfectly. One last question. Have you reached a decision about who your choice will be?"

"Yes. And no, you may not have that name."

"I understand. Thank you."

CHAPTER 41

Cait stared at the names, but only one stood out. It wasn't a complete surprise; Rachel was ambitious.

Cait wondered if Rachel knew she was on the short list of applicants. She recalled what June Hart had said about makeup not hiding the signs of aging under the bright lights on stage, and the energy it took to compete against much younger talent. *Has Rachel's time come to move on?*

Cait closed her notebook, turned out the light, and went downstairs. RT strolled in the back door as she poured herself a cup of coffee.

He smiled. "You look all made up. Nice."

She seldom wore makeup, but wanted to put a little more effort into her appearance. "Thanks." Something was different about RT this morning, she thought. Not his usual tight jeans and fitted T-shirt he wore most days, but something else.

"There you go, staring at me again," he said.

"You look different somehow. Happy."

"Why, Cait. I believe you're clairvoyant." He reached out and tugged on one of her curls. "I just sold my third children's book."

"Great. Congratulations. What a lucky little girl Mindy is to have her daddy write books for her to read."

He smiled. "Got something for you." He disappeared into the office and quickly returned carrying a single yellow rose in a crystal budvase. "For luck today."

His thoughtfulness tugged at her emotions; her cheeks flushed. "What a nice thing to do." She smiled. "Thank you."

"You're welcome. Let's sit. I have something to tell you."

Cait set the vase on the counter and pulled out a stool. "I was going to ask you to help me set up the chairs in the front room, but someone already did it. Was that you?"

RT filled a coffee mug and then joined Cait. "Nope. That was Marcus."

She stared at him. "Marcus? But—"

"He came in early. He was released last night. Rook called to let me know and to ask if I thought it would be okay if Marcus came by the house. Apparently, he was worried about the setup in the front room."

"I'm stunned. Is he still here?"

He shook his head. "He left. He set out the dishes Tasha liked to use." He pointed to plates and cups stacked near the sink. "They'll need to be rinsed."

She set her coffee down and went over to see the dishes—rose-covered china plates with an indentation to set a teacup on. The last time Cait drank from a real china cup was the last time she'd visited her grandmother before she died. "I'll have Fumié rinse them when she gets here." She sat back down and sipped her coffee. "Is Marcus coming back?"

"Probably, but maybe not today. He's on probation."

She nodded. "He's not a bad person, but he is seriously troubled." She glanced at the wall clock and couldn't believe it was eleven. "Have you seen Rachel?"

"Nope."

"I talked to a friend of Tasha's yesterday. June Hart, she's connected with the Oregon Shakespeare Festival."

"How did you know about her?" he asked.

"Tasha's date book."

RT laughed. "You got a lot of mileage from that book. First

Karl Novak, now this Hart person."

Cait rolled her eyes. She told him about the associate artistic director position and the missing confirmation letter. "Did you know about it?"

He shook his head. "No, she didn't mention it. Is it important?"

Cait wrapped her hands around her coffee mug and watched RT out of the corner of her eye. "Rachel is one of three up for that position now."

He scowled and set his coffee down. "Cait—"

"Jealousy's a strong motivator for murder, RT. If I can find that letter, I'll turn it over to Rook."

"Interesting theory, but where did you get the names?"

"From Kenneth Alt."

He stared at her. "Who the hell is Kenneth Alt? Don't tell me. You got his name from Tasha's date book."

She smiled. "Not this time. He's a director at OSF. June Hart thought I should call him." She told him about their conversation and his connection to Tasha.

RT drained his coffee. "Have you told Rook about this?"

"Not yet, but I will. RT, if Rachel gets that job, she'll leave and I'll be left to find someone to replace her." She glanced at him. "Rachel never mentioned anything about this to you?"

The corner of his mouth curled up. "Rachel stopped confiding in me."

"Since when? She purrs like a kitten every time she looks at you."

RT laughed. "She's an actress and a tease. You know that."

"So why'd she stop talking to you?"

A slow smile spread over his face as he turned to her. "She thinks you and I are an item."

Her hand froze on her coffee mug. "You've got to be kidding."

He raised his eyebrow. "Would that be so bad?"

Stunned, and at a loss for words, she looked away.

RT took her chin in his hand, forcing her to look at him. "What's going through your mind?"

Oh, God. "It wouldn't be a good idea."

"That doesn't sound like a no to me."

"It would be awkward." *You'll be leaving, and I'm not interested in a quickie affair.* She set her coffee mug down before she spilled it. "Where was Rachel when Tasha died?"

"Okay, change of subject. She was in the UK. You know that."

Right. Her brain suddenly muddled, she struggled to think. "The night of the fire . . . Rachel didn't shed a tear when you told her Tasha was dead. She was more concerned about the fire."

"That was Rachel being Rachel." He leaned over and brushed his lips over Cait's temple. "Can we just get through today and discuss this later?"

"My, my. How poignant." Rachel came in the back door.

Cait jumped away from RT.

A slight smile curved Rachel's red lips. "Don't let me interrupt. I'm here to get something off the computer." She went in the office, her heels clicking against the tile floor.

"Whatever you're thinking, forget it," RT whispered in Cait's ear. "I kinda like the idea of us being an item."

While his words spread through her body like fine wine, she was thinking how she could get Rachel's house key back. She heard the computer boot up in the office. "I need to talk to her."

"Be nice." He pecked her cheek.

Cait hesitated in the doorway and watched Rachel attack the keyboard. "Got a minute?"

Without looking up, Rachel said, "Let me print this first." She reached over and turned the printer on.

Cait's cell phone beeped. She pulled it off her belt, glanced at the screen, and turned her back on Rachel. "What's up, Ilia?"

"You should have music for the tea this afternoon. Fumié plays the guitar and sings like an angel. Want me to ask her?"

Cait recalled the haunting music she'd overheard Fumié sing. "Yes. Do you think she'll do it?"

"Leave it to me," he said and hung up.

Rachel entered the kitchen with a sheet of paper in her hand. "Walk out with me."

Outside, Cait waited until they'd rounded the corner of the house, then said, "I heard Tasha was to be the associate artistic director for *Hamlet* at the Oregon Shakespeare Festival."

Rachel tripped but quickly regained her balance. "So?"

"It's sad she died before she had the chance to fulfill her dream."

"People don't die on schedule, Cait."

What a cold thing to say. "Are you interested in directing?"

"Sure, who isn't?"

"Did Tasha tell you she'd accepted the position?"

"I don't remember. It doesn't matter now."

"Everything matters, Rachel, when an unexpected death occurs."

Rachel stood beside her Mercedes. "Is there a point to this conversation? If not, I have things to do." She pointed her key fob at her car. A sharp beep sounded.

"It's a motive for murder."

Rachel stared at her. "Don't be silly. She died from a heart attack." She opened the driver's door. "Be careful, Cait. Murder's a dangerous sport. Don't make accusations you can't back up." She slid in behind the wheel.

Is she threatening me? "Rachel, if you're concealing vital information, you need go to the police."

"You don't know what you're talking about."

"I'm talking about possibly three murders. You may have information you're not aware of."

Color drained from Rachel's face. "Three?"

"Tasha, Karl Novak, and Hilton."

Rachel gasped. "Everyone knows Hilton fell from his horse and hit his head on a rock. How is that murder?"

"That's what the police think happened. I'm not so sure."

"Excuse me, but this sounds suspiciously like a police interrogation." She slammed the door shut and started the engine, drove a few feet, and then stopped. She rolled the window down. "Why can't you be satisfied? You've inherited a nice piece of property. You're a wealthy woman now. I'm sorry about Tasha. Your aunt was a good person. I miss her."

Cait approached the car. "That's the problem, Rachel. Tasha wasn't my aunt. She was my birth mother. That's why it's important to find who murdered her."

Rachel's jaw dropped, a shriek tore from her mouth.

Cait and Rachel stared at each other for a few seconds before Rachel stomped on the gas and squealed out of the driveway.

CHAPTER 42

The caterers arrived at two-thirty with trays of canapés. Cait and Fumié rinsed and dried Tasha's dishes while volunteers set up tables in the front room. Cait worked robotically, her mind on Rachel and her reaction when she learned that Tasha was Cait's birth mother. When her cell phone beeped, she went into the gift shop to take the call.

"Hello."

"You must be busy preparing for your tea so I won't keep you long," Rook said. "Did RT tell you I called about Marcus?"

"Yes, he told me. Marcus set up the chairs in the front room and also set out Tasha's favorite dishes. But he's not here now."

"I'm glad it worked out. About Kenneth Alt. He was under the impression we worked together."

"I never said that. I told him I work in law enforcement. How he interpreted that is his problem."

Rook laughed. "I didn't tell him otherwise, so your secret is safe."

"Thanks." She liked the detective, even if he was hung up on the territorial issue.

"Did he give you what you wanted?"

She walked around the gift shop, fingering merchandise on the shelves. "Yes. I have news for you." She told him about the job at the Oregon festival, Tasha's acceptance and the missing letter, and the names on the short list as possible replacements for Tasha. "Does it surprise you Rachel's one of them?"

"No. She may be ambitious, but that's not a motive for murder last time I checked. Where did you hear about Alt?"

"From June Hart, whose name was in Tasha's date book."

He chuckled. "I'd like to see that book sometime."

"Anytime." Splashes of color on the walls from the stained-glass window behind the counter mesmerized Cait. For a moment she lost track of what she wanted to say. "Jealousy can be a strong motive for murder, Detective. With Tasha dead, the three on the short list have to be considered suspects until proven otherwise." She walked out of the room and down the hall to the front room. "I wanted to know what Rachel knew and if she had any interest in directing. Turns out, she does." She sighed. "Then I told her about my real relationship to Tasha. That didn't go over very well."

"You're like a thorn in one's side, aren't you?"

Pissed off, Cait said, "Maybe so, but how else am I going to find a murderer?"

"That's my job, remember?"

"Look, Detective Rook, Rachel Cross knows something. I'm going to find out what." She gathered her composure. "The tea starts at four. You're invited."

"I'll try to be there on one condition."

She hated conditions. "What?"

"My name is Ace. I have a feeling we're going to be seeing a lot more of each other."

She smiled. "Done, Ace." Cait snapped her cell shut. She didn't expect they'd become buddies, but if calling him by his first name was all it took for him to think of her as an equal, that's what she'd do.

Cait went to the kitchen, picked up the crystal vase with the yellow rose RT had given her, and went back in the front room and set it on the grand piano. She checked her watch: three-fifteen. She raced upstairs to change into the festive outfit she'd hung out. She pivoted before the twin mirrors attached to the inside of the wardrobe doors. Her favorite skirt swirled around her calves, its gathered tiers in colors of merlot wine and black. She pulled a black knit top over her head and tugged at the lace peeking out at the V neckline. The stretch belt in silver tones of metal links finished the look Cait desired, thanks to her friend Samantha, who had included it in the box of clothes she had sent.

She went over to the window and looked down on the vineyard and across the road toward Rachel's house. She wanted Rachel at the tea, but was afraid she'd offended her earlier and she might choose to stay away.

Later, when she went downstairs, RT was standing at the piano looking at the yellow rose. He turned and smiled when he heard her. Then he whistled. "You clean up real nice." He made no attempt to hide his approval as his eyes slid from her cleavage down to her black leather peek-toed pumps. "Since we're all dressed up, it would be a shame to waste it. Would you like to go out to dinner later?"

Hot pulses flashed through her body. *Lord, the man is good.* "Are you asking me on a date?"

He smiled. "Yes ma'am, I am."

Cait absorbed his slow smile, thinking it definitely should be registered as a lethal weapon. She admired the fit of his dark-blue suit, light-blue shirt, and maroon silk tie. "Nice suit."

Fumié and Ilia came into the front room, she with her guitar and he with his camera around his neck. "Perfect." Ilia grinned. "Now if you two would stand by the piano, I'll take your picture."

Cait and RT looked at each other. "Sure, why not?" they said in unison. RT put his arm around her waist and pulled her close.

It seemed to Cait that Ilia took his time finding the right

angle while she inhaled RT's aftershave lotion.

The doorbell chimed as Ilia took their picture. "Great. Thanks," he said.

Lauren Ballard, president of Las Positas College, was the first to arrive, along with three of her students, who would take turns reading excerpts from Shakespeare. Livermore City Council members arrived shortly after followed by a man from the Commission for the Arts. Cait lost track of names, but several people were from local wineries.

Ilia moved about the room snapping pictures and jotting on a notepad. Fumié strolled among the guests, her guitar draped over her shoulder, her soft voice radiating like a gentle mist.

"Nice touch," RT said, motioning toward Fumié. "The girl's got talent." He glanced around the crowded room. "I expected Rachel here by now."

Cait wasn't so sure. "Maybe she's waiting to make a grand entrance."

The front door opened and Stanton Lane walked in. Cait hadn't talked with him since she'd called to thank him for sending the poetry book that she still hadn't taken the time to open.

"I didn't know he was coming," she whispered to RT.

"Rachel probably invited him."

Lane was making his way over to them. "Good afternoon, Cait, RT," he said. "Looks like a pleasant group."

"I think so," Cait said.

"I was surprised to see a Channel Five News van pull up behind me," he said.

Cait looked from Lane to RT. "You're kidding. Why in the world . . . who told them about it?"

"The logical assumption is Rachel, but why?" RT said.

Cait wasn't fond of the press. She'd never forget her one appearance in court on a high-profile homicide case she'd worked on. During recess, the press got in her face and ruthlessly questioned her testimony.

"By the way, where is Rachel?" Lane asked as he glanced around the room.

"I don't know." Cait saw Bo and his family enter from the back hallway. "Excuse me."

RT followed her. "Are you going to wait for Rachel?"

"We'll give her a few more minutes." She smiled at the Tuck family. "I'm so glad you came."

"I picked a horse for you," Joy said from her wheelchair, her violet eyes sparkling.

"Oh gosh, honey. I don't know if I could stay on one."

"I'll teach you. I was really good before this happened." Joy tapped the arm of her chair.

Cait clenched her teeth. "Do I have a choice?"

"No, ma'am," Bo said and then shook hands with RT.

"How about tomorrow?" Joy said.

"Ummm. Let me think about it, okay?"

Cait had only seen Bo in blue jeans and plaid shirts. Today, he wore pressed chinos and a white sports shirt. His dark-blond hair, like his clothes, was casual and with hints of the California sun. Khandi's cream silk blouse complemented her warm cocoa complexion. Her black skirt flowed to the middle of her black boots. A long, thick braid hung down her back.

Cait pointed to the front room and the tables against the outside wall. "Canapés and tea are over there. Help yourself while I get this party started." She peeked at her watch—four twenty-five—and then took one last look around the room. When the front door opened, she expected to see Rachel. Instead, a man with a camera and a woman walked in. They had Channel Five insignias on their jackets. With everyone now seated, she focused her attention on the guests.

Cait smiled as she stepped to the piano. "Thank you all for coming this afternoon. I'm Cait Pepper, Tasha Bening's niece.

As you probably know by now, Tasha bequeathed her estate to me. But to be honest, I haven't a clue how to manage a Shakespeare festival, but I am willing to learn."

Their laughter eased Cait's apprehension. She glanced over at RT and saw him purse his lips and shrug. Still no Rachel. She continued. "I know even less about running a vineyard, but Royal Tanner is here and he's promised to educate me." She drew a deep breath. "What I do know something about is law enforcement. I was a police officer in Ohio before I became a crime analyst. However, I want you to know that I am committed to continuing Tasha's legacy." After a small spate of applause, she smiled and raised her hand to direct their attention to Fumié standing next to the food table. "The beautiful music you heard as you arrived was provided by our own Fumié Ondo."

Ilia snapped a picture of the blushing Fumié as she grinned and nodded to acknowledge the clapping.

Cait turned the meeting over to Lauren Ballard and her students, and went over to stand by the news folks. Her voice low, she asked the female reporter why a simple tea was news.

"Apparently someone thought this was an opportunity to explore rumors of another murder at this estate," the woman said. "I'm sorry, but I promise we won't interrupt the tea."

Cait forced a smile to hide her dismay and focused her attention on the Shakespeare readings, but she couldn't cover her ears to silence the humming sounds from the news photographer's camera.

CHAPTER 43

The house was quiet and empty except for Cait and RT. The tea had lasted a couple of hours, but a few local vintners lingered until almost seven, offering suggestions about learning the business of growing and harvesting a vineyard.

RT dragged his fingers over the ivory keys on the grand piano. "Relax, Cait. It's over. Everyone had a good time."

"I think so, too. But I'm concerned about Rachel."

"I know. If she hasn't surfaced by tomorrow, give her a call." He struck a chord on the piano. "Do you play?"

"I wish. Unfortunately, I lack the talent. Obviously, you play."

He pulled out the bench and sat down and played through several bars of "Wind Beneath My Wings." "I don't read music. I improvise," he told her as the last notes faded away.

Cait watched RT's hands move over the keyboard. *This macho Navy SEAL is a man of many talents,* she thought. "That was beautiful. Please don't stop."

He rose and tucked a flyaway lock of her hair behind her ear. "We have a dinner date."

"We don't have to go out. There are plenty of leftover canapés. We could open a bottle of wine, and you could show me what else you can play. Pianos need to be used or they'll get out of tune."

He wiggled his eyebrows. "Sounds like a plan."

Cait pulled trays of canapés from the refrigerator and set them out on the counter. "Rachel said the actors for *Tongue of a*

268

Bird would be here soon to begin rehearsals. It's sold out, so I doubt another rumor of murder would affect it, but I'd sure like to know who invited the media here."

He pulled the cork on the wine bottle. "They didn't stay long. Better yet, I didn't see them talking to anyone."

"I didn't either. At least the union hasn't pulled their actors out of their contract." She went back to the refrigerator for strawberry cheesecake.

"Rook's promised to have off-duty cops here in case there's a problem." RT took two wine glasses from the cupboard.

"Maybe that's not such a good idea, particularly if they're in uniform. You'll be here, and I'm not exactly a neophyte."

"Cait, that is not up for negotiation. Besides, we promised the union there would be security. Now, we're supposed to be on a date. Let's make the most of it. Let's take everything upstairs where it's more comfortable."

"I thought you were going to play the piano for me."

"I will, later. Right now I'm starved. I'd rather not eat on a folding chair." He grabbed the bottle and glasses. "You grab the trays."

Upstairs in the apartment's sitting room, Cait set the trays of food on the coffee table and peeled back the aluminum foil. "There's a microwave in this kitchen. It'll only take a few minutes to heat the canapés."

He poured the wine into the glasses and handed one to her after she returned from the kitchen. "To success."

She tapped his glass with hers and then sipped her wine. "It feels strange being in this room. I usually bypass it and go on up to the bedroom."

"You've been busy." He sat down at one end of the sofa and patted the seat next to him. "Sit."

The buzzer on the microwave went off.

Cait put the food on a tray, set it on the coffee table, and then sat at the opposite end of the sofa from RT.

RT slid to the middle of the sofa next to Cait. He grinned. "Isn't this nice?"

Cait ate one canapé and reached for another, aware of RT's warm body next to hers, then drank her wine.

He smiled over the rim of his glass. "Do I make you uncomfortable?"

She ate the canapé. "Why would you think that?"

"Maybe because you've suddenly become very quiet," he said.

"I was thinking about where the Navy might send you when you leave here."

He ate a ham-and-cheese canapé.

"Some land of vampires and werewolves?"

"You can bet it'll be top secret." After consuming a mushroom canapé and some more wine, he said, "Do you like this wine?"

She looked at her glass. "Very much."

He refilled their glasses. "This Chardonnay was made from the very first harvest of Bening grapes. I've been saving it for a special occasion." He set his glass on the table, took Cait's glass from her and set it next to his, then held his hand out to her and pulled her to her feet. He touched his lips to hers and nibbled on her lower lip.

Cait kissed him back, taste for taste, need for need, as warmth from the wine and RT spread through her. He tilted her head back with a lingering kiss that left no doubt how much he wanted her. A lifetime of undiscovered sensuality stirred and awakened in her body.

He kissed her neck. "Let's go upstairs."

Unable to resist, she let him guide her to the stairwell that would take them to the third floor. Her hand shook as she fumbled in her skirt pocket for the key to unlock the door.

As soon as they stepped out of the stairwell, RT pulled her

against him, fumbled with her belt and dropped it on the floor. His breath husky, he said, "You've got a strange hold on me, Caitlyn Pepper. I don't understand it, but it's impossible to resist."

Oh, God. What's wrong with me? Why don't I stop him? Her heart pounded; she began to fall apart at his touch.

He stepped away long enough to pull her sweater over her head and drop it to the floor next to her belt. "You are so beautiful," he whispered in her ear. His hands slid under her camisole and caressed her skin.

Cait trembled, her breathing quick and strained. She wanted to hang on and never let go. He'd left his suit jacket downstairs, but his tie hung loosely around his neck. She pulled it off, unbuttoned his shirt, dropped both on the floor and ran her fingers over his muscular chest with just the right amount of curly black hair. His kisses were hot and wet; he unzipped his trousers as he backed her over to the bed. Lowering his head to kiss the valley between her breasts, he pulled her skirt down and tossed it. "Kiss me," he said, his voice a husky command.

A small moan rose from her throat under the sweet seduction of his hands.

CHAPTER 44

Cait's cell phone rang early Saturday morning. When she rolled over to reach for it, she knocked Lane's poetry book off the bedside table and onto the floor.

She blinked a couple of times to clear her eyes and then saw the call was from Shep. "Good morning."

"Did I wake you?" he said.

She tossed the covers back and sat up. "No." She glanced the clock: half past eight. "How are you?"

"I'm good. Sorry. I keep forgetting about the time difference."

"I was up, just not wide awake. Are you at work?" she asked.

"Not yet. I worked late into the night. Thought about how we used to shoot the breeze to kill time while we sat in the car expecting something to happen."

Her voice softened with remembrance. "Seems like a long time ago."

He laughed. "It *was* a long time ago, Cait. How was your tea party?"

"Okay. The people were nice enough."

"Told you so." His voice turned serious. "Listen, Cait, what I called about . . . the chief wants to know if you're any closer to catching Tasha's killer."

She stood and paced in front of the bed. "He just granted me a two-month leave, Shep. Why is he asking about that now?"

"I'm only the messenger."

"I know. Look, I went ahead and drafted my letter of resignation." She went to the window and looked down on the glistening vineyard. "I'm vacillating about sending it. The decision is driving me crazy. I should just do it . . . get it over with."

"I wish I could help you make that decision. Use those couple of months. For now, concentrate on finding a killer."

"You're right." The sun danced through the stained-glass windows, splashing the walls with color.

Neither spoke for a while, and then Shep asked, "Have you got any leads?"

"Maybe. Detective Rook and I went to the high school. Karl Novak, the dead PI, and Rachel Cross were high-school sweethearts. They're the couple in that old snapshot I told you about, the one from Novak's office."

"Yeah, right. Talk to her. She might know something about the killer, particularly if she stayed in contact with Novak."

She walked back to the bed and sat down on the edge. "I will, but she didn't come to the tea because of a conversation we had earlier."

"Try anyway. Sometimes people know things they don't know they know until it's brought up."

"All right." She hesitated. "Shep, do you think the department would let me buy my gun?"

"Not a chance. It's department property. It would be easier to buy one there."

She chewed on her lower lip.

"You want your Glock as a keepsake of your time spent with the department, don't you?"

"Am I that transparent?"

"Afraid so. Get yourself another gun for protection. Maybe a small twenty-two-caliber Glock."

She picked up the poetry book that had fallen on the floor and started to set it back on the table when a folded sheet of

paper slipped out. She opened it. "Oh, my God. The OSF letter."

"What?" Shep said.

"Shep, I just found the letter from the Shakespeare festival in
Oregon. They sent it to Tasha confirming she got the artistic
director's job." She laughed. "It wasn't a rumor."

"Good. Now what are you going to do with it?"

"I'm not sure. Give it to Detective Rook, I guess. You know
what this means? I've been thinking all along jealousy and
revenge played a part in Tasha's death."

"You've got one of the best instincts in the business. Let me
know what comes of it. In the meantime, I'll tell the chief your
hunt for a murderer is progressing."

After they hung up, Cait took the letter over to the window.
It hit her then that Stanton Lane must have seen the letter. She
frowned. *Why didn't he tell me? Did he put it in the book for me to
find?* When she started to refolded the letter, she saw writing on
the back.

She couldn't believe what she saw.

CHAPTER 45

Cait massaged her temples. Why had Tasha accepted the associate artistic director's job and then changed her mind? Had someone coerced her into recommending Rachel? Did Kenneth Alt know? She checked the date of the letter: March ninth. It had been typed twelve days before Tasha was murdered.

She paced between the bed and the bay window.

Her cell phone buzzed. She didn't want to talk with anyone right now, but when she glanced at the screen she was surprised to see the Columbus Police Department number. "Hello."

"Cait, Chief Flynn."

"Chief, I just got off the phone with Shep."

"I know. My intent wasn't to hassle you to make a quick decision, but to offer assistance or advice if you need it. Don't send your resignation letter until you are absolutely sure it's the best decision for you. Are we clear on that?"

"Yes, sir. Thank you."

He cleared his throat. "Okay. Shep mentioned your gun. He's right. It belongs to the department. Hold on a moment."

Cait recognized the voice she heard in the background.

"Dot wants to know if it's okay to call you to discuss the frat case," he continued.

"Of course. I want to keep up with it."

"Good. I'll pass your number on to her. Be safe, Cait."

After they hung up, Cait sat at the desk with her laptop and reread the draft of her resignation letter. Only days ago, she thought she was prepared mentally to resign from the police department, but after Shep's call and now the chief's, she hesitated.

Two months. I've always been one to make quick decisions, not delay the inevitable. So why am I vacillating now? Because my future hangs on my decision.

She closed the laptop, stood, and headed to the bathroom. Thirty minutes later she was headed downstairs with her handbag and the OSF letter. She paused in the kitchen doorway when she saw RT sitting at the kitchen counter writing on a yellow legal pad. She tried to frown to cover the flush of heat she felt through her body and the tightening knot in the pit of her stomach at the sight of him.

He must have mistaken her frown for anger because he raised his hands over his head. "Honest to God, Cait, I thought last night was consensual."

She grinned, thinking he looked good enough to nibble on for breakfast. "Relax and read this." She handed him Tasha's letter.

With a look of confusion on his face, he looked at it. "Oh, that letter. You found it." He smiled. "You had me worried there for a moment."

"It was in Stanton Lane's poetry book all this time. Turn it over."

His brow furrowed as he read Tasha's note. "This doesn't make sense." He handed the letter back to her.

She tucked it in her handbag and took out her cell phone. "Let's see what Stanton Lane has to say about it."

"It's Saturday. He won't be in his office."

She dug in her handbag and found Lane's business card. "I'll try his office first, but I have his home number on his card."

She punched in Lane's number.

Surprised when his secretary answered, she said, "Is Mr.

Lane in? It's Cait Pepper."

Lane came on the line immediately. "Morning, Cait. Enjoyed your tea party yesterday."

"Thanks for coming. I'm surprised to find you in your office but promise this will be quick. I found the letter from the OSF board to Tasha. It was in your poetry book."

"Really? How forgetful of me," he said.

She rolled her eyes at RT. "I assume you saw Tasha's note on the back and know she changed her mind about taking the job."

"Of course. I was as confused as you sound, Cait, but she refused to discuss it with me."

"I wish you'd told me about it."

"I'm sorry. It slipped my mind. Tasha wanted to get her thoughts straight before acting on the OSF offer."

"Do you think Rachel knows?" Cait asked.

"If she does, she didn't hear it from me."

That's what she wanted to know. "Do you think Tasha was getting pressure from someone? Why else would she change her mind?"

Lane hesitated. "I know she was afraid, but she wouldn't talk about that either."

"Did she think Hilton was murdered and thought she could be next?"

"She insinuated as much, but as I said, she wouldn't discuss it with me. I wanted her to go to the police. This was the one and only argument we ever had. Cait, I've not mentioned this to anyone, not even the police"—his voice cracked—"but the more I thought about it the more I was convinced it was that damn directing job that got her killed. Not a heart attack."

"I think you're right. Were you aware she wanted to buy a gun?"

"No, but if she had, I think she would have used it to protect herself. She was a gutsy lady."

"Then for heaven's sake why didn't she have a lock on the bedroom door and a security system installed?" Cait asked.

"I can't answer that except to say she was too trusting. I advised her to hire a private security firm but she never did. I loved her, Cait, but she had a stubborn streak."

She felt sorry for Lane and wanted him to know the truth about RT. "She did have someone—Royal Tanner. He's here on pretense: stage manager." She glanced at RT.

"But, I thought . . . oh, dear God. All this time I thought . . ."

"Don't worry about it. RT understands." She smiled at RT, who now stood next to her rubbing her back. "He knows he's a poor substitute for stage manager."

"I'm embarrassed. I should have been told," he said.

"Mr. Lane, will you call me if you remember anything about the last time you saw or talked to Tasha?"

"Of course I will. I'm glad we talked about this. Watch yourself."

"I will." She snapped her cell phone shut.

"Poor substitute? Give me a break." RT tipped her chin up and kissed her on the lips.

The back door swung open. "Oops. Sorry," Ilia said, and backed out.

"Get in here, Ilia," Cait said. "RT's just being playful."

Ilia grinned and walked back into the kitchen. "I've got pictures for you from yesterday. What happened to Rachel?"

Cait called the LPD and learned Detective Rook was in conference. Just when he was beginning to come around and let her in on the case, she didn't want to withhold evidence. The letter from the OSF was important. After about an hour, RT drove them into town to see Rook.

"I do have other talents," RT said out of the blue.

She didn't know what he was talking about, but then her

cheeks flared with remembrance of last night.

He laughed. "Growing grapes. What did you think I meant?"

"I knew that," she said, trying to hide her flushed cheeks.

Fifteen minutes later RT pulled into the police station and parked. They went up to the front doors and pushed the buzzer.

"May I help you?" a voice answered.

"Cait Pepper to see Detective Rook. I have an appointment," she lied.

"One moment." The door finally clicked to let them in.

They had just sat down when they heard a door open and a woman storm out, her heels snapping on the marble floor like bullets as she rushed to the front door.

"Do you think Rachel saw us?" Cait said.

RT shook his head. "No. She was too angry to notice us."

Detective Rook approached them. "I didn't know we had an appointment."

RT and Cait stood. "Sorry, my mistake. Why was Rachel here?" Cait asked.

He raised his eyebrow. "You know better than to ask."

Cait liked to push the envelope. Sometimes it worked, sometimes not. Today was not one of the better times. "I have something to show you."

Rook motioned to a door. "I hope it's good news. Let's go in here." He unlocked the interview room and turned on the light. "Have a seat." The door clicked shut behind them.

Cait and RT settled into chairs across the table from the detective.

Cait opened her handbag and took out the letter. She slid it across the table to Rook.

Rook picked it up. "Tasha's letter of confirmation," he said as he read it.

"Turn it over," Cait said, eager to see his reaction.

His brow furrowed as he read Tasha's note. "Does Rachel

know about this?"

"I don't think so. I asked Lane, but he said he didn't tell her." Cait told him about her talk with Rachel before the tea. "She skipped the tea."

A slight smile crossed his face. "You must have offended her. By the way, I'm sorry I couldn't make it."

Cait nodded. "It's okay."

Rook laced his fingers together on the table. "I did a little digging and learned Novak broke up with Rachel and started dating a new girl on the cheerleading squad. This girl won the spot that Rachel had held for two years."

Cait moved to the edge of her chair. "Ouch. I bet that didn't go over well."

"That's not all. There was an accident. The girl fell during rehearsal and broke her neck. She's been in a wheelchair ever since. Rachel reclaimed her spot."

Cait stared at him. "Really?"

He nodded.

She waited for him to elaborate, but when he didn't she said, "So, are we looking at a pattern here?"

Rook shrugged. "I don't know."

Cait studied her fingernails. "What are we going to do about it?"

Rook tried to suppress a smile. "We? I'm the detective on this case."

With a sigh, Cait picked up her handbag and stood. "That incident happened thirty years ago. Who holds a grudge that long?"

"Depends," RT said, "on the green-eyed monster."

Rook rose. "Appreciate your coming in. I'll keep this letter, if you don't mind."

CHAPTER 46

Traffic had picked up by the time Cait and RT were back on the road. She watched a group of bicyclists in yellow jerseys ahead of them. Feeling depressed about Tasha's letter and note, she said, "I wish I had time to play in the sun like those guys."

RT looked over at her. "You will. How about we go to the ranch? Joy has a horse picked out for you to ride, remember?"

Cheered up, she replied, "I'd love to. We can ask Bo to show us where Hilton fell from his horse."

"It's been months since then, Cait. I doubt we'd find any evidence."

"I know, but it won't hurt to have a look."

A few miles out Mines Road, RT slowed and then drove under the arch to the ranch, dropping his speed to keep the dust down. "I'd like to bring Mindy out here sometime to meet Joy."

"You should send Joy one of your children's books."

He smiled. "Good idea."

RT parked off to the right of the barn. "Bo still carries a burden of guilt for Hilton's death. He may act tough sometimes, but he's sensitive about inheriting the ranch. He's worried some of the neighboring ranchers will wonder if he had something to do with the accident."

"He said as much when I was here." She thought the situation was similar to what Detective Rook told her about his brother, the Navy SEAL who died while on assignment with

RT, and how RT admitted he'd been haunted with guilt for not being able to save him. "Innocent people are always first to blame themselves when there's nothing they could have done to prevent a tragedy."

RT frowned and stared hard at Cait, his lips pursed.

Bo and Khandi approached the Hummer. "Afternoon," Bo said. "You folks come to visit or just content to hang out in that fancy vehicle?"

RT and Cait opened their doors and stepped out. "Hey," RT said as he and Bo shook hands.

Bo slipped two fingers beneath the rim of his hat and pushed it back. "Nice tea party, Cait. Thanks for inviting us."

"I'm glad you could make it."

"Would you like to come up to the house for something to drink?" Khandi asked.

Cait looked at RT. He shrugged. "Thanks. Some other time," she said. It surprised her how much she'd come to like the ranch. "Would it be okay if we visited Faro?"

"Don't see why not," Bo said. "Let's cut through the barn."

The scent of hay and earthy undertones of animals permeated the barn. Cait noticed a saddle she hadn't seen before hanging on a post next to Faro's stall. The leather was worn in a couple of places but buffed to a shine, the seat embroidered in colorful patterns of leaves and flowers. When she saw the initials HB burned into one side, she got a sudden chill.

"Bo, I don't remember seeing this here before," she said.

"It's Hilton's," Bo said. "I cleaned it up a bit and buffed out some scratches."

Cait ran her finger over the initials, as if expecting an answer to Hilton's death. "Did the police examine the saddle when they were here or search Faro's stall?"

Bo stared at her from beneath the brim of his hat. "No. Why would they?"

To be thorough in their investigation. "Okay if I have a look in the stall?"

"Suit yourself." He opened the gate and stepped aside to let her enter.

"Smells of fresh hay and disinfectant," she said.

"A clean stall is a vital requirement," he said. "The stall will be ready when Faro's ready to come in."

Khandi slipped her arm around Bo's waist. "We always honor Hilton's guiding principle: cleanliness is next to godliness. Effective stable management keeps horses healthy and happy in an unnatural environment." She smiled as she swung her arms out to imply she meant the barn.

Impressed, Cait stood a moment before entering the stall. She appreciated that she wouldn't have to muck around in horse manure. The chance of finding any evidence of tampering at this late date was nil, but it wouldn't hurt to have a look, if only to satisfy herself. She crouched on her heels and poked through the hay. Shadows were a deterrent and she had to squint to see.

"If you smell like shit when you're done in there," RT said, "you're walking home."

She ignored him and widened her search. She brushed at a speck of white, assuming it was either dust or a crumb. Instead, it was a silver stud. She picked it up, examined it, and then stood up.

"What's that?" Bo asked.

"Jewelry." She showed it to Bo.

Bo groaned. "I have a new hand. He likes jewelry." He dropped the stud in his shirt pocket.

Instead of kicking the hay around with the toe of her shoe, Cait dropped down on her hands and knees, her attention focused on the sides where she'd noticed the fresh hay had missed some of the edges.

After a while, something caught her eye. If the sun hadn't

settled on a section across from the window, she might have missed it. A speck of blue nestled in the hay. She assumed it was another stud, but when she separated the hay she picked up a tiny blue pill and put it in the palm of her hand.

"Got something else?" Bo asked, worry in his voice.

Cait got to her feet, walked over to Bo and held out her hand. "What's this?"

Bo took the pill and shook his head. "Shit. Don't recognize it, but let's go to the clinic."

"Good job," RT whispered as they followed Bo and Khandi out the rear of the barn.

In his clinic, Bo looked through his bottles of pills. "Didn't think so. It's not one of mine. Most medicines I keep come in liquid form."

"Maybe your new hand likes more than jewelry," Cait said.

He frowned. "Everyone who works for me knows the rules. No eating, no drinking, and no drugs in the barn. Hilton set those rules, and I enforce them. I'll look into this."

"Do you remember who was around the morning Hilton fell?" Cait asked. "A delivery person maybe, another rancher?"

Bo shook his head. "I don't recall." He looked at Khandi.

Khandi shrugged. "I was up at the house. If there'd been a delivery, I would have been called. That day, when Faro returned without Hilton, one of our hands was worried and went looking for him. He found Hilton and called us on his cell phone." Her chin quivered. "It wasn't long before the place was swarming with people—police, medics, neighbors. Hilton was well known; everyone loved and respected him."

Cait thought Khandi was about to cry.

Bo pulled Khandi close and hugged her. "It's okay, honey."

"Someone was here," a voice said from the doorway.

Cait whirled and saw Joy in her wheelchair. She smiled.

"Who did you see, honey?" Bo asked.

"No one, but I heard a voice."

Cait stooped in front of her. "What did you hear?"

"Just mumbling, really."

Cait breathed deeply. "Joy, could you tell if it was a male or a female voice you heard?"

She shook her head and looked at Bo. "I don't know."

"Maybe someone who came to ride?" Cait urged.

"I don't think so."

"How many voices were there?"

"One, I think."

"What do you think this person was doing?"

Joy shrugged. "I don't know. Visiting Faro, I guess."

Cait's pulse raced. "Why do you say that?"

"Because Faro was the only horse in the barn. The others were in the pasture. I talk to all the horses."

"Joy, was a car parked by the barn?"

She shook her head. "I was outside the barn in the back. My wheelchair doesn't move too well on gravel in the front."

Cait glanced at Bo and RT. "Someone might have seen Joy, got nervous and left." She looked back at the girl. "Did you hear an engine, like a car starting up? Or maybe someone on horseback?"

Her eyes lit up. "Yes. A car. But that was after I heard footsteps running. I'm sorry."

"Oh, no, honey, don't be sorry," Cait said. "You're our star witness."

"You think someone wanted to hurt Faro, don't you? And Hilton too."

Cait fought back her emotions. This precocious child was so eager to help. She wanted to wrap her arms around her. "Don't you worry. That's what I intend to find out."

After Khandi took Joy back to the house, Cait said, "She's an amazing ten-year-old."

"Yes, she is." Bo held his palm out with the blue pill. "What do you want to do with this?"

"I'll take it." Cait pulled a tissue from her handbag, wrapped the pill in it, and put it in her pocket. "I think someone sneaked into your barn and drugged Faro by hand or slipped something in his food. I'd like to see him now, and then I'd like to see where Hilton fell."

CHAPTER 47

After they left the ranch, RT said, "Too bad we didn't find any evidence where Hilton fell, but that pill you found in the stall could be more incriminating than a wire that might have caused Faro to fall."

Cait took the tissue with the blue pill from her pocket. "I think so too. This pill could prove Faro was drugged." She tried to calm her excitement. Every clue was a piece to the puzzle, no matter how seemingly mundane. Cait would shift them around in her head until she found a fit and then a solution.

"It would have to be a strong stimulant and act damn fast," RT said. He glanced over at her. "And given by someone who knew Faro and Hilton's riding habits—when he rode, where he rode."

"I should have asked Bo about that." She drummed her fingernails on her handbag. "I wonder—"

He shot her a look. "What?"

She spread the tissue and stared at the blue pill. "I read an article a while back about horses that were given Viagra to make them run faster. Bunches of people in Italy were arrested for clandestine racing and betting." She turned to face RT. "What do you want to bet this pill is Viagra?"

RT laughed and shook his head.

"What's so funny?"

His voice shook with laughter as he struggled to be serious. "Your choice of reading material."

"You'd be surprised what I read in the name of research. It so happens the article was about a wide-ranging investigation that took a couple of years to solve. The police found horses were doped with Viagra and other drugs before both legal and illegal races. The horses went crazy."

"Well, if that pill in your hand is Viagra, there should be some kind of marking on it."

She held the pill up to the window. "Bo would have noticed."

"Not necessarily. After you found that earring stud and then the pill, he was more concerned about his help being careless."

Cait thought of her ex as she held the diamond-shaped pill up to the light. Roger was thirteen years older than she, an age when the body begins to falter. He'd tried to hide his Viagra; she'd found it but never let on she'd seen it. She squinted as she turned the pill over. "It's faint, but I can still make out V-G-R-five-zero." She looked at him. "It is Viagra. There's only one reason for this pill to be in Faro's stall."

RT grinned. "I wonder how many of those pills it would take for a horse . . ."

"Get serious." She wrapped the pill back in the tissue. "I need you to do something for me."

"Should I be worried?"

She rolled her eyes. "Find an excuse for us to visit Rachel at her house."

"I could probably do that, but why?" He waited for an oncoming ancient pickup spewing blue-black exhaust from its tailpipe to rumble by and then turned in their driveway.

She told him what she'd seen in Rachel's medicine cabinet when she looked for aspirin. "It's fun to find answers in the most unexpected places."

"True. Makes our jobs interesting."

Cait counted four vehicles parked in front of the house. Ilia's yellow VW and Fumié's Jeep were parked off to the side on the grass. Two blue and white vans parked near the vineyard belonged to the vineyard workers. But Stanton Lane's orange Land Rover and the shiny new black Mercedes Coupe made her pulse skip a beat.

"I wonder what's going on," RT said. He parked by his trailer.

She pulled her keys from her handbag as they walked back to the house. The front door stood ajar. "I don't like this."

RT reached to the small of his back as he pushed the door the rest of the way open with his foot.

Ilia walked in from the hall. "Hi. You got company."

"The door was open," Cait said.

Ilia said, "Rachel and Stanton Lane must have forgotten to shut it. They're upstairs."

Cait stiffened. "What are they doing up there?"

His face flushed. "Uh . . . I asked, but Rachel said it was okay. She has a house key."

"Don't worry about it, Ilia." She started for the stairs with RT at her heels.

"*Everybody* has a damn key to this house," RT said.

Rachel's angry voice reached them as they approached the second floor. "You lawyers are all alike. Shakespeare had it right. 'Kill all the lawyers.' "

Cait almost choked when she saw Rachel and Lane searching the bookshelves. "What's going on?"

Rachel spun around; blonde tendrils slipped from her high hairdo. "Looking for Tasha's date book. I didn't think you'd mind."

Yeah. Right. Cait's hands clenched at her side in tight fists. "On those shelves?"

"Well, you've locked the door to the upstairs. Tasha had a habit of writing tons of notes, things she meant to tell me about but too often forgot to. I want to make sure everything for the festival is taken care of. You should appreciate that since you're new here."

How dare she come up here as if she owns the place. "This apartment is off limits. I would appreciate it if you would remember that." Cait glanced at Lane, who looked guilty of trespassing. "You needed legal assistance for your search?"

Lane's face flushed. "It won't happen again, Cait."

You bet it won't.

Rachel planted her hands on her hips. "Stan was at the house to see Ben. I dragged him along for company. Tasha never locked her doors. She considered it inhospitable."

"If she'd been less friendly, she might still be alive," Cait said.

Rachel glared at Cait. "What's that supposed to mean?"

"If it's not clear by now, I don't have time to explain it to you. I've been through her date book. I didn't see any such notes."

"You're angry, aren't you, because I skipped the tea," Rachel said. "Ben hasn't been feeling well. I thought I should stay with him."

"I'm sorry to hear that," RT said. "How is he?"

"He's fine now." She pulled on Lane's sleeve. "Let's go."

RT and Cait followed them downstairs and out to the front porch.

"Oh, by the way, Rachel," RT said. "I could be called up to leave any day now, but I'd sure like to see Ben before I go. Okay if we stop by sometime . . . maybe in a day or so?"

Rachel hesitated. "Fine. I'll tell him."

CHAPTER 48

Tongue of a Bird actors began to stream in Sunday without fanfare. After meeting Cait and Rachel, they went about their business with professionalism and lots of humor. Because the cast was small, they didn't require a large wardrobe, which was good because space was limited in the Blackfriars Theater where they would be performing.

Cait and RT caught a dress rehearsal from the back row of the theater. The literal story was about the search for an abducted girl, but the play was rich with other layers. Everything went on inside the main character's mind, where the search becomes an inner flight. Regardless of the difficult subject matter, humor played an important role in the story. Cait lost herself in the other worlds of the play—metaphysical, spiritual, and psychological—where the characters lived.

Afterwards, she thought about the play as she and RT walked back to the house. She was spellbound by the play's internal journey. She found it interesting that you entered it through your head and exited through your heart. Now she understood why Tasha wanted to open the season with this particular play—it was poetic in its use of language and managed just to tell the story without theatricality getting in the way.

They sat at the counter eating chicken-salad sandwiches Cait prepared. "That was an emotional play," RT said, "one I wouldn't normally go to see, but I kept thinking of Mindy and how young and vulnerable she is."

She looked at RT and saw a faraway look in his eyes and thought about Mindy perched on the front steps with Velcro. "She's lucky she has your parents to look after her while you're away."

"Yeah, she is." He finished his sandwich and pushed the plate away. "I called a locksmith for the house and the theaters. I suggest you not hand out new keys any time soon."

She licked mayo from her finger. "Except for you and Marcus, if he comes back."

Someone knocked on the back door.

RT jumped up. "I'll get it."

Cait finished her sandwich and took their empty plates to the sink to rinse. When she turned around, Marcus was standing with RT in the middle of the room. His khaki pants were neatly pressed, a soft blue shirt tucked in at the waist and buttoned up, and his hair natural and sun bleached without a trace of mousse. "Hello, Marcus," she said as she dried her hands on a towel. His face appeared thinner and his eyes sunken, but he made direct eye contact with her.

"I'd like to come back to work," he said.

She glanced at RT and saw him smile, but took her time deciding if she really wanted him back. "You understand there will be rules."

"Yes." He handed her a folded sheet of paper. "Detective Rook said to give you this—conditions of my probation."

She took the paper and unfolded it. Aware of his eyes on her, she took her time reading it. On the bottom of the page, Rook had handwritten a note asking her to call if she had questions or changed her mind about having Marcus at the house. She refolded the sheet and looked up. "If you want to work for me, I'll expect respect. And I won't do everything the same way Tasha did."

He nodded.

"There would have to be an attitude adjustment."

He shifted his feet and nodded again. "Yes, ma'am."

"I won't tolerate dishonesty."

"Yes, ma'am . . . I mean . . . no, ma'am."

Cait bit the inside of her cheek to keep from smiling. "Understanding that, you still want to work for me?"

"Yes, ma'am."

She rubbed her chin as if in deep thought. "One more thing: my name is Cait."

A slight grin crossed his face. "I can do that . . . Cait."

"There would be a salary adjustment."

Marcus's shoulders slumped. "I understand."

Cait shook her head. "I don't think you do. I was thinking of an increase. You'll no longer be my secretary; you'll be my assistant manager, if that's acceptable." She smiled. "I appreciate the work you do, Marcus. I really do."

Stunned, Marcus stared at Cait and then at RT.

RT held his hands up, palms out. "Don't look at me. She's the boss."

Marcus smiled. "Oh, thanks, Cait. I won't let you down."

Cait sighed. "You're welcome. One more thing. If you know anything even remotely connected to either murder, no matter how trivial, now would be a good time to tell me."

Marcus stood tall, head up, shoulders back, and looked her in the eye. "I'll tell you what I told Detective Rook. I swear I had nothing to do with any murders, but I suspected something was wrong when Tasha died. I drove her to the doctor for her annual physical. The doctor told her she was in good health. But soon after, she began to act . . . I don't know . . . secretive."

"How do you mean, secretive?" Cait asked.

"That wasn't her way with me. We used to talk and she would discuss ideas she had for another theater or teahouse. She made me feel my input was important. Then suddenly, she appeared

worried but afraid to talk about it. Sometimes I caught her staring at me. It freaked me out. I asked if I'd done something to
offend her, but she said no and to mind my own business." He
brushed his hand over his eyes. "She'd never spoken to me like
that before. Ever."

Cait understood this was tough for Marcus to talk about, but
she needed answers and thought if she pressed him a little, he
might offer some insight into what it was that had troubled
Tasha. "Go on."

He picked at his fingernails. "She never accepted the police
version of how Hilton died. She said Faro would never hurt
him unless something spooked him."

Cait looked at RT with a raised eyebrow.

"When Tasha asked what I thought about what happened to
Hilton, I reluctantly agreed it couldn't have been an accident.
Maybe that's why she went to see that PI guy, but I don't know.
She never said, and I'd never heard of him until that . . . that
incident in the garage."

Cait held her hand out to Marcus and they shook. "I believe
you."

Later that afternoon, as Cait and RT walked up the front steps
of Rachel's house, he whispered, "Make nice, Cait. It was only
yesterday when we said we'd stop by, so don't expect to be
embraced with open arms."

Her body tingled with suppressed energy. "I'll be as wily as a
wolf."

RT groaned. "Sure you will." He punched the doorbell with
his finger.

Cait's first impression of the tall muscular man who opened
the door didn't match the faltering voice she'd talked to on the
phone the couple of times he'd called looking for Rachel. He
wore blue jeans and a bright orange sports shirt with some sort

of logo on the pocket. His gray-blond hair was cropped military style, similar to Stanton Lane's.

"RT," the man said after an awkward moment.

"Hey, Ben, how ya doing?" RT offered his hand. "I hope you don't mind our stopping by like this, but I could be out of here tomorrow and wanted to see you before I go." He touched Cait's arm. "I don't think you've met Cait Pepper, your new neighbor."

Cait smiled and held her hand out. "Hi, Ben. It's nice to finally meet you."

He took her hand. "You, too."

She felt strength in his hand when he gripped hers. She handed him the bottle of Chardonnay from the Bening estate RT suggested they bring. "A neighborly token."

He took the bottle and glanced at the label. "Thanks." He opened the door further and invited them in, then led them across a room that smelled of the same pipe tobacco Cait had noticed on her previous visit.

She paused to admire the soaring thirty-foot ceiling. Since Ben appeared reserved at the door and clipped on the phone, she hoped he'd open up if she admired his house. "This is a fantastic room."

"We enjoy it." He motioned toward a grouping of leather sofas and chairs. "Have a seat. I'll let Rachel know you're here."

Cait and RT sank into one of the sofas. She leaned close and whispered, "I don't think Ben likes me."

"He's a physicist, one of the more serious types," RT said. "I've met a few who weren't very socially polished."

Ben returned and sat across from them in a well-worn chocolate-brown leather recliner. "Rachel will be in shortly." He picked up a pipe from a side table and tapped the bowl against an ashtray. He looked at Cait. "So you've taken over the Bening estate. Know much about running a place like that, the theaters and vineyard?"

Taken over? Interesting expression. "I know a little about Shakespeare, but I admit to knowing nothing about growing grapes. As far as the festival goes, I'm counting on Rachel to educate me."

He stuck his pipe in his mouth but kept his eyes on Cait. "Think you'll stay or settle up with your inheritance and return to . . . where are you from?"

What an odd question to ask after just meeting me, Cait thought. "Ohio. My plans aren't finalized yet."

"You must have a job waiting for you back home. What is it you do?"

Apparently, Ben and Rachel don't communicate much. "Didn't Rachel tell you? I work in law enforcement."

Ben frowned, took his pipe out of his mouth and stared at it as if it was some foreign object. "Oh. She must have told me and I forgot."

Confused by the direction of this strange conversation, Cait looked hard at Ben. He didn't look sick, as Rachel had claimed. She was grateful when RT took over.

"How's retirement treating you, Ben?" RT asked.

His eyes drifted to RT. "Lacks challenge, except maybe for the sheep. Don't know why I thought it would be easy work. When the labs ran out of funds for the project I'd spent three years working on, I decided it was time to go. They expected me to sit behind a desk and become a paper pusher." He shook his head. "I couldn't do that." He gnawed on his pipe stem. "Instead, I push sheep around."

Cait doubted he'd attempt to push Rachel around.

RT smiled. "It must be nice having Rachel home."

"It is, but I would never stand in the way of the work she loves. She gets restless and is easily bored. Even with me."

"I'm never bored with you, darling." Rachel waltzed into the room, the first time Cait had seen her without stilettos. The jewels on her flat gold sandals glittered in the sunlight streaming across the room. "Ben, be a dear and open the wine they brought. I left it on the kitchen counter. And bring some cheese and crackers."

Ben set his pipe down and left the room.

Docile as one of his lambs, Cait mused. "Please don't go to any trouble for us. We won't be staying long."

Rachel sank down in a chair next to Ben's and tucked one leg under her. "A little afternoon drink will do us good." She smiled at RT. "Have you heard when you're leaving?"

RT crossed his legs and arms. "Any day now. Today, tomorrow. That's the military way."

"Ben must be feeling better," Cait said.

Rachel brushed a hand down her short skirt. "I think he mainly suffers from boredom. He needs to get out more, maybe take up golf."

Ben returned with a tray of filled wine glasses and a small basket of cheese and crackers and set it on the large coffee table in reach of everyone. "Help yourself." He handed a glass to Rachel and then took one for himself before sitting down.

RT and Cait reached for a glass at the same time. "To good neighbors," RT said.

While Cait sipped her wine and listened to RT trying to converse with Ben, she was also aware of Rachel's eyes on her over the rim of her glass. She decided to stir things up a bit and leaned forward in her seat. "Rachel, I finally found the letter from the OSF board, the one about Tasha being selected as associate artistic director."

Silence filled the room.

Ben jumped to attention.

Rachel lowered her glass. "What letter is that?"

Is she playing dumb, or doesn't she know? One can never tell with Rachel. "I assumed you knew," Cait said. "The letter confirming she had the job."

Rachel moved to the edge of her seat and dropped her other foot to the floor. "Well, I didn't. No matter, I don't see how it concerns you."

"It does if you get the job now. I'd lose your help with the festival. I know it hasn't been filled since Tasha died, but—"

Rachel shook her head back and forth until a lock of hair fell over her face. She shoved it back. "I don't understand. What are you implying?"

Cait glanced at RT and then Ben. "Tasha changed her mind. She intended to turn it down but apparently died before she had a chance."

Rachel's glass slipped from her hand, spilling wine in her lap. She ignored it. "You're wrong. If Tasha was offered that position, as everyone assumed she would be, she'd grab it and run all the way back to Oregon." She glared at Cait. "I don't know what game you're playing, but I want it stopped now."

Ben grabbed a couple of napkins from the tray and shoved them at Rachel. "Excuse me," he said. He stood as if to leave the room.

Rachel dabbed at the spilled wine on her skirt. "Stay, Ben."

Ben hesitated.

"How do you know this?" Rachel said.

"That Tasha changed her mind? She wrote her intentions on the back of the letter." Cait took a deep breath. "Rachel, she wanted you to have that job. Unfortunately, she was murdered before she had a chance to tell Kenneth Alt."

Rachel paled. "You're lying. Have you talked to Kenneth? How do you even know him?"

"We talked on the phone." Cait thought it wasn't her place to tell Rachel she was on the short list. She glanced at Ben and noticed he looked drawn.

"It's the truth, Rachel," RT said. "I read the letter. I saw

Tasha's note."

"The letter was in Stanton Lane's book, the one he and Tasha shared," Cait said.

Her eyes as large as saucers, Rachel looked at Ben. "Ben, there's something I haven't told you. There's more to Cait's interest in this. Tasha wasn't Cait's aunt. She was her biological mother."

Cait's stomach knotted with Rachel's blunt announcement. Apparently, it surprised Ben, too, because he wasn't looking so good.

Ben swayed and reached for the back of the chair.

RT jumped up. "Ben? What's wrong?"

Ben's hand went to his chest. Ashen faced, he reached into his shirt pocket.

"Ben, your nitro," Rachel said.

He slipped a pill into his mouth. "Angina," he said, breathlessly.

Cait sat frozen on the sofa. *Angina? What's he doing taking Viagra?*

"Sit down, Ben." RT tried to steer him to a chair, but he resisted.

"Better if I stand. I'll be fine. Give me a minute." He left the room.

Cait studied Rachel and noticed dark puffy circles beneath her eyes, deep lines etched on her brow, and spidery veins at her temples and around the outer edges of her eyes. Beauty was losing the battle against aging. She felt an unexpected jolt of sympathy for her. "Rachel, how long has Ben had heart problems?"

"Since he was twelve."

"I think we should go," RT said, "unless there's something we can do for Ben."

"Ben took his nitroglycerin. He'll be okay." Rachel glanced

down the hall where Ben had disappeared. "Please stay. Cait, I want to clear up some misunderstandings."

Uneasy, Cait thought Rachel looked as if she'd lost steam.

RT returned to his seat next to Cait.

"Tasha would have made a terrific artistic director. She studied every aspect of the theater. She had incredible stamina and commanded the stage as though it was her natural home." Rachel massaged her temples. "While I've spent half my career living in her shadow, being her understudy. I felt like a consolation prize. Still do."

"I'm sorry," Cait said, for lack of anything better to say.

"Don't be. I get enough sympathy from Ben. The reality is, we've gotten to the age when actors have to consider the next phase of their careers. Shakespeare audiences are intelligent. It's hard to fool them when we're trying to portray a certain age for our roles."

This was a softer side of Rachel that Cait hadn't seen.

"I thought it was important for you to know since you didn't know her. You would have liked each other."

"Thank you for sharing that with me," Cait said. "I appreciate it."

Rachel turned her attention to RT. "Will you come back sometime?"

He smiled. "I hope to. Livermore has a lot to offer."

Cait knew it was time to leave, but she still had a mission to accomplish. "May I use your bathroom? Must be the wine."

Rachel nodded. "I think you know where it is."

Cait excused herself, closed and locked the bathroom door. She turned the water on to cover the noise of opening the medicine chest. She didn't see the Viagra until she moved several items aside and found it tucked behind a box of Imodium. She quickly read the label: VGR50, prescribed for Ben Bauer two years ago. *If this is what upset Faro, then it must still work,* she thought. She unscrewed the lid, slid one blue diamond-shaped pill into the palm of her hand and then tucked it into her shoe. In her hurry to replace the lid, she dropped the bottle in the sink. Her breath wedged in her throat. She grabbed the bottle, turned the water off, snatched some toilet tissue, and dabbed the pills with the tissue.

The floor squeaked outside the door.

Cait froze. She waited, then dropped the pills back in the bottle and returned it to the cabinet. She flushed the toilet, counted to ten and opened the door. Rachel and RT were waiting for her by the front door. Ben was nowhere in sight.

After they said good-bye and were belted in their seats, RT asked, "You okay?"

She nodded and rolled her window down to let the breeze cool her flushed cheeks and help calm her racing heart. She took her shoe off and recovered the pill, then reached in her handbag for the one from Faro's stall. When she compared them, she said, "Both are stamped V-G-R-five-zero."

RT glanced over at the pills. "Doesn't prove the one from Faro's stall came from that particular prescription. What concerns me more is that Viagra is inadvisable for someone with heart problems. Ben had to know that. Why would his physician prescribe them for him?"

"Who knows, but obviously someone found another use for them."

CHAPTER 49

When Cait and RT left Rachel's house, they drove into town to Roundtable Pizza. While they waited for their order, they sat at a corner table and discussed how best to handle the latest development about the Viagra. Cait wanted to call Detective Rook right away, but since it was Sunday, RT convinced her to wait until Monday.

"Tasha was right," Cait said. "Hilton was murdered. Finding that pill should convince Rook to reopen the investigation into his death. It's obvious the murders are related." When RT didn't respond, she said, "What's the matter?"

"If only Tasha had called me after Hilton's death, things may have turned out differently. Maybe I could have done something to stop the other killings."

"But you were out of the country."

He stared across the table at her. "How do you know that?"

Oops. "I just assumed that's when you were hurt," she said. "You were teaching . . ."

"I never said I was out of the country."

Cait felt heat rise in her cheeks. She never could lie. "Rook may have said something."

"Like what?"

"RT, he mentioned you knew his brother and that that was how the two of you became friends."

Lips pursed, he studied his fingernails. "I don't like to talk about it, but since it's out in the open now . . . I was in charge of the mission we were on. Bad stuff happened. Some shit head cut our rope as we were repelling down this cliff. Unfortunately, Ace's brother didn't survive the fall." He looked up. "Here comes our pizza."

In her years as a cop, Cait had perfected the ability to stay awake late into the night and keep her senses alert while trying to solve a crime. She could respond instantly if summoned, which is why, when the apartment phone rang near midnight, she answered with a clear head.

"Hello?"

"This is Ben. I'm sorry to call so late, but something's come up. Since you work in law enforcement, I think it would be to your advantage to meet me at the Elizabethan Theater."

She straightened in her seat and closed her laptop. "Now?"

"It has to be now if you want to catch a murderer."

Now this is creepy. "Where's Rachel? Is she with you?" A chill swept through Cait.

"No. I'm alone and I need you to come alone."

"Ben, come to the house. We'll talk here."

"No! Please! Don't you see? It has to be at the theater because the theater is to blame for everything that's happened. What started here has to end here."

Oh, God. Cait jumped up, dragged the phone cord across the room to the bed, grabbed her handbag, located her cell phone and opened it to call RT. "Ben, what do you mean the theater is to blame?" Nothing about the call felt right to her. Earlier he'd had an angina attack. Had she said something while at his house that stirred a hornet's nest?

"Everything will become clear when you're here. I promise."

"I'm not dressed," she lied. "Give me a few minutes."

"Make it quick. Remember, just you and me. Do not tell RT." He hung up.

Stunned, she replaced the phone in its cradle. Ben's voice had been firm and steady, not as if he'd been drinking. She punched in RT's number on her cell phone. When the call went to voice mail, she wanted to scream.

"Dammit." She checked the time again: seven after twelve. *It's too late for him to be on his rounds,* she thought. *So where is he?* She disconnected and tried again. This time she left a message: "Where are you? I had the weirdest call from Ben. He's expecting me to meet him *now* at the Elizabethan Theater. Something about catching a murderer. I'm to go alone. He specifically said not to tell you. Call nine-one-one, then get over to the theater as fast as you can. I have to go." She switched her cell to vibrate and clipped it to her waist.

She kneeled and pulled her duffle bag out from under the bed. The Mag light and Leatherman knife were all she had for weapons. She took them out and dropped them on the bed and then slipped into her black Windbreaker and old tennis shoes. She clutched her keys in her hand, dropped the knife in her pocket, grabbed the Mag light, and after one last look around, raced downstairs, sending a silent prayer to RT to check his messages.

With the moon hidden behind clouds and fog, Cait cautiously headed down the darkened path toward the theater complex.

She recalled every word Ben had said on the phone, then thought back to yesterday when she and RT were at his house. She remembered he looked drawn when Rachel told him Tasha was Cait's birth mother. Could Ben have murdered Tasha? The more she thought about it, the more feasible it seemed. He was a scientist; he had the knowledge to administer drugs and probably the resources to get them. He also had opportunity. He could have used Rachel's key to Tasha's house; Tasha never locked her bedroom door. But that didn't explain Hilton's or

Karl Novak's murder.

With Cait's hand on the gate to the theater complex, something shot out near her feet.

"Jesus, what—"

Her heart raced as she struggled to find the switch on the Mag light. When she saw a rabbit dash from behind one of the earthenware jugs, she flipped the light off and opened the gate.

The gate squealed. She froze, waited and listened before crossing the brick courtyard. A sudden gust of wind swirled around her; shifting shadows and fog cloaked the theater ahead of her. She expected one of the shadows to rise up like a ghost and grab her throat.

The theater appeared out of the fog like an eerie memorial park. An owl screeched in concert with her heavy breathing. When she realized there were no lights around the theater, she hesitated. Had Ben turned them off?

She crept closer to the theater until she reached the side door. Her hand on the handle, her cell vibrated. She grabbed it from her waist and glanced at the lit screen. "RT," she whispered. "I'm outside the theater but the lights are out."

"Do not go in. Wait for me," RT said.

"Did you call nine-one-one?"

"Yes. Dispatch will call Rook."

"Okay. I'm going in," she said.

"Don't do it. I'm on my way."

She thought she heard him groan, but dismissed it and tried the door handle. The door opened. She cautiously stepped inside the theater, flattened herself against the wall, and clipped her open cell phone to her waist. From her vantage point, the rows of seats were dark shadows but nothing appeared menacing. She stepped away from the wall.

A powerful spotlight burst in her face, piercing like needles in her eyes. She raised her hand to shield the glare. "Not funny,

Ben. Cut the damn light."

"Are you alone?"

"Yes. Why the theatrics, Ben?" Two things she knew from countless confrontations: never show fear and don't let your opponent get the upper hand in conversation.

The light tilted away from her face. "Patience, Cait. First, you have to join me up on stage. Soon everything will become crystal clear."

"You're scaring me, Ben. What's going on? How did you get in here?"

"Come up the stairs, Cait. Now!" The sharp edge in his voice cut like a knife.

Cait tightened her grip on the Mag light behind her back; her left hand grasped the knife in her jacket pocket. "Not until you explain why we're here in the middle of the night." She had to take her hand out of the pocket to shield her eyes from the intense glare of the high beam that had crept back across her face.

"You're trying my patience," he said. He raised his right hand for her to see what he held.

She remained where she stood; there was no questioning the power of the weapon in his hand.

His voice as dry as fallen leaves, he said, "Like mother, like daughter. Everything was easy for Tasha, while poor Rachel was the one who really deserved the lead roles. Everyone was out to backstab her."

What's keeping RT? "Why would anyone want to backstab Rachel?"

His raw laugh sent chills down Cait's spine. "Ever since Karl Novak, that SOB, I've made it my business to know everything about my wife and what upsets her. Tasha should never have left the Bening estate to you, a stranger. It should have been left to Rachel."

That was not something Cait had considered. She stayed where she stood and kept her eyes on the gun. "Ben—"

"Shut up. I *will* shoot you if you don't get up here on the stage now so we can settle this. We'll talk, and then I'll decide whether to let you live or die."

Sure you will, like I'd have a chance. "No one needs to get hurt." She wanted to keep him talking, to stall until RT and the police got there. "Does Rachel know you're here?"

"Rachel doesn't keep tabs on me. I worked everything out myself. After you left our house, it became clear what had to be done." He laughed. "There's only one way this can end."

With a leap of faith, she said, "Like when you murdered Tasha? Rachel wouldn't want you to kill anyone else." Talk was her only weapon, unless she got a chance to use her knife.

He didn't take the bait. "There are six steps up to the stage. Start counting," he said.

Her mouth dry and scratchy, Cait said, "Don't shoot, Ben. I'm coming." Her toe caught the edge of the first step. She stumbled. She felt a muscle twitch in her right leg. It vibrated like a violin string.

"Hurry up. Count them."

She was sure she was on her way to certain death. "Two . . . three . . . four . . . five." She stopped at the last step. The light bore into her face, making her sweat. She wanted to smash it in his face.

"One more," he said. "I like confrontations up close and personal, don't you?"

He's sick, she thought. "Close enough to watch me die?" She took the last and possibly fatal step onto the stage.

A rustling noise came from Cait's left. She wanted to turn and look, but didn't dare take her eyes off the gun in Ben's hand. *Hopefully, the police are here.*

"Ben may or may not kill you, Cait. But I might." Rachel

stepped from behind a scenery panel on the left side of the stage with a gun pointed at Cait's chest.

Jesus. Both of them? She flexed her fingers around the knife in her pocket.

Ben whirled, his gun now pointed at Rachel. "Rachel? What the hell are you doing here?"

Cait gasped. *Good Lord. They're going to shoot each other.*

Ben lowered his gun. "How did you know?"

"We've been together a long time, Ben. You can still surprise me, but I'm pretty good at reading your mind." Her eyes slid to Cait. "Someone has to tidy up this mess. I've also been doing a lot of thinking and have reached some serious conclusions."

Cait's eyes darted back and forth between Rachel and Ben. *Did I see movement in the wing behind Rachel?* To draw their attention away from there, she threw her arms in the air as if to surrender. "I'm unarmed. Shooting me won't do anything for you except put you on a wanted list."

"Really, Cait, you look silly," Rachel said.

"What have you got to gain by killing me?"

Rachel's gun wavered for a moment. "I haven't killed anyone, not intentionally. Hilton wasn't supposed to die. I'm sorry the accident didn't go as planned. I wanted him to fall off his horse and be disabled so Tasha would stay home and care for him. Like Joy's accident that left her in a wheelchair."

"By giving Viagra to Faro?"

Rachel gasped, her eyes darted to Ben. "You're crazy. Where would I get Viagra?"

"From the medicine cabinet in your bathroom," Cait said.

Ben stepped toward Rachel. "You killed Hilton? Oh, Rachel . . ."

Rachel turned her gun on Ben, stopping him in his tracks. "Get over it. It was an accident. If it hadn't been for that damn rock—"

Cait inched closer to Rachel, hopeful of tackling her. "Then you could have been the next associate artistic director."

"I have friends in high places," Rachel said. "I'm on the short list." Her voice quivered. "I truly was heartsick the night of the fire, when RT broke the news about Tasha." She glared at Ben. "Why didn't you call and tell me when she died?"

"You were out of the country," Ben said. "I thought your work was more important."

Cait couldn't believe what she was hearing, but with their attention on each other, she might have a chance to take one of them down and get their gun.

"We'll deal with this later at home," Rachel said. "Let's settle what's before us now."

Rachel's gun swung back to Cait. "In case you're wondering where RT is, he's been delayed. He'll be okay, but he may have a headache for a while."

Cait froze. *Oh, God.* "What have you done, Rachel?"

"I want to talk about Tasha," Rachel said.

Okay. Talk is good. But where are the police? "Ben murdered her," Cait said.

Rachel's eyes watered, her gun wavered. "Ben? No. Tell me it wasn't you, Ben."

Ben's gun dropped to waist level. "I did it for you, Rach. You were always complaining how Tasha was everyone's darling. She got the best roles, roles that should have gone to you. The last straw was that director's job for . . . that play . . ."

"*Hamlet,*" Cait said.

He nodded. "Yes. I wanted to make sure Tasha didn't get that too. I wanted it for you, Rach, because you wanted it."

"Oh, Ben," Rachel moaned.

It became clear to Cait that Ben also murdered Novak. "But why kill Karl Novak, Ben?"

Rachel paled. "No . . ."

Ben laughed. "He was blackmailing you, Rach. He threatened to spread lies and pictures throughout the Shakespeare community about that stupid cheerleader business way back in high school. Seems like I've spent my life protecting you."

Rachel stared at him. "You knew about that?"

The moon peeked out of the clouds over the open-aired theater. Cait sensed movement again, this time from the rows of seats behind her. To draw their attention from the seating area, she asked, "What pictures are you talking about?"

"Pictures of a certain cheerleader's so-called accident," he said. "Novak was the high school's photographer during senior year. He had a habit of sticking his nose where it didn't belong. After all these years, he threatened to take his pictures to the police. I couldn't let him do that." He looked at Rachel. "Yes, I knew. When you reignited your affair with Novak and then wanted out, he couldn't take the rejection and called me. We met late at night in Tasha's garage." His eyes red-rimmed, he glared at Cait. "You were supposed to be out of town." He raised his gun and stepped closer to her. "I offered Novak money, but he didn't want it; he wanted revenge." He looked at Rachel. "Very revealing pictures. He took videos of the two of you in his house. I don't think I need to tell you what they showed."

"Oh, Ben. Why didn't you tell me?"

Cait feared that if the police didn't appear soon, the whole stage would erupt in gunfire, and all three of them would be dead. Ben's eyes burned with intensity. Cait couldn't be sure if it was from hate or love for Rachel.

"I took care of Novak," he said, his gun close to Cait's heart. "Time to end this."

Cait heard the familiar click of a trigger being pulled back. Staring at the blackness of the gun's muzzle was like staring down a dark tunnel. She considered jumping into the orchestra pit. "If you shoot me, Ben, the police will look everywhere for you: at your house, airports, car rentals. You can't escape."

"Put your gun down, Rach," Ben said. "Let me do this."

Tears spilled from Rachel's eyes. She shook her head as if in a trance. "No."

He reached for her gun. "We'll go anywhere you want. You'll see. Now give me your gun."

Ben's voice seemed to snap Rachel from her trance. She turned her gun on Ben. "No. I can't let you kill anyone else." Her voice shook. "I don't want to do this, Ben, I'm sorry, but . . ."

Her gunshot resonated throughout the theater.

Ben slumped to the floor, his eyes wide in disbelief. "Rach . . ."

Detective Rook ran onto the stage from the left wing, his gun steady on Rachel. "Drop it! Now!"

Half a dozen police officers raced down the aisles, their weapons drawn.

Caught in the middle, Cait said, "You took your time getting here." She looked for RT but didn't see him.

"Be grateful we're here," Rook said. "You were seconds from being the next victim."

In a split second, Rachel's gun was on Cait. "Everyone back off! I swear I'll shoot her! I have nothing to lose!"

Cait believed her. From the glassy look in her eyes, she realized Rachel had turned the corner from sanity to insanity. Like Ben.

Detective Rook ignored Rachel's warning. Instead, he kneeled down beside Ben. He put his fingers on Ben's neck, then looked up at Cait with a subtle shake of his head, his eyebrow cocked, his eyes boring into hers as if transmitting a message.

"Oh, my God. Is he dead?" Rachel screamed.

Rook removed Ben's gun from his hand and rose. "Get the

medics in here, quick."

Cait understood Rook's subtle message. "Rachel, there's a chance, but Ben needs immediate help." With her eyes on the gun in Rachel's hand, she pleaded, "Everything Ben did was out of love for you. Now it's your turn. Don't let him die."

Rachel stared down at Ben, seemingly mesmerized by the pool of blood collecting on the floor next to him.

Cait saw tears roll down Rachel's cheeks and drip from her chin.

In the next instant, Rook grabbed for her gun, but Rachel drew her arm back, wildly discharging a bullet.

The officers charged up the stairs.

Rook held his hand up at the officers. "Stay back!"

Cait sucked in a breath. The bullet had grazed her arm before plunging harmlessly into the empty rows of seats. She clapped her hand to the wound as rage pumped through her body. The scrape was superficial, but it burned like hell. She kept her eyes glued on Rachel, eager for an opportunity to take her down. Given the chance, she'd do whatever it took to survive and protect the officers and Rook.

"Is Ben dead?" Rachel moaned.

"He will be if paramedics don't get to him soon," Rook lied.

Cait charged at Rachel, catching her off guard. She slammed her down on her back, but Rachel twisted her arm out from under Cait and fired several more wild shots. Officers dodged behind stage props as ricochets chewed chips from scenery panels.

Cait pried Rachel's fingers from her gun, then yanked it away and tossed it to the nearest officer. With her last bit of energy, she flipped Rachel onto her stomach, roughly pulling her arms behind her back. "Dammit! Somebody cuff her!"

A pungent tang of cordite hovered over the theater. An officer stepped forward and snapped cuffs on Rachel's wrists and pulled her to her feet.

Cait gasped for breath and forced herself up. "I have to find RT. Rachel hurt him to stop him from coming here."

A sudden commotion from the bottom of the stairs had Rook and his officers positioned with their weapons on the intruder.

RT staggered up the stairs, breathing hard. "Cait. Are you okay?" A look of deep-seated fury, almost savage, crossed his face when he saw her wounded arm. "You've been hit."

Cait ran to him, wanting to grab him but afraid she'd hurt him. "I'm okay . . . better than you look." She ran her fingers across his head looking for an injury. "What did she do to you?"

"It takes more than a knock on the head to keep me down. But you need to be looked at." Coiled with rage conveying shades of frustration and anger, he glared at Rachel. "Bitch."

Paramedics advanced toward them.

"Look at him first," Cait said, pointing to RT.

RT brushed them aside. "I'm fine. She's the one who's been shot."

Rachel yelled over her shoulder at Rook. "You should have killed me, Detective, when you had the chance."

"I prefer live suspects," Rook said. "They give me more satisfaction than dead ones."

Rachel's eyes sparked like a serpent's—sharp, piercing, and treacherous. " 'Out of my sight! Thou dost infect my eyes,' " she snarled at Rook as an officer Mirandized her.

"What the hell did she say?" Rook asked.

Cait smiled. "That, Detective, was from *Richard the Third*."

CHAPTER 50

It had been a hectic few days. The house phone rang nonstop. Reporters and TV crews knocked on the doors. Cait and RT made half a dozen trips to the police station for interviews, until Cait had finally had enough and invited Detective Rook to dinner. She didn't like cooking, but she knew how to celebrate and set a table with delectable offerings with the help of Trader Joe's market in downtown Livermore.

The day after the dinner, Cait and RT strolled through the vineyard, prolonging his departure that morning. "It was nice of Rook to offer me access to the shooting range in Dublin so I can keep my skills up," she said.

"He's a nice guy, but there is a public shooting range just outside Livermore, the Livermore-Pleasanton Rod and Gun Club. You could go there and save a trip to Dublin." He grinned. "He's either got the hots for you or hopes to persuade you to join the LPD. I hear they're hiring again."

She laughed. "Oh, please. As if I don't have enough to keep me busy for the next century. I'm going to call June Hart. She and her husband may be ready to leave Oregon and come work for me. They could park their RV in your space."

He raised his eyebrow. "Where would I stay when I come for a visit?"

"Hmm. I think I can accommodate you."

A breeze carried the fragrance of eucalyptus and wisteria. Cait and RT clasped hands as they continued to walk through the vineyard. "You'll remember to feed the cat, won't you?" RT said.

"How could I forget when he's always underfoot? Now that I officially resigned my job and plan to live here, I'm thinking about getting a dog as a playmate for Velcro."

"Get a big one," he said. "If Tasha and Hilton are looking down, I'm sure they're smiling and are very, very proud of you, Cait." He brought the palm of her hand to his lips and kissed it.

"I hope so. I'm okay with being her daughter." She squeezed his hand. "If it weren't for Tasha, I wouldn't have met you."

"And I wouldn't have met a sexy law enforcement officer from Ohio."

They grinned at each other as they turned and headed down another row.

"Detective Rook got permission to loan me a police radio until I can buy a gun," she said.

"There you go. Next thing you know you'll be on payroll."

"Ha. I never thought I'd say this, but I'm ready for a change in my life. I've learned a lot about myself throughout this whole experience." She touched a swollen grape bud with her fingertip, smiling at the miracle of nature.

"That makes two of us," he said.

Surprised, she looked at him. "Really?"

"Really. I'm adaptable."

Cait wanted to ask what he meant, but decided to let it go. "Marcus says ticket sales have skyrocketed. I think we might have a sellout for the rest of the plays."

"That's good. You and Marcus going to be okay?"

"Yeah. I believe so. We've both changed. After what happened with Rachel and Ben, Marcus has been like my shadow. Bo's agreed to stable Marcus's horse at the ranch in exchange for work. Between the ranch and here and frequent visits to his mom, Marcus won't have time to drop in at the Dirty Dog

Saloon. That place should be burned down."

"I know," he said.

They stopped at the edge of the driveway and looked out over the valley. "This is a beautiful place for Shakespeare," Cait said. "I hope Fumié and Ilia stick around long enough to help with the festival. They're great kids. I asked Rook if he'd take them on a ride-along sometime. He agreed to."

"That was nice of you. I called and said good-bye this morning." He chuckled. "He's still in awe over how you hit on that Viagra angle."

She grinned and lightly punched him in the ribs. "Maybe you both should expand your reading interests."

He pulled her to him and kissed her. "Point taken."

Cait inhaled his aftershave lotion and wanted to hold onto him, but he took her hand and guided her back up the driveway to where he'd parked his Hummer and trailer.

"Karl Novak seems to have fallen through the cracks," she said. "Even the guilty should have someone to grieve for them. Doesn't he have family?"

"An ex-wife is all Rook's been able to come up with. But don't feel too sorry for him. According to Rook, a look at his computer revealed tons of e-mails between him and Rachel. Unfortunately, he fell into her . . . shall we say . . . steamy sex drive and then coaxed her into admitting guilt for that cheerleader incident in high school. The police may never know how Rachel managed to bring the pyramid of cheerleaders down, even with Novak's pictures. It's a moot point now, anyway."

"They deserved each other."

RT checked his watch.

Cait caught the look and flinched.

"Have you considered keeping Stanton Lane on as your attorney?" RT said.

"I have and I will. All he's guilty of is allowing Rachel to pull his strings like a puppeteer."

He nodded. "Good. I actually liked Rachel, until that green-eyed monster took over and ruined her life."

"I wanted to like her, but she was a difficult woman," she said.

"In the end, she killed Ben to save your life. The courts will probably give her life instead of the death penalty."

"Did she really kill him to save my life? Or to give the performance of her life?"

RT wrapped his arms around her and hugged her close. "Unfortunately, we'll never know." He kissed her. "Let's put all of the bad stuff behind us."

Cait wanted to take him back to the house and hang a Do-Not-Disturb sign on the front door. "Do you remember what day it was when Stanton Lane called to tell me I inherited a vineyard in California?"

He looked puzzled. "I don't think I ever knew."

She grinned. "April Fool's Day."

He laughed. "I should be able to come up with something funny to say, but damned if I can." Then he sobered. "Some joke, huh?"

"Seems like a long time ago."

RT tipped her chin up and kissed her soundly on the lips. "Cait, my life would not be an easy one to share."

Cait wondered where he was going with this.

Instead of explaining, he pointed to the sky. "Look. A golden eagle. An omen of good things to come."

She saw the eagle soar overhead in liquid movement. "Ilia says there's a golden eagle habitat on top of Brushy Peak."

"We'll hike up there and see for ourselves when I come back." He touched her cheek with the back of his hand. "I have to go."

"I know."

Long after RT's Hummer disappeared from Cait's view, she remained sitting on the front step, thinking how her heart had uncurled and allowed RT into the deepest, most intimate areas of her being. Letting him go was difficult, but she understood. He had a job to do and a daughter to rear.

When her cell phone rang, she considered not answering, wanting to savor RT's last touch on her cheek without outside interference. But the incessant ringing continued without going to voice mail.

"Hello?"

"This is not good-bye," RT said. "I promise."

Don't miss the next exciting
Shakespeare in the Vineyard Mystery
Sour Grapes
Read ahead for a preview!

SOUR GRAPES

CHAPTER 1

The security alarm woke Cait Pepper from a deep sleep. Night still clung outside the bedroom window. She bolted upright in bed, tossed the covers back, and reached underneath for her green canvas bag. Heart racing, she grabbed her 9mm Glock with one hand and her Maglite with the other. Barefoot, she tiptoed down the stairs to the second floor of the apartment. With her ear to the door she listened before opening it, and then slowly slid the bolt back.

Cait stepped out, flicked on the flashlight, and swung her gun back and forth in front of her. She cast the bright beam over the sitting room until satisfied no one was hiding there. Shadows seemed to mock her as she made her way down to the first floor where she hit the light switch on the wall at the foot of the stairs. Light spilled across the front room and hallway as the alarm continued to scream in her ears. Scanning the room, she backed over to the digital keypad on the wall next to the front door and punched in the code.

With the alarm silenced, Cait rattled the front door handle, confirmed it was locked, checked the windows, and then slowly moved down the hall to the rooms that comprised the Shakespearean gift shop. She flipped on the lights, stepped into each room, checked the locks on those windows, and then continued to the kitchen at the back of the house.

Something brushed against her ankles. She gasped and jumped back; Velcro the cat dashed past her and disappeared into the dark kitchen. As she fumbled at the wall for the light switch, someone pounded on the back door. Startled, she hit the switch, flooding the kitchen with light.

Jim Hart, her property manager, motioned to her through the window. Relieved to see a familiar face, Cait rushed over to unlock the door and let him in.

"I heard the alarm. Everything okay?" His thinning gray hair stood on end as he scanned the kitchen.

She crossed her arms against the chill in the air and nodded. "Yes, I think so. Probably a malfunction. You heard the alarm way over at your RV?"

"Sure did. Surprised me too. I thought June would have a heart attack. I can look around the house before I go back if you want."

"I checked every room except the office, but thanks for coming over," she said. "The new alarm system probably needs adjusting. I'll check the office and then go back up to bed." She glanced at the wall clock, a big round one with Roman numerals: 3 A.M. "Sorry the alarm woke you. You better go comfort June so she won't worry about us."

Jim stepped further into the kitchen. "Won't take but a minute to check the office. Sometimes these new-fangled alarm systems go off for no reason."

Cait turned the light on in the office. Jim rattled the outside door while she checked the window. "All clear," she said. After Jim left, she went back upstairs to bed, still shaky but satisfied no one was in the house.

An hour later the alarm sounded again.

Cait shot up and out of bed. "I don't believe this." She went through the same procedure, only this time her gun and flashlight were in easy reach on the bedside table. She slipped into her robe and slippers, went down the stairs to the second floor, and then down to the first. Surprised Jim Hart wasn't back pounding on the door, she punched in the code on the keypad, went through the same procedure as before, and then returned to bed. *Maybe Tasha's ghost set the alarm off or this old house is settling in. Still, at first light I'm calling ADT.*

When Cait inherited the Bening Estate from Tasha Bening, her mysterious aunt, she had been a cop and then a crime analyst in Columbus, Ohio. The estate—a Victorian house, Shake-spearean theaters, and a vineyard—was in northern California, forty-five miles east of San Francisco. Along with her inheritance came awesome responsibilities that meant she had to move to California. If she chose not to move, the estate would go to a foundation for the arts that Tasha had set up.

Cait had never heard of Tasha Bening and assumed Tasha's attorney, Stanton Lane, was mistaken until she read a copy of the trust he'd faxed to her and saw that she and Tasha shared the same middle name—Tilson. She flew to California assuming she would settle the inheritance quickly and then return home.

She assumed wrong.

During the weeks since Lane's urgent phone call, she'd resigned from her job and helped solve three murders. Cait hoped the tragedy of those weeks was behind her, and she could move on to manage Tasha's beloved Shakespeare Festival and Hilton's vineyard. After the incident with the security alarm during the night, Cait wondered if Tasha would still be alive if one had been installed in the house. Both theaters had security systems but neither had been activated. Now they were plugged into the central panel in the house. If someone tried to enter the theaters, an alarm would be tripped at the house, and the digital display would tell her which theater had been compromised.

Cait called ADT first thing in the morning and was assured someone would be out before noon. She sat at the kitchen counter with June Hart, steaming cups of tea before them, discussing the alarm incident and *Hamlet*. The play would be performed this coming weekend at the Elizabethan Theater while *Macbeth* was playing at the Blackfriars Theater.

"Thank God for you and Jim," Cait said. "I'm grateful you decided to retire and come here to help me with the Shakespeare Festival. After everything that happened last month, I thought I'd have to refund everyone's money and shut the theaters down."

June smiled, her earnest blue eyes on Cait. "Why would you think that? From what I've heard, you managed *Tongue of a Bird* like a pro."

Cait stared into her cup. "That's only because everything was already in place. I didn't have to do anything. The play ran like a well-oiled machine. But for *Hamlet* . . . Tasha was supposed to be the associate artistic director for it at the Oregon Shakespeare Festival."

"Nonsense. Don't you dare go there, Cait Pepper. What happened to Tasha was no fault of yours. Or hers, for that matter." She shook her head. "Too much drama, on and off the stage. Unbelievable. But I don't recall there ever being a murder within the industry until poor Tasha." June placed her hand on Cait's arm. "Things will get better. They always do."

Cait sighed. "Let's hope so. This inheritance seems like a kiss of death. Don't get me wrong, I appreciate it, but it's difficult to ignore everything that happened in the short time I've been here." A smile tugged at her lips. *Except for RT. That was a good thing.*

"Fate," June said. "There's always that element of fate, no

matter how hard you try. You know that. You were a police officer, trained to expect the unexpected. Your situation here is no different than if you walked into a bank during a robbery."

The doorbell rang.

"That's probably ADT," Cait said.

A tall black man smiled and held out his ID. "ADT."

Cait glanced over his shoulder and noted a white and blue panel truck in the driveway, then compared the man's face to the one on the ID tag. "I'm glad you're here." She held the door open for him to enter.

She explained about the late night alarms.

"I'm sorry," he said. "Would have freaked me out too. I'll check the system and make sure it doesn't happen again."

"Great. I'll be in the kitchen if you need me." Cait left him by the security panel at the front door and returned to the kitchen where June was talking with Marcus Singer, her assistant.

Marcus drew himself up straight when Cait walked in. "June told me about the alarm going off during the night."

Cait glanced toward the front room. "Probably a malfunction."

"Sure hope that's all it is. There's been enough trouble around here." Marcus swept his hand over his spiked sun-bleached hair. "We're going to have a lot of people milling about this weekend, in the house too because of the gift shop. Do you think we have enough volunteers to help Fumié with the sales?"

"We should be fine," Cait said. "Fumié promised tickets to friends from Las Positas College in exchange for their help."

Marcus turned to leave. "I'll be in the garage if you need me. I still have work left to do on the platform before the Green Show."

Cait watched him go. She marveled at the change in Marcus, an ex-con Tasha had taken on as her secretary. In exchange for trusting him and giving him a second chance in life, he had done everything for her that she asked, even driving her to appointments because she didn't like to drive. When Cait inherited the estate, it hadn't been that way, at least not in the beginning, and not until they came to a mutual understanding.

"Ma'am?"

Startled from her thoughts, Cait jumped at the deep voice. The ADT man stood in the doorway.

"Nothing is wrong with the keypad," he said. "It's functioning like it should. I'm going outside now. I'll walk the perimeter of the house and check the security lights. Might be a short setting the alarm off."

"Thanks. I don't want to go through another night like last night."

"Could be a mouse," June said after the man left.

Cait shivered. "*That* would be bad. More tea?"

"No, thanks. I want to see what Jim's up to."

Worried that the Harts would go back on the road now that they were retired and living in an RV, Cait asked, "Do you think Jim will become restless being here?"

"Not a chance, unless you kick us out." She stepped close to Cait, her voice low as if afraid of being overheard. "I know Jim told you he was a carpenter, but that's just one of many hobbies. Jim and his partner ran a small security firm specializing in stolen art. He still keeps his nose in the business, but only as a silent partner. He's like a modern-day Indiana Jones."

"Really? I would never have guessed."

June grinned. "That's because Jim is a very private, modest person. He would never have told you himself."

The back door opened. "Ma'am, would you please step outside. I want to show you something," the ADT man said.

Cait's heart lurched. *Probably not a mouse.*

Cait and June followed the man around to the west side of

the house where he directed their attention to two windows outside the gift shop. Pry marks scuffed the wood beneath one of the windows. A deep gouge had been cut out of the other.

"Fresh marks," he said. "Someone attempted to open these windows and tripped the alarm."

Cait's breath caught as she stared at the damage.

"And then there's this. I stumbled over it on the ground." He pulled an object from his tool belt and held it out to her. "Not your usual burglar's tool, if that's what it was used for."

Cait took the object, frowned, and turned it around in her hand. "It's heavy and very ornate." She carefully fingered wood splinters protruding from the end of the metal piece. "I wonder what was broken off the end." She looked down at the ground and surrounding shrubs. "Maybe it's here somewhere."

"I found this too." Again he reached into his belt and held up a knife. "Found this in one of the rose bushes. Those sharp thorns would have torn someone's hand pretty bad unless they were wearing gloves."

Dismayed to see his hand gripped around the hilt of the knife, she thought, *Smeared prints.*

"Ma'am, you need to call the police."

ABOUT THE AUTHOR

Carole Price attended The Ohio State University and worked for a national laboratory in northern California before turning to writing mysteries. She graduated from Livermore's Citizens Police Academy. As a volunteer for the Livermore police, she has many opportunities to work with the officers; it continues to be a thought-provoking learning experience.

She frequents the Oregon Shakespeare Festival in Ashland where she fell in love with the Bard.

Carole is a member of Mystery Writers of America. She and her husband reside in the San Francisco Bay Area in the middle of wine country.